THESE CAN'T BE ICES

‡

CORI DI BIASE

THE APPARENT SUBLIME
MONTANA

The Apparent Sublime
www.apparentsublime.com
info@apparentsublime.com

Printed in the United States of America

Library of Congress Control Number: 2013947413

Lightning Source paperback ISBN: 978-0-9895360-9-7

Design: Paul Vargas
www.omniality.com

THESE CAN'T BE CHOICES

To my mother
And to my father
Who taught me words
And their meaning

CHAPTER ONE

Ben woke sick and suddenly with the burning, nervous fear. The thought of something vital undone or forgotten. The feel of danger now too close to avoid. A familiar panic. Before he could remember himself he was sitting on the edge of the bed and everything swam and lurched in the suddenness of motion. He tried to recall what had happened the night before. It wasn't every morning he woke up feeling like this, and he wished he didn't now.

He couldn't remember that he'd done anything stupid, or done anything that would embarrass himself. Aside from stumbling as he stepped off his bar stool to leave. He could go back to that place.

The back-lit block white numbers of the clock radio made a slapping sound as they rolled over to four o'clock. It was as cold as it ever got in Washington in August. The streetlight came in around the edges of the curtains, and through the cracks between them. Or maybe it was already false dawn. He knew he wouldn't sleep again, no matter how much his body wanted to. He couldn't get to work before seven. He couldn't be there alone, and no one else would be there before seven. He would have to eat and shower. He could do that now, or just before he left. That would take half an hour. Maybe less. That left him with two hours to kill. Free time. Time to think. Already he thought of drinking.

Ben pulled on the plaid shirt from the day before, left on the floor at the edge of the bed. He liked the cold. Turning on the light, he caught a glimpse of himself in the distant bathroom mirror. Thin. Old. Nearly fifty and standing leather. He would exercise. Do push-ups and sit-ups until he felt sick to his stomach. Twenty minutes. He would do those now and eat and shower later. Less time, but still too much. No matter how many push-ups he did his chest would still look sunken. Hollow. Like those old pictures from after the war. The Jews in the camps. Not that bad, but he worried that's what he looked like. He worried people would take him for almost dead, and they would never leave him alone.

Shutting off the light, he did push-ups on his fists on the hardwood floor. He would give himself coffee later, but this would wake him up. Five, and he could feel the blood in his system, pushing out the whiskey and the stiffness. Ten, and he could feel his arms and shoulders beginning to register the pain. Twenty, slowly. Methodically. Not letting himself rush, making every movement harder. Everything had to be hard, or else it was empty. Thirty, and everything began to feel impossible. It was an illusion. His mind tricking his body into weakness. Ten more. Forty, and he brought a knee quickly under his body to hold himself up.

Sit-ups. These he could do forever. Forty. Sixty. Sometimes a hundred in the morning, before he'd had anything to eat. He could feel the whiskey still making him heavy and slow, but the movement helped. By the time he finished, he thought he might throw up. His body flooded with an acid sickness. He wanted to curl up around his stomach, but it was better to stand and breathe very deeply. He stood like this for a while, lost in the good pain of new strength.

After a time he walked through the living room and into the kitchen, past old furniture and bare walls. It was mostly empty space, but he had what he needed. He knew the kids who lived in the city with government jobs all wanted to live in big old buildings like this. To him it was mostly useless. Apartments were bigger in this part of town. Row houses of old family-sized apartments, now swallowed up in a neighborhood most people didn't want to walk through. But he didn't mind. It was bigger than he needed, but it was cheap and there were no schools around. No one bothered him, even though he was white. He had the look of poison, he thought. Not powerful, really. Not intimidating. Just something about him that made them want to keep away.

Washington wasn't a bad city. Some of it was very beautiful when he took the time to walk around. Sometimes he walked all over the city on Sunday, and it made him happy and gave him something to do. Even when he could not see it, it made him happy to know it was there.

He turned on the bare light in the kitchen. It hung on a chain from the high ceiling over the stove. It was too bright, but there was nothing to do about it. The kitchen was painted white, but in the light it was brown and worn. He always meant to find a fixture to go around the bulb. Thick glass, to dull the light. He never remembered to use his time in the afternoon to go to a hardware store. It would be nice if it weren't so bright, but he would be done in the kitchen soon anyway.

He put water in an old metal percolator and put it over a high flame while he cleaned out the basket. He had a large tin of store brand coffee, still half full. He scooped out five teaspoons. It was more than they said he should use, but he liked it darker. He remembered when they would include a scoop in the coffee can. A little blue plastic scoop. They didn't do that any more. Maybe they hadn't in a while, so he just used a teaspoon. He put the basket in the water and the lid on the percolator. He stayed in the kitchen to wait for it to boil, or else it would boil over. There were no dishes to do. The deep-basin sink was brown, stained with the coffee he'd washed down the drain, but it wasn't worth cleaning. He shut the light off and leaned on the counter and waited.

The frantic gurgle of the percolator stirred him from wherever he'd drifted and he turned the flame down to just before it would go out. He thought about going back into the living room to sit in his chair. The coffee only needed six minutes to cook, so it was easier just to stand in the kitchen until it was done. He liked the kitchen. In the soft blue light of the gas flame. It felt alive, but secret. There was nothing behind the narrow back window but a brick wall, three feet distant. No other apartments to look in on his. But it felt better when it was dark and secret.

With the coffee finished he poured a cup without waiting and taking out the basket like his mother always told him to. He did not mind the grounds at the bottom of the cup. He would wash out the cup or just chew on them if they got into his mouth.

He walked back into the living room and sat in an old high-backed rocking chair that he'd found on the curb walking between work and his apartment. He had seen it there one morning, and he wanted to take it then but he could not be late for work. So he waited until the night, hoping that the trash would still be on the curb when he walked home. He was glad to find it there at the end of the day. He didn't go out at all that night. He sat in the chair after he'd sprayed it with ammonia and wiped it with paper towels. He woke up feeling very clear and not at all nervous the following morning, and the next morning after that. And on the third night, when he'd gone to the bar, he'd been too happy about the chair to think straight or to control himself. He'd drunk too much, been too friendly. Been too loud. He'd felt too happy and been too comfortable and he'd forgotten that anything could be a mistake. He'd talked too much, and finally he'd gotten angry. The deep disappointed angry he got when nothing was how it should be. When no one was friendly, and there was nothing right for him to say. Now he could never let himself go back to that place.

The new place he went to was better. It was away from his apartment. A twenty minute walk. Away from his work. It felt close and warm and good inside. No one bothered him. It wouldn't matter too much if he left it behind, but he hoped he wouldn't have to.

Sitting in the chair, he could feel the last of the acid sickness from the sit-ups, and he could feel the soreness of his muscles. It felt good, so he sat and did not want to get up. He thought he might put a little sugar in his next cup of coffee. He didn't need it, but sometimes he let himself have just a little sugar. It was so cheap, and there was nothing else to use it for. He kept it sealed to keep out the bugs, but he still usually had to break it loose. Especially now, in the summer, when it was hot and damp. For his next cup he would use sugar, but he didn't want to get up out of the chair to pour it. Not for just another minute. He was happy sitting in his chair.

He might read at night. Never in the morning, but sometimes if he stayed home he would read at night. History, usually, because he didn't like novels. He didn't like reading things he didn't know. Things he didn't expect. He knew what happened in history, and it felt good and it made him happy to read it. The library wasn't far from work. Sometimes he would go to the library instead of eating lunch from the carry-out. Everyone would ask where he'd gone, but he didn't say.

He stood and took his cup to the kitchen. He opened the sugar container and broke off a small piece with his fingers and put it in the bottom of the cup. He poured coffee over it and let it dissolve without stirring it. It would be even sweeter at the end of the cup, which was like a reward for himself. It was stupid to like sweet coffee and he would never use sugar at work with someone else around. But this was his place and he could do whatever he wanted. Even the little bit of sweet in the first mouthful of coffee tasted very good. He went back and sat in the chair with his coffee in the almost-dark, and he was glad he could start getting ready to leave soon.

‡

The boy woke to the feel of the car as it slowed and turned onto the blacktop of the two-lane. He looked out the window of the passenger side. The frost on the long fields shone like something precious and living under the late fall moon. The sky was clear and starless. The hills far in the distance were an outline in the night and the boy thought that if he could run and run across the field it would be like a new world for him to discover. But he didn't remember getting in the car.

The clock on the dash read 3:30. The boy couldn't remember being awake at 3:30 too many times. He could never remember being in the car this late.

His mother was driving the car. She was smoking with the window down but the boy wasn't cold. He was wearing a heavy coat, and under it a sweater, but nothing under the sweater. He realized the sweater itched his skin and then it was everything he felt. His mother didn't see him wake. He moved in his seat to try to keep the sweater from itching him, but that only made it worse.

"Go back to sleep, baby. Everything's okay. Just go back to sleep," his mother said. "It's too late for you to be awake." She was trying to sound happy but her voice was cracking, dissolving at the edges. He didn't know what her problem was.

"Where are we going?"

"We're going to see your Grammie and Gamps. For a vacation. Just for a little while."

The boy knew they didn't go on vacations at night. On a school night. But he didn't know how to ask that. "Where's Dad?"

"Dad's not coming." Her voice was sharper now. Stronger. "Your Dad's going away for a while. Daddy and Mommy talked about it last night. While you were sleeping."

As she spoke they passed a dirt road that disappeared into the woods. The boy knew that road could go anywhere. It could go for miles, and before it ended there might be another road. And another. It could go on forever, to towns they'd never been to, one road after another. He could tell by her voice that she was lying. Lying to him like she always lied.

"Where's Dad?" Dad would tell him the truth.

"I told you Dad's not coming. He and Mommy talked about it."

He hated the way she said "Mommy." He was too old to talk about "Mommy." It made her sound stupid, and he hated it.

The boy watched out the window. They slowed, driving through a small town. There were no lights on anywhere in the town, and only a cluster of buildings around one intersection. A sign at the intersection pointed left for Coudersport, and straight toward Olean in twenty-three miles. They were still far away. He tried to settle into his seat but his sweater was itching him so much.

"This sweater itches," he said.

"I packed a bag for you so you can get changed at Grammie's house. Until then there's nothing to be done about it."

"Do I have to go to school tomorrow?"

"No. I told you, we're going on vacation. No school for a few days."

The boy put his hands under his sweater to try to hold it away from his body. He sat back in the seat and stared out the window. The hills crowded closer around the road and everything felt warmer and safer. He could see the white frost on the trees and the road curved back and forth, like it was slowly rocking him. Everything was still. Frozen still as they drove past. He fell in and out of sleep for the rest of the drive, and it was always his sweater that woke him up.

The lights were on at his grandparents' house. A light in the kitchen. A light over the front door. The house was far away from everybody, and that's how his grandparents were sometimes. The kind of people who lived far out in the country and never talked to anyone. He could smell their house before he even got out of the car. The way it would smell inside like old people and old, sick air.

"Get your red backpack out of the wayback and wait a minute in case Mommy needs help with anything else." It was sharp, deep cold outside. He zipped his coat up while he stood next to the car and his mother handed him his bag, and one of the ones that she'd brought.

The porch under the front door was rotting away, and they had to watch which boards they could step on and which might break under them. His mother didn't knock. She pushed the door that always stuck on the bottom and made the house shake when you opened it. They walked through the mud room and through the living room with a small television and a couch and chair and pictures all around that it was too dark to see, and into the kitchen where his grandmother and grandfather were sitting and drinking coffee. His grandmother stood and hugged him and cooed over him and said stupid things, while his grandfather sat at the table and watched and didn't say anything.

"Say hello to your Gamps."

The boy walked over and held out his hand. He liked the way he was supposed to say hello to his grandfather. It felt like the way a man should say hello. His grandfather took his hand and shook it and the boy could smell whiskey on his breath. His father put whiskey in his coffee sometimes, too.

His grandmother and his mother took her bags up the stairs. He would sleep on the couch, which he liked. He wished he could change out of the sweater, but he didn't want to talk about it in front of his grandfather. His grandfather was wearing red and black flannel and old khakis and he hadn't shaved. His chin and his cheeks were thick with white and gray and his eyes were set deep back into his face. The boy wished he knew something that they could talk

as if in the same spell that had made
. And neither she, trapped in her pos-
y the watching of her, saw his father's
from the door handle.

muted crack of flesh against flesh and
ngth to move them. His father's hand,
f slowness. Able to break the spell that
break the enchantment of possession
ly toward him. She fell and crumpled

watched for a moment like taking one
shed. His father turned to walk out of the
ft to care about or worry about behind
the still and quiet house, the boy saw his
d blank and simple. Now broken from its
t had been vicious. Now staring blankly,
at him.

‡

sh-ups before he showered. He shaved and
button-down plaid shirt that had come to
vould put on coveralls once he got to the
er what he wore. But this felt like the right
He was glad to be into the routine of getting
ything would be clear to him for a while, and
ave to talk too much at work.
arly, even if he didn't have to. He liked that
nd if he had to work he felt like he might as
ht he'd started on a car that he could finish
d, like the kind he'd worked on as a kid. He'd

about together, but his grandfather never talked. That was probably
good, the boy thought.

His mother and his grandmother were upstairs putting bags away
and he could hear them talk and talk and talk. They never stopped.
He couldn't hear what they were saying, but it never stopped.

They came back downstairs and they were still talking. His
mother had sheets and a pillow and a blanket in her arms.

"It's time for us to get to bed." The boy stood and followed her
into the living room to the couch. "Say good night to your Grammie
and Gamps."

He turned in the doorway of the kitchen. "Good night, Grammie
and Gamps." He walked into the living room where there was only
his mother and it was private so that he could get ready for bed.

His mother put a sheet down and tucked it behind and underneath the cushions. She laid another sheet on top and tucked it into
the back and left it loose in the front. She laid a blanket on top of that.
She put the pillow down over the head of the blanket and sheets. The
boy took a black t-shirt out of his bag and took off the sweater and
put on the t-shirt. He didn't like to sleep with a shirt on, but he didn't
want to sleep without it in case he didn't wake up before other people
would be walking through the living room. He took off his jeans and
got under the covers and his mother kissed him on the forehead and
said "Good night, sweet prince," like she always did and he hated
how it made him feel good and calm and ready to sleep.

He rolled over on his side and listened to his mother and his
grandparents talking in the next room. He could only hear parts of
it. Mostly what his grandfather said, because he didn't ever like to
whisper. "How long?" "What happens after that?" "Then where'll
you go?" The boy knew they weren't on vacation. He knew it wasn't
good. He thought maybe he should try to escape. Or maybe tomorrow
he could find a way to call his father. His father would always tell him

what was really happening. He thought about how maybe he could escape, and if he could survive on his own and find his way back to his house, or if he could use the phone without anyone hearing. With the sounds of their whispers from the kitchen like something weighing him down he drifted to sleep.

When he woke again there was a thin light—the first light of morning—and a hand on his shoulder. Shaking him awake. He cleared his eyes and he could see it was his father standing over him. He didn't know how. His father was leaning close to him and the boy felt his breath. There was a rich endless smell that he knew was the smell of whiskey. The boy hadn't had the chance to call him and tell him. The boy didn't know how he knew.

His father whispered to him. "We've got to be real quiet. Is that your only bag?"

"Yes."

"All right. Pick it up." The boy picked up the bag, and even though he was getting big his father picked him up in his left arm. His father was strong, and the boy knew he was too strong to ever let anything hurt them, and that now his father could tell him what was happening and everything would be clear again.

His father walked back toward the door, and tried to walk lightly on the loud old floorboards. As they crossed the front room, everything lit up around them and the boy buried his face in his father's shoulder to keep out the sudden brightness.

"Put him down and get out of here." His grandfather's voice. The boy tried to open his eyes and his father kept walking toward the door. "You're not welcome here."

"I'm not staying." The boy's father kept walking, but he turned around to back out of the room. The boy tried to turn and look back, and even in the still too-bright light he could see that his grandfather was old and frail.

learned about the newer ones. He'd been to a class about all the features and the computer systems. He knew how to work on them, but he never really liked it. He did his job very well, but the newer ones never really felt like cars. They were like something fake.

Ben kept his eyes down when he walked. It was stupid to look people in the eye. Most of them were just people, on their way to work. But he was different. Where he was from. What he looked like. It was reason enough for some people to want to give him trouble, and reason enough for everyone to wonder why he was here. There were mothers with children on the way to the nearest bus stop. People on their way to work. And Ben was on his way to work.

All the buildings were the same. Brick row houses with walk-up stairs and a half basement. On some of the blocks, a few of the houses were painted brightly in purple or yellow or blue. Mostly they were dark, old red. Someone had taken the time to make those blocks look special, to make them look a certain way. Maybe they'd tried to talk to their neighbors. Knocked on doors until they came to know better. But now the paint was peeling and no matter the color it all looked like it was rotting from the inside. It looked worse now, to think that someone used to care. There was trash on the sidewalk and no one smiled except to laugh too loud.

Ben walked the long way around to get to the shop. He walked an extra block north, and came toward the shop from a different direction. It was still five minutes before opening, and there probably wouldn't be anyone there. Ben liked it better if no one knew the direction he came from. He stood waiting next door, outside of a Chinese carry-out that wouldn't open until eleven for lunch. There was thick metal siding over the windows and bars across the door of the shop and the bright white and red of the paint had faded so slowly yet so completely as to make it seem it had never been anything but old and worn. Ben thought that if he didn't know the shop was there, if he were driving by fast enough, that it might have blended into everything else. He stood facing the street.

Sometimes, when Ben stood still and tried not to think, it would strike him, suddenly, that everything around him was big, and full, and constantly in motion. It was strange to realize he lived where he did, and that he belonged here as much as anyone, or as much as he belonged anywhere. He'd grown up in the country. In a small town, and it seemed natural to him that a place should be still, or that there might not be a torrent and a maze of life and motion and everything always around him.

Where he grew up, the mornings were almost always cold. Even in the summer. As if in darkness and in the sleeping stillness the world itself had taken a damp chill in its bones and in its joints. There would be a haze in the air, like a mist of waking. An unfocused blur. In the morning it was as though all of life had forgotten them, forgotten that place. There was no sound at all. No motion. If there was a car on the road it sounded foreign and maybe like a threat, and it was natural to wonder why it was going, and where. The noise of it was strange and exciting, like evidence of far-flung, imagined places.

But here it was different. In this place that was home but didn't feel like it. Noise belonged here, more than he did. Noise made sense, and it all fit together and felt like reassurance. Like a metronome. Evidence that the light hadn't gone out. The chill had not descended past ever being lifted. Even the sirens and the yelling and the never knowing what came next. It all made sense. It was better for him. Here, now. It was better for what he was. What he'd become.

Roger was taking his keys out of his pocket as he came around the corner. Roger was early man on today. He was the only one aside from Ben that would show up on time. Ben liked Roger. Roger was big, and his skin was fantastically black. A deeper black than Ben thought skin could be. Roger gave Ben a lot of shit, but he never asked questions. He never wanted to know anything except what was happening with a car, or when a job would be done. He was the assistant manager, and he always knew how to talk to everybody. Ben knew that was what you had to do in a job like that, and he was glad it wasn't his job.

"Another early morning, huh Cornpone? Wassa matter? Didn't make it out to the barn dance last night?" Ben didn't mind how Roger talked to him. He didn't know what to say, or how to joke back, but it didn't matter if he never said anything at all. "Okay, chatterbox, let's head in."

Roger unlocked the padlocks under each of the heavy metal guards in front of the windows while Ben followed behind him and pulled them up. Roger unlocked the gate and inside there was a reassuring, normal smell of spent oil and tire-rubber. There was a reception desk covered in old newspapers, unfiled order forms and customer receipts, covered over with an open appointment book. Ben walked to the small locker room behind the bathroom to change into his coveralls.

Ben liked working. Not having to think. Everything was easier when he knew what he should and shouldn't do. What was right or wrong. He worked hard, and he worked well. Better than anyone else in the shop, but he didn't care about that. It was easier to work, and to be good at what you did.

By eight most everyone was in the shop except Vic, who owned the place and only ever came in to check up on Roger and the rest of them. Ben was most of the way through work on the carburetor of an '82 Custom Cruiser, an old wood-paneled station wagon with faded, sick-yellow paint. He'd had to wait because the parts weren't in, but they had come in from a scrap yard in Springfield just before closing the night before. They were harder to get because this was one of the models with a genuine Olds engine, before the Olds started carrying the same engine as all the other GM cars. Ben liked that, and he liked knowing it. It was like history, except no one else cared. Ben stood under the lift and lost himself in the easy complexity of the old mechanics.

Roger walked from end to end in the shop. He spoke with one customer after another. A man in a suit. A woman from the neighborhood. "We'll have that up and running for you by five at the latest." When he spoke to customers he spoke softly and his voice was even and solid, and it was like a different language. A different person he would become. Ben didn't understand it, and it made him feel there was something about Roger he ought to fear. "If it's ready any sooner we'll give you a call."

For lunch he walked across the street to the carry-out. There was a confused mill of people, like always. No line, just a crowd of people waiting that the woman somehow kept track of from behind dull, milky, bulletproof plastic. Ben walked slowly to the window, careful not to cut in front of anyone. He ordered through a small window that was a foot below his height. He put money on a rotating service tray. After a moment, his change came around on the other side. He moved to stand as far out of the way as he could.

The food came in a white plastic bag. He checked for a plastic fork, napkins and hot sauce, and walked back toward the shop. He sat eating the greasy, heavy noodles while the rest of the guys talked.

"Telling you. This new kid they got on the mound, what's his name? He's going to take the Nats to the Series this year." Enrique had been talking about baseball most of the day. "He's the real deal. About time, too." He was slender and emphatic, but the subject made him reverent. Almost still as he spoke.

"Listen, man." Roger shook his head. "I grew up in this town. Been here since the Nats were Senators. It ain't the way sports works here. We don't get to have the World Series. Super Bowl neither. Like a Senate seat. It'll never happen."

"No, man. You ain't seen the new kid."

Ben stopped listening. He could do that, now, today, because what they were saying didn't matter. He didn't understand sports, and he didn't care about them, but he could hear in the sound of their voices that what they said wouldn't matter to him. There would be nothing to hurt him or surprise him in what they would say. If it changed, if something in their voices changed, he would hear it.

"I saw him last year. He's not new. The 'Skins have a new quarterback, so you can go on about that until they're oh-and-four on the season. You from Florida, right? Why don't you do like those Tony Montana motherfuckers down there and root for the Marlins?"

Enrique shrugged. "Can't root for a team in a town you don't live in. People look at you like an asshole. Anyway, home games here are cheap as shit."

Ben's father had watched sports. He'd liked football the most, and Ben remembered sitting and watching games with him. But he'd never learned about the sport. He'd barely even watched the games. He'd watched his father, and he listened to the sounds from the TV, and from his father cheering or getting angry while he watched. He would still remember the closeness and the feel of it when he heard the empty, hollow sound of a game when the announcers were quiet.

"What about you, Ben?" Tony was large. Muscular. Bigger than Roger. Ben listened to what he was saying like he'd never stopped. "You down for this Nationals nonsense?"

"I don't follow it." It was quiet. He knew he was supposed to say more.

"Ah, shit. Cornpone probably ain't even see a TV till he moved here. Too busy playing that cow flop bingo."

Tony asked, "What the fuck is cow flop bingo?"

"It's what these cracker motherfuckers do for kicks in the sticks. They go out to a pasture, however big. They section it off into squares like a checker board, then they number the squares." Ben didn't mind when they made fun of him. It made them know they could forget him.

"How many squares?"

"The fuck should I know? Depends on the size of the field or whatever. Anyway, can't be more than ten unless someone gots to take their boots off. So then they put this cow in there and set it loose, and they all stand around chewin' on hay or whatever, waiting for the cow to take a shit. When it does, whoever's square it shits on wins the prize."

"No shit. They really got that?" They all looked to Ben.

"Yeah. They used to play with the whole town for charities."

"What'd you win?"

"I don't know. I never did."

"Whoever she was, she was probably related." Roger slapped Ben hard on the back. "Time to stop talking bullshit and get back to work."

They all stood from the table. Enrique smiled to himself. "Bullshit. Yeah. Right."

‡

Ben left work at the same time as everyone else. He'd gotten there earlier, but he didn't mind. In a week he would put in fifty to sixty hours, but he never got overtime. It was part of the arrangement. Part of how he could be working at all, so it didn't bother him. He didn't have any other place to be, so it didn't matter.

Ben was going to the bar, to the bar he'd been going to. When Roger asked if he was going anywhere special he'd shrugged and said, "Home." He didn't like to lie. Not to a specific question. But it was better than having Roger with him at the bar. That could never happen.

He walked down the wrong street leaving the shop, away from his apartment and the bar, just like he had coming to work. After a few minutes he turned toward the bar. Ben never enjoyed the evening walk. It was still hot, and he just wanted the day to be over. He knew he should just go home. He stopped at another carry-out for a sandwich he could eat while he walked.

The place was called NY Express, and it was in the basement of a brownstone next to an empty lot. The neighborhood was empty. Deserted. The bar could play music as loud as they wanted. Ben walked down the steps and through the door. It was half full, and still had a quiet afternoon feel. Ben didn't know why they called it NY Express, and he didn't care enough to ask.

The regulars were at the bar. Ben thought he recognized them. Black men in their forties and fifties. Ben liked that they were older. They played old black music. The kind he could listen to. He liked it here. The place was long and narrow and got darker toward the back, away from the high basement windows and the lighting around the middle of the bar. It usually didn't get busy that far back, and there was a view of the rest of the bar and the people coming in. That was where he always sat.

They were playing doo-wop when he came in. The Five Satins. Ben's dad had even played them sometimes, even though he didn't like black people. Ben didn't care one way or the other, but he'd known a lot more black people than his father. Some of the old men at the bar nodded as Ben came in. Maybe they thought it was funny that he kept showing up. The bartender looked nervous to see him. The bartender was tall and thin. Never downright rude, but Ben knew he made him nervous. The bartender was always nervous about everything until the bouncer showed up around eight.

Ben settled into the cushioned stool, half in the shadow. The bartender brought him a glass of bourbon. Maker's Mark in a low, heavy tumbler. The first few times he ordered it the bartender had put it in a brandy glass with a stem, or a shot glass. Ben didn't send the drinks back, but he made sure to ask specifically the next few times for a regular glass. It felt better drinking whiskey out of a glass like this.

He tipped his glass up to the bartender and put a ten on the bar. The bartender would have run a tab for him, but Ben didn't like it. It was easier just to pay as he went. The first, and then another sip of whiskey settled over him and he could feel himself drifting out of everything else and sinking into the place. It was just the right place to be. After a while, and another drink, the music sank into everything. Tied it all together, like a simple machine. Ben tapped his finger lightly on the bar, in time with the beat. Ben liked these times in a bar where everything fit together. Everything made sense, and everything seemed perfectly fine. He drank off another glass and he could feel it was going to be a good night.

After a while one of the old guys whose name he never knew sat next to him. There was some part of a thought, like a suspicion or a memory that wouldn't come clear, that he shouldn't want the old man near him. But the fear was distant now, because everything was fitting together just right. The old man being there was just part of how everything was working, and it was working fine. The fear was distant. Like a storm behind a range of hills. So he let it drift by.

"William Howard Taft!" The man spoke slow and had a head of short gray hair so thin that he looked bald from a few feet away. He was wearing a black, mid-length leather jacket and in his features there was something misshapen, almost deformed, that made him look like he was always squinting half his face against the world. "It's an honor to have you in this establishment, Mr. President. It isn't often a humble company such as our own, presently, has the chance to mingle with royalty."

"Presidents aren't royalty." This wasn't new. For Black Jacket, Ben was always President Taft. Ben didn't know why. It was the same as always, but tonight he'd had more to drink.

"Hell no. Enshrined in the Constitution, Mr. Taft. Inalienable like a motherfucker." Black Jacket sat next to Ben and looked out at the rest of the bar. "These motherfuckers don't even know what it means, Mr. President. Don't even know what inalienable means." He was still for a moment, considering this. "Give them something, and they'll drop it on the ground. Straight up. Nothing at all." With the whiskey in him, Ben liked the company. He was part of something, if he could keep it under control. "Hey, Jimmy!" Black Jacket yelled across the bar to one of the men he'd left behind. "Hey, Jimmy. Come on over. I've secured us an audience with a genuine white head of state."

Jimmy was often called into the President routine. He was heavy-set and always looked impatient, even when he laughed. "Man, why don't you leave that cracker be? Stop talking that President shit and buy us another drink." Black Jacket signaled the bartender for a round, and pushed forward Ben's almost empty glass. The bar had gotten louder. It was dark out now and there were more people and the music got louder with the talking, which was loud and happy. It was a thrill for Ben, like driving too fast in a car. It could all spin out of control. It could all get bad, too loud and out of time. Ben saw the bouncer leaning by the door and everything stuttered awkwardly when he looked too far across the room. This was good, now, because no matter how loud or fast or badly anything moved, it was all moving in time, sounding in time. One perfect unit. None of the pieces out of step.

Black Jacket held up his glass, which was somehow iridescent blue. "To his lordship Mr. Taft. May he preside forever in peace and harmony."

"To who?" asked a short man standing behind Jimmy.

"Taft, man! William Howard! A genu-ine President of the U-nited States."

"Man, fuck that slave-owning motherfucker." The rest of the crowd at the center of the bar was in on it now. Laughing. Cheering it all along, whatever it was.

Black Jacket shook his head. "Dumb bitches, Mr. President. I apologize for these dumb bitches that don't know a slave-holding President from an anti-bellum man like yourself." This injustice seemed to hurt. Ben thought to reassure him, but for now he knew to keep quiet.

"They all might as well've owned slaves," the short man said. "'Cept for Lincoln and Clinton, it was all the same."

"You think Obama got slaves?"

"Slaves by another name, man. That's all it ever is. Probably Clinton, too."

Black Jacket nodded at the awful truth of it. He patted Ben on the back, sharing the disappointment. "Then here's to Mr. Lincoln." Black Jacket held his glass up toward Ben.

"Drunk motherfucker." Jimmy turned back toward the bar and the nervous flow of everything that had been building up around them drifted away again. Black Jacket stared at his drink, deep in thought. Ben felt his pulse starting to slow. It was loud, but everything was easy for a while and Ben listened to song after song, forgetting everything but the music. He bought Black Jacket a drink.

"Goddamn senseless thing to live like that," Black Jacket said with a heavy wet slur. "Goddamn. Tell me, Mr. Taft. How are we supposed to go on with all this? I don't know how a man can live. Without knowledge? And so much anger you can't ever let go. Goddamn." Black Jacket began to sing along, quietly, almost under his voice. "Take happiness with the heartaches, and a dee dum dum wearing a smile." Ben's dad would do the same thing, sometimes. It usually meant that he was happy drunk, not wild or angry. Just quiet, singing drunk. Ben felt comfortable and warm and like there was something here that was his alone.

Another group came in through the door. They were loud. Not louder than everything else, but Ben could hear them over the rest of it. Like one song played on top of another. And with them everything shifted wrong. Everything fell out of step.

They were white, but that wasn't it. There were three of them. Dressed angry. Looking angry. Standing bent against the world, like having something to prove. They were older, but not that old. In their forties, maybe. Ben could see the wear on them. The edge. And with them was a woman.

She came in three steps after them. She was dressed like she belonged with them. A short black skirt and a tight, low-cut blouse. And she looked good. But she didn't fit. She was trying too hard to stay with them, to hold on to them. They didn't care about her. She was a temporary amusement. They could leave her behind without even noticing.

They stood by the wall across from the bar. She stood next to one of them, the tallest. She tried to take his arm. He shook her off and pointed her toward the bar. She leaned in close to the bartender to make the order, one hand on his. He smiled and nodded and served up three beers and a glass of whiskey. She brought the three beers first and each of them took one. She went back for her drink, then stood by the tallest man but didn't try to touch him.

"Friends of yours?" Black Jacket had stopped singing when they came in. "You shoulda stuck with the friends you had." The bouncer had looked like he was sleeping, but now stood alert.

The men by the wall were talking loud. Ben couldn't make out what they were saying. Except "Fuck you," the tallest was saying to one of the others. They were laughing, but it sounded wrong. The woman stood by them. The tallest one pushed one of the others, and he fell back into someone at the bar. Everyone was looking at them, but only the woman saw. She put her hand on the arm of the tallest one and leaned in close to him. He pushed her back, hard, toward the bar. The bouncer was up and standing over them in a second. The bouncer told them to leave, talking to the tallest one in a voice of pure authority. No taunt. The man stood deciding. Ben could see him thinking, weighing his options. Almost ready to step over the edge.

"Fuck it. We're going." The tallest one held up his hand to the bouncer as they finished their drinks. He handed his empty to the bouncer as they walked out. "Keep the bitch, too. Make her work it off if she can't pay."

The woman held a hand over her face, as if she could disappear behind it. The men walked out, still talking loud, and she sat at the bar. Everything looked back to normal. But it was hushed, cooled. Waiting for the next wrong thing. Ben felt sick to his stomach and his heartbeat shook through his breath and his fingers. The woman sat at the bar, fixing her makeup. Putting herself together.

"Don't you worry, Mr. President." Black Jacket stood up from his stool. He walked from man to man at the bar, slapping them on the shoulder, sharing a conspiratorial word. Putting everything back in place. He continued until he got to the woman. He sat down next to her, and put a hand on her shoulder, leaning close to talk to her. He didn't hesitate for a moment; didn't wait to be asked. The woman was grateful. They talked and he smiled when she laughed. Ben didn't understand it. He realized that the pace of everything was wrong, moving too quickly or too slowly. Or something else was wrong that he couldn't decide or discover. Black Jacket stood the woman up. She wasn't steady on her feet, but he held her close to him and she seemed to fold into him like she'd done it a thousand times. He walked her to the back of the bar and sat her on the stool next to Ben. He sat on the next stool down. "Allow me to introduce my exalted colleague, the Honorable President Taft."

"Pleased to meet you, Mr. President," she said, holding out a hand. Her voice was softer, somehow, than Ben had expected. She still had fear, but she was good at hiding it.

"You, too," Ben said. They were both looking at him. "Is everything okay?"

"Looks like it's better now. They're all gone, and there wasn't a fight."

"Nah, girl, they weren't gonna fight." Black Jacket easily put a hand around her shoulder and she leaned against him. Ben saw for the first time that she was older than she had looked from across the bar. The light showed the etching along her face and eyes, like a trick of shadow. "They jus' wanted some free drinks, and to act like fools. What you doin' with them, anyway? Nice girl like yourself should be spendin' time with the upper crust, like Taft here, and his esteemed Cabinet."

"You're probably right." She ran a finger gently down the edge of his cheek and he smiled bashfully. "I guess I just never got the invitation."

"Well now you do, girl. You know right where to find us."

Ben drank off his glass and tried to get the bartender's attention.

"So what's a President doing in a place like this?" She leaned toward Ben, resting her arm on the bar. Close to him. He could feel the heat from her hand like the feeling of a feather on his skin. Almost nothing, but he couldn't keep it from his mind. "Don't they build libraries and mansions and stuff like that for you guys?"

"I wasn't really a President."

She smiled like a record skipping. "I know that, sweetie. I was just kidding along with you guys."

The bartender came with Ben's whiskey. He went into his pocket for his wallet. "Do you want something?"

"I'll have another, sure. Thank you, sweetie."

"Make it three." Ben wanted to drink now, but he waited for the other two.

"So why do you call him Taft?" She turned toward Black Jacket, but moved over on her bar stool closer to Ben. Everything was happening faster than Ben could make sense of it.

"Well you see, baby, you just need to know a little about William Howard Taft. The original." Black Jacket leaned back and got bigger as he spoke. "He was president just after Roosevelt, right? Theodore. He was Teddy's Vice President. And not him or anybody else ever thought he would be President. Didn't even want it, his own self. But Teddy wanted to choose the next guy, and he chose Taft, and weren't nobody gonna tell him no.

"So take my esteemed colleague. No one's ever gonna think he'd be President. Or probably anything else. But along comes a natural born leader of sufficient grace and charm, such as yours truly, and now he's about the whitest president in this whole joint. Whaddaya think about that?" Black Jacket laughed and the woman laughed and clapped and Ben was happy they weren't really talking about him.

Their drinks came. Whiskey for the woman, served neat like Ben's in the same low, heavy glass. Some new concoction for Black Jacket. The woman sat straight ahead on her stool, but still just as close to Ben. "To you, Mr. President." She held her glass up over her head but lost her balance, slipping off the stool. She caught herself on one leg, and the rest of her weight fell against Ben. He put a hand out to steady her and it rested on her hip. She turned and looked at him, making a show of smiling as she pushed herself closer. He let her go and turned away. She slid back onto her stool, but was still sitting too close. "So what does he do if he isn't a President?"

"Hell if I know. He don't talk much."

She turned back toward him. "So what's the story? You just a senator, or what?"

"Mechanic. I'm a mechanic." He took a long drink. She was still looking at him, as if there was more to say. "That's all. I know it's nothing special."

"Oh, sweetie, I'm not making fun of you." She smiled again, but this time it was real somehow. Her first real smile that he'd seen, and he felt it inside of himself. He took another drink. "There's nothing wrong with being a mechanic. That's what my dad was."

Ben nodded.

Black Jacket stood up behind her. "I gotta go over and see this fool. Y'all be good, now."

"Thank you, sweetie," she said, without turning around. She wouldn't stop looking at Ben.

"So, what do you do?" It was the only thing Ben could think to say. He could feel her eyes on him. He took another drink.

"I'm a hairdresser. I work at one of those chain stores. Over on Dupont. I have to work in a place like that because none of the black girls trust me with their hair. I can do all that stuff they do, but none of them trust me. So I give buzz cuts to interns and students."

"How did you get over here?"

"Well, I live over in Shaw, which is pretty close I think, and those assholes brought me here. This place was closer to the Metro." She was playing with a ring on her finger. Taking it off, putting it on. Twisting it over and again. Ben could feel a new drunk settling in. Not a good feeling. Just heavy and raw. It was bad. That was a fact, and he knew it somewhere in the back of his mind. But he didn't care. Tomorrow got further and further away. "I should never have been hanging out with those assholes." She reached out and put a hand on his arm and looked at him, now again with a kind of manufactured sincerity. "They're not my friends or nothin'. They're not like the guys I go around with. I was just at this bar after work and I saw them and they talked to me and I started tagging along. It was fucking probably stupid. But I thought maybe it would be fun." She toyed with her ring in silence for a while longer. "They were fun at first." She looked at him nervously. He stared ahead at the bar, trying not to look back at her. "So what about you? You come here all the time?"

"Sometimes."

"You celebratin'?"

"No, just here. Sometimes I go out after work." He tried to think of something more to say. He was supposed to say more. But he couldn't think of anything, and the weight of saying nothing got heavier and heavier until it was like a panic. And he could barely speak at all.

"I'm kinda celebratin'. Nothing in particular. Just taking the night off. Celebratin' for the sake of celebratin'. Normally I can't go out 'cause of my daughter."

"Why aren't you with her?" It didn't sound like he thought it would. She folded her arms and he could feel her go stiff where she was still leaning against him.

"She's up with my parents. Up in Maryland. She's up there for a couple days before school starts. So this is like my night off."

"Are you having fun?" He tried to look at her, but he couldn't. He bent his face toward her, but kept his eyes down on the bar. Nothing made any sense. Everything was happening automatically, and everything was impossible to decide. He looked down at the shape of her legs, crossed one over the other. He looked at the bell of her hips.

"I guess. It depends."

"Depends on what?"

She ran her fingers over his cheek the way she had for Black Jacket. But slower. He wanted to turn away, and he wanted to pull her closer. He wanted to kiss her, and he could taste bile in his mouth. He pressed his eyes closed and he could see the length of her body there for him, open to him. Not afraid. Uncomplaining. A pool of blood slowly gathering. He opened his eyes and she smiled a real smile.

"You want another drink, Mr. President?"

Ben signaled for the bartender, who brought two more glasses of whiskey.

"You from around here?"

"No. New York. Not the city. A little town up past Binghamton."

"Country boy, huh? No wonder you're so quiet. Did you like it?"

"I guess. As much as I had to."

She smiled again and put both hands on his arm. "I don't even know what that means." She laughed and leaned back on her stool. If he'd let his arm go she would have fallen back on the floor. Like a pendulum she swung back toward him, resting her head against his shoulder.

"You don't know me," he said. It was the first thing that had felt right to say since he'd met her. He knew it was a true thing to say.

"I know you a little. We've been talking."

"You don't know me at all."

"I can get to know you."

He started to say that she didn't want to. That she wouldn't want to know him. But it all sounded stupid, even in his head. It all sounded like a bad movie. He wanted to warn her. She didn't seem bad. He wanted to warn her but there was nothing to say but things he could never, never say. He felt sick, and exhausted, and had nothing left to say or do.

"Do you want to go?" she asked.

He nodded. He didn't want that any more, or any less. He drank off the rest of his whiskey in a swallow, and hers was already gone. He stood, and almost fell getting off the bar stool. She fell backwards, into him. Standing there, he could feel the curve of her against him, and he could see it all played out. She laughed like nothing mattered. He steadied her to stand on her own. She took his hand, and he almost pulled her through the bar. Black Jacket was trying to catch his eye, but he wouldn't look at him.

Out in the night it was cool. It was past midnight. The whiskey was like waves in his head, but there was something clear about the night. The cold of the night made an island in his mind. Something that made sense, and would make sense tomorrow and the next day. He liked it out in the night.

"Sweetie, wait. You're walking pretty fast. I'm just in heels." He stopped and she held up a foot to pull off her shoe and put it back on. She stood next to him, holding herself up on his shoulder just as if she always had. A wave took him over and he looked at her. Really looked at her. There was something girlish about her, despite her age. She was thin. He thought she was dressed like a whore, but that it wasn't how she had to look. He thought maybe she could look different. Her chest was small, and her face was small and fragile. She saw him looking at her and he turned away.

"It's okay," she said. "It's okay to look if you like what you see." She leaned toward him, closing her eyes. He pulled away.

"We shouldn't just be standing here." He pulled her to keep walking, but he made himself walk slower. They walked down the wide street, and sometimes he would see figures in the shadows. He thought maybe they were real, but he wasn't sure. He wanted someone to come. To threaten them. To challenge them. He wanted to kill someone, or die. But the streets were almost empty here, and the figures in the shadows didn't even look at him.

"This way, sweetie." She pulled his arm to the right at an intersection, off onto one of the smaller side streets. They walked in silence, and the neighborhood changed around them. He walked through here sometimes. It was better here. There were new stores, and a restaurant moving in not too far away. Mostly when he walked through here on the weekend it was college kids, or maybe they were professionals. They all looked the same on the weekends. But they were all white. It must be turning into a better neighborhood. He didn't speak to her as they walked, but it didn't feel wrong. It didn't feel like he had to talk. He could feel her hand in his, and it didn't feel bad.

They walked a few more blocks until she pulled on his hand. "This is it, sweetie." They were standing at the foot of the stairs. As they stood there, she looked like a little girl. She smiled now. Sweetly. It was a real smile. Everything about her was real, and she held his hand in both of hers, squeezing it nervously. "Don't you want to ask me my name?"

"What's your name?"

"Maria. What's yours?"

"Ben."

"It's nice to meet you, Ben." She squeezed his hand tighter. She held it up to her lips and kissed it. He tried to understand, but he was exhausted. He thought he could have slept in the street if she'd just let him lie there.

"'Everyone needs a ruff over their heads.'" Ben read it from a poster in the window of the first floor of her building. A cartoon dog licking the face of a ridiculously smiling child.

"My daughter put that up. Sophia, when she was just a little kid. Her way of telling me she wanted a dog. She never even got the dog, but we never took the poster down either."

Ben nodded. He didn't know what else to do or say, and he thought that now he should probably go.

"Don't you want to kiss me, Ben?" She closed her eyes again and leaned toward him, her mouth half open. She looked stupid standing there like that and he almost laughed, but instead he kissed her. He kissed her hard. Driven by an instinct. He put his arms around her and held her close to him. He felt strong. He could feel the strength in his arms and in his chest. He could feel her against him. He ran his hand down her back, hard. He held her at the bottom of her skirt and he could feel the curve of her flesh and the heat and the need of her. His other hand was on her neck and he kissed her harder. He wanted her entirely. Holding her hard, her flesh seemed to him the way it would seem to an animal. Like meat. Like live flesh and blood that he could tear, and consume and that would sustain him until it was gone.

He pushed her away. Her lipstick was gone, and she looked simple and girlish in the street with her skirt pulled halfway up.

"I can't," he said. He walked away from her without looking back.

‡

The boy could see the differences in the kids who lived far out of town. The ones who lived on farms in the country, or just out in the middle of nowhere. Everyone could. It was easy to tell with most of them. Easy to see in their eyes. On their skin that was darker with dirt. Sometimes when the boy's father would take him out for a drive they would see all the houses in the country. The farms. The old houses with rotting cars lined up in the front yard, one against the other. At night, the light hung over the front door. It made the boy feel lonely in all of the darkness. The yellow glow from the kitchen. The boy could see how it would make anyone different. The boy could see how it made them wild, like they were.

Satch was the worst one. Satch wasn't his real name, but it was the only thing anyone ever called him. He wore clothes that were dirty from work on the farm. He smelled like a farm, and kids told stories about what went on in his family. About how his dad hit them. Satch and all of his younger brothers. Hit them or maybe worse. They told about how they were part of some religious cult. They didn't go to church, but the father was like a preacher for all of them. Satch had long dirty-blond hair and the boy thought it was probably greasy to the touch.

Sometimes when the lunch room was full there would only be seats left at the end of the table close to Satch. The boy would sit near Satch if he had to, but he wouldn't look at him or talk to him. The boy didn't want anyone to think he was sitting with Satch, but he couldn't sit too close to anyone else and have them make fun of him. So he would sit and look down at his food and try not to look at anyone.

Satch didn't notice the boy when he sat down. Satch didn't seem to notice anything the way most people did. He always seemed half-confused, or hypnotized, like the boy had seen once on TV. Satch always brought food from home, and he would look down at the crumpled paper bag and the boy couldn't tell what he saw or didn't.

Satch would have different food than everybody else. Never sandwiches or fruit or chips in a bag. He would have cold meat wrapped in tin foil. Sometimes still on the bone. Or cooked vegetables that looked gray and wilted. Green beans that smelled so bad the boy would have to bury his nose in his sleeve.

Sometimes Satch would talk. Not to the boy, directly. Not to anyone, and the boy didn't know if he was supposed to hear it or not, or if Satch even knew he was there. His voice was slack. Numb. The words spilled out unformed and uncertain like drool from the side of his mouth.

Sometimes Satch would swear. These words came out sharper, and the boy could hear the words clearly. He could almost feel them. His father said words like that, and sometimes the boy would say them in his mind or late at night and with the lights out and under the covers in bed. But Satch said them out loud, in school. The boy would hide his face under his hands and try not to look like he was laughing.

Satch bent low over his food, the way a dog ate. "Thisfucking shit." He would get a fork from the cafeteria, walking the wrong way into the lunch line after he'd already sat down, but he would never use a tray. The table would look greasy and wet from where he'd sat. "Howmysposta eathisfuckingshit?"

The boy covered his mouth with his hand and tried not to look like he was laughing. Satch saw him and he smiled. He kept talking and swearing. And the boy would laugh harder and harder.

CHAPTER TWO

"Know what your problem is, Cornpone?" Roger stood over Ben, as he had all morning. Ben could smell and feel his breath as he talked. "If you want to know. You got that pent-up rage. Or pent-up something." Ben was under a car on the lift. Roger leaned on it with his elbow over his head, a clipboard in one hand. "Or maybe it's just some kinda white dude thing. Protestant work ethic or some shit. I mean, mosta these dudes, the only way they show up to work lookin' like you're lookin' right now is if it's payday, and even then they won't hardly work." Ben felt like hell, and he knew he looked it. "You, you're lookin' half dead from Monday night, and you're working a sweat all Tuesday morning." Roger idly watched the others in the crew as he spoke. Ben didn't mind. He would rather have been alone, but Roger's voice kept him from thinking.

"Don't get me wrong, Cornpone. I appreciate someone workin' around here. I don't mean to sound ungrateful. Better a crazy-ass white dude than three of these fuckin' Mexicans. But I'm tellin' you man, it points to some inner demons. You come in like this. All raggedy lookin', and working harder than I've ever seen anyone work. It points to some deep-seated dissatisfactions. If you want my advice, you gotta love yourself some, brother."

"How should I do that?"

"Shit. How should I know? Go buy yourself a new possum rifle. Something." Roger laughed, taking up and sipping the coffee that he'd rested on the front bumper of the car. "Sleep in when you're so hungover you're still drunk. Start there."

Ben had woken up sick, and had gotten worse when he tried to do push-ups. He couldn't finish, and he couldn't eat. He couldn't do anything at home. Even sit in his chair. He'd tried to go back to sleep, but he felt electricity running through him every time he closed his eyes. The sick, welling fear of the person he'd become the night before. It upset him, because he'd liked that place.

Ben liked being a mechanic in this neighborhood. Most of the guys who came in had old cars. The kind most people would throw away, but also the kind you could really fix. None of the other guys wanted to be bothered. The newer cars were easier, mostly. You plugged them into a computer and that was that. This was a car you could fix, and you'd never have to throw away. He was working on an old Malibu. The model from 1965. It looked almost like a sports car, but blunted. This one was brown, but the paint was bleaching out. It was a good car. This was the same model—almost the same year—that he'd worked on with his father. One of the first cars he'd ever worked on. Some of the best times he'd ever had with his father. Easy times, almost as good as hunting. Even if his father got mad. If he scraped a knuckle or got his finger caught, or if nothing worked the way he wanted it to. Then he would yell, or hit the car with a tool, or worse. But it wasn't as bad as when he was really angry. It didn't run that deep. Once, he'd knocked the car off a stand of cinder blocks he'd used to prop it up while Ben was still half underneath it. But Ben wasn't hurt, and it wasn't that big a deal.

His father would have known what to do with that girl. Maria. His father would have known exactly what to do with her. Right from the start. Ben had never been any good with girls, but his father always was. It would make his mother angry, his dad had been so good. But everything made her angry, anyway. If his father drank around town, she'd be angry when she heard about it. If he drank farther away, she'd be angry because she said he was sneaking around. There was always something. But his dad had traveled for work sometimes, driving a truck, and there was nothing he could do about it.

Ben hadn't seen his father much before he died. He died before Ben got out. His dad would make visits for a few years. Not at first, but after a few years. And then he stopped visiting and would call, but Ben knew he was sick. Then he stopped calling after he got too sick, and after that he died. Ben thought it would have been nice to see him after he got out. But maybe not. Maybe it was better. His father wasn't perfect.

In his worst times, Ben's father would come to him, even when he was very young. He couldn't talk to Ben's mother, so he'd talk to Ben. Now that he was older, he could see how afraid his father had been. Afraid he'd become a failure. Afraid he hadn't made it. Afraid he'd never make it.

His father had talked about that all the time. About how he could make it, or if he ever would. He'd heard his father talk that way for so long, since he was so young, that he barely stopped to think what it meant. Maybe his father didn't know either. Maybe it was just an idea that could never have been real. Maybe it was too much to ask of himself. Too much to ask of life. Or maybe it was just how he talked when he got drunk.

Ben didn't think of any of that for himself. He didn't have to wonder if he'd made it, or if he ever would. It wasn't real for him to think that way. This was as good as it would get. It was as good as it had to be. It wasn't very good, but Ben knew how much worse it could be. This was fine. All he worried about was how not to lose what he had.

It might have been different. If he'd turned out differently, or if he hadn't done what he'd done. But it was stupid to think like that. It was stupid to wonder how anything could ever be different from what it already was. It was better just to know that he'd already made the worst mistakes. Now he didn't need to worry about what could be better. It was simpler like this.

Maybe he should have felt bad, the way his father did. Maybe he should regret it all. But that was too long ago. It might as well have been someone else. Everything went wrong when he was a different person. But that person was gone. Now there was only Ben, living the rest of it until he died. It wasn't failure. It's just how things were.

"What's up, Cornpone? You meditatin'?"

"Just working on this car." He felt like he'd been asleep, but he knew he hadn't stopped working.

"Well, me and the fellas are going across the street for carry-out. You comin'?"

The thought of food made Ben feel sick, but he knew he had to eat. "Yeah."

‡

The boy had gym class every Monday, Wednesday and Friday. The boy knew it, and knew it was always the same. But he wouldn't always remember. In seventh grade there were more things to remember, and thinking about it made everything feel endless and dangerous. When he was home everything about school seemed far away, and when he was getting ready in the morning he would be tired and wouldn't think about what day it was. There were things he knew he had to remember to bring for every class, and he would try and try to remember. When he forgot something he needed, when he would have to sit in class and be the only one without a book, the feeling of it would burn in him and he thought he would never, never forget. But at night and in the morning while he was getting ready it all disappeared. The thought of it was gone, like it had never been there.

When the boy forgot his gym clothes he would have to play in his regular clothes. Everyone looked at him and he could feel them and see them and he didn't know why he forgot but he usually did. He would ask to sit out but the coach wouldn't let him. Sometimes he would even have to play in his boots.

At the beginning of the school year, while the weather was good and they could still go outside, they would play soccer, again and again. They would pick team captains from the best players, and they would try to act just like the coach while they picked one kid after another, and the boy was always one of the last ones they would pick. The boy didn't want to be picked. The boy didn't want to play, but he had to, and someone had to pick him.

He would always be the goalie. After they picked, all the other kids on his team would walk away and leave him standing closest to the goal, and then he would have to be the goalie.

When the ball was on the other side of the field, he could almost like it. It was nice to be outside, and from the field you could see houses that people lived in, and people doing whatever they wanted to do. Free to walk around and do whatever they wanted in the middle of the day. He would imagine what it would be like to walk up and down the main street on nice days, or stay inside if it was cold. To watch television, or go to the Double D for a hamburger for lunch whenever he wanted. He watched a fat woman come out of her house with her dog and walk away from town toward where the road got thin and rough and it was mostly woods on either side. She would walk up a hill into the woods with the dog, or along the side of the road. She could walk on a path up deep into the woods and hear nothing but the sound of the wind in the thick pine, and walk as far as she wanted. She could do whatever she wanted, and it made the boy imagine something that was almost like magic.

Once he had taken a bus ride in the middle of the day to another town to go to a different kind of school for part of the day. It was only him and a few other kids on a small bus, and he got to sit alone and look out the window while the other kids talked and talked and laughed. But they left him alone and he watched as the bus drove through one town after another, and there were always people out on the streets. Walking down the sidewalk.

The boy would make up stories about the people he saw. One after the other. The old woman pulling a grocery cart who'd cashed her check to buy food for her son. The man in the suit who would stare people right in the eye when they tried to rip him off and who would always be smarter than them and never back down. The boy would imagine himself, walking down the street. He would make a story for himself, and it could be any story he wanted.

After the ball went past him into the goal, the boy thought he remembered yelling, and the sound of running toward him. But it hadn't meant anything at all. Not until the ball was in and everyone looked at him like he'd ruined everything. They called him names and one of the boys pushed him hard and he fell down inside the goal. On his hands and knees he could feel the softness of the grass. He could feel the moist earth. It had rained a few nights ago. It was cool and rich and he could feel the earth under his hands like a living thing. Digging his fingers into the grass as they walked away toward the middle of the field to start the game again, it felt like the flesh of the earth. Like holding together one great, long living thing. Digging his fingers into the feel of it as the other kids gathered at the middle of the field in a blurred mass, he imagined pulling away the grass and the earth. He imagined what there would be if he could pull away the skin of the earth.

There was no reason for him to be in the locker room after class. There were grass stains on his jeans from where he had fallen. He didn't have any clothes to change into, and if his mother noticed the stains she would be angry, but maybe she wouldn't notice. The boy didn't want to talk to anyone. He stood in the far corner of the locker room away from everyone. He opened the door to one of the long lockers that was taller than him, and he stood behind the open door and he thought maybe they just wouldn't bother with him.

They joked and laughed and pushed each other and he didn't look at them but it was like they were all one thing. Laughing and happy and always thinking the same and acting the same and being the same and all of them doing and saying the right thing. All of them right and all of them okay and all of them happy. They didn't mind being naked. They didn't mind taking their shirts off and being in the shower. They would laugh. They would yell and push each other but it didn't matter, because they were all okay. They were all the same, and they were all okay. Not different bodies. Not different flesh. Not different. But all one. One creature with only one thought. One long and convulsing form. One animal, like a monster.

He stood behind the door of the locker and he remembered what it felt like to imagine being free. Being away from this. Being free in the day to walk a dog, or go to the store, or not go anywhere or see anyone. The thought of it was in him like a faint and fading warmth, and he tried to hold it without killing it. Without snuffing it out entirely.

He could feel them standing there. Three of them. Four. Five. It didn't matter. One of them meant all of them, eventually.

The closest one pushed the locker shut and the boy felt naked and wanted to be away. To be covered and hidden. "Nice job out there, goalie." It was the closest one. Shirtless, with the others gathered around him. Eyes on him and twisted mouths and arms and bodies. *"Yeah, retard. What's your problem?"* Another mouth. Another voice, but all the same. A hand reached out from the confused mass of them and it pushed the boy back against the wall. He might have fallen but he was huddled too far into the corner and he fell against the wall. He could feel the pocked concrete under years of heavy coats of paint.

He stood up, but the monster was all around him, now. He held his arms up to block punches to his face but other arms emerged to strike his torso and his stomach. There were too many arms. Too many sneering, laughing faces. It was too much. Too big.

He swept his arms from side to side. Quickly, frantically. Trying to push away the countless hands that punished him, hit him, grabbed him, pulled him. He swung his arms like swatting at a swarm of flies and he ducked his head and nothing was in control anymore. Nothing was his to decide, and his arms swung wildly back and forth and he sunk against the wall and slid down against it, crouching lower and lower into the corner. He could hear screaming. The monster screaming. Howling its anger and its hatred. Screaming because this time it would never stop. This time it would tear him apart.

The bell rang and suddenly it felt quiet. He opened his eyes. The other boys had backed away, but he was still flailing his arms. Still screaming. Like his arms and his lungs and his mouth had been taken. Like they belonged to someone else. He tried to stop. To bring his arms to his sides, to stop screaming. He was breathing hard. The sound of it in his throat was a desperate, heavy moan. He couldn't stop the sound of it in his throat. He wrapped his arms tight around himself as if to keep everything about him from falling to pieces on the ground. He saw the other boys drifting apart. But they kept their eyes on him, like animals watching a coiled threat.

The boy saw their hatred. Their disgust. It was pure, and it was clear, and it was honest. But there was something else. Something on their faces, or behind their eyes, or in the receding sinews and tethers of the one monster that had broken apart and now faded away. There was something else that drove them away. The boy couldn't understand that it was fear.

‡

His father had told Ben that there was something wrong with every woman. That it couldn't be helped, and that there was no use going on and on looking for the perfect one, because there was something wrong with every one of them. All you could do was decide if what was wrong with the one you had was something you could live with.

His father had told him after he'd come in late one night. His mother had woken Ben with her yelling. His father had yelled back, and it got worse and worse, until finally it all broke loose. Both of them yelling like they were singing together, and then the breaking sound of his fists that sounded louder when he remembered them. Sometimes his mother would cry out, but usually by then she was quiet. And then everything was quiet. Then it was over. It never lasted long. But Ben had been scared after it was over. Ben was too young, and hadn't understood that it was over and that there was nothing else to be afraid of. Ben's father came into his room and was very gentle with him. Ben could smell the whiskey on his breath, but it didn't bother him. His father spoke softly and smoothed his hair, asking him what was wrong. Ben couldn't talk, so his father did. Softly. Gently. He said that they'd had an argument, but that it was over, and that everything was fine now. And he talked like that, softly, for a few minutes.

Once Ben had calmed down, his father joked with him and laughed with him. That was when his father had told him about women, and how it just couldn't be helped. Ben had asked why his father put up with it; why they couldn't just leave? His father told him there were worse things. There were always worse things. And not everything was bad, so there was no sense in leaving.

Ben wondered what was wrong with Maria. But he would never have to find out.

Ben hadn't been back to the bar since that night. He hadn't drunk at all for a couple nights. Then he stayed in and opened a bottle of Maker's that he'd found at one of the Cut-Rate stores that were mostly just cheap booze that he couldn't stomach. But he didn't drink too much. Just two drinks, or three while he read.

His mother hadn't been all bad. Ben's father was right. She was loud and hysterical sometimes, but not all the time. Sometimes she and Ben would have very good times, the two of them together. If his father was away on a long haul, or just away. Ben knew sometimes she was afraid, and so was he. They would play cards together, or watch television, or she would read to him. Anything to keep noise in the house. They both felt safer with noise in the house when his father wasn't there.

Sometimes his mother would talk about moving. About all three of them moving together and going to the city. She never said which city. Just the city. She'd never lived anywhere but the town they lived in. His father had moved around, here and there, but his mother never had. Now that he was older and he knew more, Ben wondered if she would have been able to survive in the city, and he thought probably not. She'd never had to be strong like his father. But then he thought maybe anyone could adapt to anything if he had to, and find a way to keep going.

There wasn't anything in the town where Ben had grown up. It was nice to think about how quiet it was sometimes, but there wasn't anything there. There was an old wood mill in the part of town behind the school, and there was a gas station. He used to think just walking to the gas station was something to do, even though the town wasn't anywhere near the highway and you only saw the same people there as anywhere else. You might see one of the guys who lived in the backwoods coming in to fill up his truck and a few old gas cans so he wouldn't need to come back. That was something. And there were a couple bars. One of the bars—the Double D, with a sign like a branding iron—was the only restaurant in town, with booths on two sides of a small room off to the side. Sometimes his mother might take him there, if she knew his father was out of town and if she felt like giving Ben a treat. His father would never want to go out if he was home. He had to eat out most of the time, he said. When he was home he wanted to eat at home, like a family.

Maybe Ben's mother would have been happier in the city. Maybe she would have been happier here. There were things to do, and she could have met more people. Ben's father always said she needed to have more friends for when he wasn't around. And she could walk around like Ben did, and look at the monuments. And there was probably other stuff she would have liked that Ben hadn't even thought of. Maria would probably know what kinds of things there were, but probably they were different now than they had been back then.

She'd died before he got out. His father had told him one day. Not even when he was on a visit. But it wasn't worth thinking about. It was her fault. Her weakness, and there was nothing anyone could have done to stop her. It was everything that was wrong with her, and there was only her to blame.

‡

Between classes the school hallway was loud and confused. The boy felt lost in it. The boy thought the other kids were all bigger than him, and they were loud and he couldn't tell where one of them ended and another began. He hated the way they yelled and pushed. He hated the way they laughed. It sounded angry, like the start of something bad.

This was his first year in this building, and he didn't like it. It was his first year with a locker and having to change rooms between classes. He didn't like it, and he didn't like the way everyone was loud and there were too many people, and everyone pushed everyone but no one seemed to care. All of them together.

When he stood at his locker he still wasn't alone. They would push him walking past, and there was never enough room. It was always too loud. But standing at his locker was when he always saw the girl.

Her last name was next to his in alphabetical order. Her hair was tight black curls. She would wear skirts above her knees or jeans that were exactly the shape of her. Her face was small and her mouth and her nose and her eyes were small and fragile, like something he had to be careful not to break. She wore thick-framed black glasses and she would say she didn't like them. But he did. When she was alone she was quiet and kind. But she was popular and she acted like all of them did when they were together in a group. And when they were together they weren't different people anymore. And when they walked together they would laugh and talk too loudly and they would push back and forth. When she was with them she was gone. Swallowed up. But when it was just her, alone, it was different. He would watch her and she would smile. He would think of things that he could say to her and he would imagine that if he said them she would smile and laugh. And she would hold his hand. When she was alone and he looked at her being alone and quiet he could imagine that all of it was real. That was who she really was, but he was the only one who knew.

She had friends that would come to her locker. They would stand together and he would stand behind the open door of his locker and look at her so that he knew she couldn't see him. Her locker was neat on the inside, and she had pictures of herself and her friends and of actors from magazines taped to the door. Everything in his locker was in a pile at the bottom. Books. Old papers. He would stack whatever he was leaving on top of what was already there and take what he needed from underneath. But her locker was neat and she'd even had her parents bring shelves that she could use to keep everything in order. She was always small and quiet while she was standing at her locker, looking at her books or her pictures and waiting for her other friends. When she was with them her face looked big and loud, but while she was waiting her mouth and her eyes and her face were small, and that was when he loved her.

He could imagine if something horrible happened, or if there was an emergency and he could save her. If there was a man with a gun or a knife, and the man would take her hostage and hold his arm tight around her neck so she couldn't breathe. Like in the movies or on shows. Then the boy could sneak up behind him and ambush him and save her. Or if the building was burning and she was trapped. If there was smoke and fire and she was almost burned to death, he would be the one who was brave enough and strong enough to save her. Or if something was falling over, like the bleachers in school when they were standing up on their side the way they would when the janitors had to clean the gym floor. If they were falling over and she was there and couldn't get out of the way, he would be strong enough, and he would stand over her and catch them and hold them while she got away. She would see who he really was. Everyone would see who he really was.

When it was close to the time that the bell would ring again, all of her friends would show up and she would stop being small

and quiet and beautiful and she would become a part of the group.
A part of the monster that would consume her and change her and
make her laugh and talk and it would make the boy afraid. They
were mostly boys, and they were mostly older, and they gathered
around her but they didn't know who she was because she wasn't
really her when they were there. He knew they would destroy her, all
of them together. She wouldn't be there at all. But there was nothing
he could do to save her.

‡

For weeks Ben would try to remember the night with Maria.
The series of events. At first he could almost remember them. It
came back to him like an old-time movie. A silent movie. Everything moving too quickly. Words out of joint with the pictures.
Things happening for reasons he couldn't understand. But then
there would be her face. Her smile or her body. And he wouldn't
need to try to understand.

The more he thought about that night the harder it was to
remember. The memory crumbled in his hands like old paper. It
fell to pieces. Fragments that had no order and made no sense at
all. Shards that would mix with pieces of his imagination and he
couldn't tell them apart, or he didn't want to try. She had her hand
on his shoulder, standing on the sidewalk. She leaned into Black
Jacket in the bar. He pushed her skirt up over her hips and pushed
her back against the wall. She drank a drink like his and said she
wanted to leave. He cupped a hand over her naked breast. He was
there in front of her apartment, but didn't leave.

He knew the difference between what happened and what
didn't. He wasn't crazy. He could remember the memory of that
real night, and how it really happened. But that was just history, like

reading it in a book. It was right, he knew. It was fact. But the facts didn't feel like anything.

Ben was standing looking up at a warped rotor but doing nothing. Just thinking. He didn't know for how long. He wished he could take it out of his head. All of it, and be free to work. He went to lower the lift, but he almost tripped over a young boy. The boy was looking up at him and he was dressed nicely in new clothes and he shouldn't have been real. But it was real, and it was happening.

"What are you doing?" the boy asked. He looked like he was eight. Or maybe nine. Ben looked around. There were no parents around. Probably outside. Some mother, outside on her cell phone. Ignoring her kid. And now it was his problem.

"I'm fixing this car."

"I know. But what?"

"What?" Ben took the controller for the lift off the wall to get the car to just the right height.

"What are you doing on the car?"

"The brakes. I'm taking them off and then putting new ones back on."

"You're replacing them?"

"Yeah. Stand out from under the car. Over there." The kid moved back a few feet. Ben looked around but there was no one else near him. Maybe they were at lunch. He wanted Roger to come by. "You need to get farther away."

The kid didn't move.

Ben lowered the car and picked up a power wrench off the table along the wall. The kid had moved up close while his back was turned.

"You need to move farther back." Ben tried to sound authoritative, like he remembered a teacher sounding, but the kid didn't listen. Roger walked by, maybe back from lunch, but he didn't notice the kid and he didn't help get him away.

"Our other mechanic has a tool like that, but it's bigger. It's on a cord that hangs from the ceiling." Most of the power tools in the shop were cheap, and Ben knew it. But it made him feel stupid to hear the boy say it.

"You just need to stand back." Ben held the boy gently by his shoulders and moved him back.

"No!" The kid squirmed out of Ben's hands and stood where he had been before. His voice sounded like Ben had hurt him. Ben wanted him just to leave, but he was probably back far enough anyway.

Ben loosened the bolts around the rotor. When they were stuck he would hit them with a wrench to knock loose the rust. He put the nuts in his right hand pocket, with the nuts from the wheel in his left, and put the rotor off to the side. The kid had wandered off, and it was just as well. Ben cleaned off the assembly around where he'd removed the rotor and checked that everything else aside from the brakes and the rotors was in good shape. He could finish this today because these brakes and rotors would be in the stock on hand.

He walked over to get the parts and he could see the kid on the other side of the shop, standing under a lift with the controller in his hand. He was moving it up and down. There was no one else around. Ben didn't know why there was no one else around but he wasn't thinking about that anymore.

The kid went to put the controller back in its cradle when he saw Ben coming. Like Ben hadn't seen him playing with it, or there would be nothing he could do. Ben took the boy by his shoulders, hard, and shook him. "What the fuck do you think you're doing?" Ben held him tight by his shoulders, up off the ground. Ben felt like he could snap him. Crush him, and he thought maybe he should. Ben saw fear of him in the boy's eyes and he imagined the boy crushed under the lift. He could imagine the boy screaming, and he could imagine everyone coming to blame him. Everyone gathering around him and pointing at him and looking and never letting him go. Saying it was his fault, and making everything worse. And all the boy could do was be afraid of him. Ben thought of Maria and he saw the boy in his hands that he could crush if he wanted to and he hated them both.

Roger took Ben by the collar and pulled him away from the kid. "What the fuck?"

"He was under the lift, playing with it. I told him not to. I told him to get away. He could have died." Ben pushed Roger off him and walked away, back to work on the car.

"It's all right, son. It's okay." Ben heard Roger talking to the boy. Talking just right. Calming him, making him safe. Another language. Another way that he could be. "Is your mom around here, or your dad?" As they walked out toward the lot Roger took a baseball cap with a logo out of a box on the shelf. "Whattaya think if we set you up with a racing cap and get you back to your folks? You and your pop watch NASCAR?" It was easy for Roger. He knew what he was supposed to do.

He should have done it sooner.

‡

Ben's dad took him hunting, when he got old enough. Just for a year or two, after he turned twelve. Ben liked the feel of the rifle in his hands. It fit very well. It was the right size for him. The right tool.

They would go out in the fall. During Thanksgiving week. They'd go out early, just before the sun rose. They'd already be out and in place when the light came up. When the black gave way to the gray and to the mist. When the gray of everything became the gray of bare trees and the brown of the wild grass and the cut stalks of the corn-field. The green of the pine trees and the sinking brown of the dirt and the mud. In the dark every noise would be a shock. Every noise would seem as loud as anything could be. The gray morning light dampened the sound of the woods and the field. They would crouch in a natural ditch by the field that carried runoff in the spring. Ben would feel it through his jeans, but his coat was warm, and his father had long hunter's pants that matched the brown wood camouflage of his jacket and kept out the wet.

Ben and his father would sit still through the dawn. It would take the deer a while to be up and around. They would wander in the half light at night, but not in the morning, while it was still cold. They would wait for the sun. But Ben and his father had to be there before they were up, so they wouldn't scare them away. So their scent would drift off from where they walked, and they wouldn't make any noises while the deer were up and walking. Ben's father said the deer would come to the cornfield out of habit and because there were still leaves and scrap to eat.

The first year they went, Ben's father hadn't let him shoot. Ben didn't mind, and he was glad that his father killed a deer and that Ben hadn't let him down and that he was there to see his father so happy. But the next year his father said he could shoot. Ben would get the first shot either of them would take, and his father would be ready with a second shot in case he missed, even though it would probably be too late. Ben's father had taken him shooting at targets and he had gotten pretty good. But live animals were different from targets, and there was only one way to learn.

The breeze blew lightly off the field, and took their scent away with it. The sun was up and the mist was burning away quickly. Ben was already set up with his gun facing out on the field. He could shift to take aim anywhere across the field. He wouldn't make any noise.

His father didn't say anything, and Ben knew it was the right way to prepare. The mist was almost gone when they saw the first deer coming out of the woods on the far side of the field. Directly upwind. Ben took aim where they were, but he knew to wait. They would come closer, and he would see them all, and he would see which one was the best one and he would get the best shot he could. The third deer out of the woods was a twelve-point buck. That was good. It was the best one in the herd.

Ben let them walk out to the middle of the field. It scared him every time one would jerk its head, or step too quickly. He was scared they had smelled him, or that they might get spooked for no reason. He was scared he would miss his shot and that everything would be ruined. He was scared it would run, and once one of them ran they'd all run together. But the deer always put its head back down and ate. Or walked a few steps closer. Three more steps and stop. Two. Stop. Four. Stop. They were in the middle of the field before the first one of the herd started to turn. She wasn't running, just walking slowly in a different direction. It meant they would start to walk away from him, and once the buck turned he would have a better shot. There would be ten seconds— maybe twenty—that would be the best chance he'd have. After that it would slowly get harder and harder, or disappear in an instant.

The buck turned and took two steps, then stopped to pick at a half-eaten cob on the ground. Ben breathed the sharp air into his lungs until it hurt, until he thought he would choke and every muscle felt wrong and out of place. He breathed out slowly, and all the being scared went with it. And all the hurt, and the chill and the damp around his knees, and the numbness where his leg had fallen asleep, and the tremor in his hands and his finger and he watched through the scope and without even realizing he pulled the trigger.

The gun snapped back. Not hard, but he lost the deer in the scope. He put the gun down and looked and all the deer were running. He hadn't heard the shot, but he heard the echo now, and the buck he'd shot at was standing there. The buck took a step, then lost his front legs. Then it collapsed all at once. Everything was quiet. Everything was still. The deer had run off and the breeze had stopped. Nothing grew in the cold. Ben didn't even breathe. Ben thought that if he could keep from breathing, that everything would stay exactly like this, forever.

Ben's dad broke the stillness as he wrapped both arms around him from behind. He picked him up in a bear hug. He was laughing and he shook Ben back and forth and back and forth and Ben was laughing, too. But he said, "Cut it out!" and tried to push himself free. His father let him down and they walked together to get the deer. The shot was perfect and the deer was dead when they got to it. Ben was like a hero after that. His father told everyone about it for weeks, and whenever they ate meat from that deer Ben got to decide how his mother cooked it and his father would thank him for getting food for the family. There had never been anything like it.

Ben's father had a big gun collection. All kinds of different guns. Ben didn't know what happened to the collection after he died. Maybe they sold them to pay bills. The only thing that was left was an old hunting knife that Ben had kept ever since he got out. His father had used it for everything. His father kept it strapped to the back of the left hip, on a belt between two loops so he could move it out of the way to sit. Ben barely ever looked at it, but he liked knowing it was there, at the bottom of a drawer. It was like a connection to his old life. Just enough of a connection.

‡

Ben was in school. In a dream. In confusion he could not understand and could not question. In the clothes he wore to work. Ben was back in school. Junior high. But he was already big. He was already old.

There were children all around him, pressing up against him, pushing by him and by each other. They were loud. Deafening. He couldn't hear anything else. But he couldn't hear them either. Like sounds from under water. He couldn't see their faces. He couldn't reach down to touch them. To push them away.

In a classroom. In the back row, sitting in a desk chair. He couldn't see or hear the teacher. She was too far away. He couldn't get comfortable in the seat because of the knife on his belt. He couldn't get the teacher's attention to tell her. When he tried to speak it was like someone choking him. He was too young for the class he was in. He was in a class with seniors, and he was only in seventh grade. He tried to be excused, and he tried to sit still but the knife was in his way.

He was standing in the library with the knife in his hand. Out of its sheath. The sheath was gone. It wasn't on his belt. There was no place to put it safely. They were all gathered around him. All of the other students and teachers, all in a circle. It was the library so he tried to be quiet but he couldn't whisper. If he tried to be louder he would yell. But he couldn't even whisper.

They were all yelling at him. He couldn't tell them not to be loud. Not to make noise in a library. He couldn't tell them. He tried to show them the knife. To show them that he had it and he couldn't put it anywhere safely. He tried to get their help and to get them to talk quietly, but everyone yelled. Even the teachers were yelling at him. He showed them the knife and they were afraid and he was like a monster but really it just made them angrier. It just made them hate him more and more. One after another they put their hands on him, but he couldn't reach them or talk to them. They were yelling but with their hands on him they were all still and quiet and they held him with one hand after another and another and he couldn't get away. When they put their hands on him they all had her face. Her face was everywhere, looking at him. And in her face he saw she was angry. And in her face he saw she was afraid, and almost gone.

Ben snapped awake in the bathroom, throwing up in the toilet. He was cold all over. Sweating. It felt cold. He threw up but he wasn't sick. He remembered the dream and he threw up again. He tried to wash his mouth out, and wash the taste and the memory and the feeling of it all away. He was cold, so he turned on the shower and stood under the water; so hot it almost burned him. It felt good. He stood under it until the water ran cold.

Ben got dressed and made coffee and sat in his chair with the lights dim. It was just past five in the morning. There was still too much time. He felt tired but he didn't want to go back to sleep. He wanted to stay up. He drank the coffee as fast as he could get it down, and when it was gone he could feel the dead spots on his tongue where he'd burned it. He wanted the day to start. He wanted something to do.

He closed his eyes sitting in the chair, but he wouldn't let himself sleep. He thought about Maria. It was good he hadn't gone with her. He wished she was here now, to rest her hand on his forehead. To say "shhh" so quietly he'd have to hold his breath to hear it. To stand over him as he slept and to keep everything else out and away from him. To be in his dreams. To be all of his dreams. Naked, and lovely, and loving him. Curled up soft and small in his arms, in their bed. To feel the warm length of her along his body. Half asleep, she'd say, "I love you I love you I love you," slowly and softly, like saying it in a dream. Saying what she really felt without hiding anything at all. And there'd be nothing to protect himself from, nothing to fear. She'd be sleeping, protecting him, dreaming of him and he was strong but he would never hurt her. He could put his hands and his lips on every inch of her but there'd be no reason to hurry. They could take as long as they wanted, and nothing would go wrong.

Ben woke again and it was time to go to work.

‡

Satch never looked at the boy when he talked. They never looked at each other. "That Missus Scott'sa stupitbitch." The boy would laugh and laugh even though he didn't have a class with her. "Sh'aughtta try suckinmy dick." But Satch never looked at the boy, and the boy never looked at him.

The boy would try to say things, too. "This sucks shit," he said, holding up his sandwich, but he could barely say it before he started laughing. But Satch heard him and he smiled.

"Oughta try thisfucking shit, then. It'sall shit." Satch would smile and the boy would laugh and laugh.

"Fuck it," the boy said, and started laughing. The word in his mouth was like a spell. Or a weapon. It made him nervous to have it. It made him breathless to hear himself say it. To feel it said. It made him feel strong and powerful. He knew he was becoming a man.

‡

Ben waited until ten after seven before Tony got to the shop. Ben had forgotten that Roger was taking the day off, and that it would have to be Tony or Enrique that opened the shop. Tony was late, and he yawned as he pulled the keys out of his pocket. He saw Ben walking toward him.

"The hell I gotta come here if you were gonna be here already?" He picked through the unfamiliar key chain. "Ain't no goddamn organization in this fuckin' place. That's the problem with any business that fails to grow. You know? Organization and communication."

"I don't have keys."

"Take these keys. Fuck it. I'll go back to sleep."

"I can't."

"Seriously. Take the fucking things." Tony held the keys out, but Ben wouldn't take them. He stepped back. "Fuckin' beautiful. Really. Don't bother telling me." Tony opened the grate over the door, and the main door. "I'm going inside to sleep. At least make yourself useful and open up the rest of the grates over the bays." Tony threw the keys at Ben, and he caught them awkwardly.

Ben opened the grates and left the keys by Tony's feet on the reception desk. It wasn't against the rules for him to use the keys. Just to be in the shop alone. There wouldn't be any trouble for this, but he would keep quiet about it just in case. He went to the back and put on his coveralls.

Roger had come up to him after the kid and his family left. The kid he'd yelled at. Ben was expecting him to.

"What the fuck, man? The fuck were you doing to that kid?"

"Just getting him away. He wouldn't listen. He would have gotten hurt."

"So you freak out on him? Why not just take him out of the shop? He's not s'posed to be back there anyway."

"I told him. He wouldn't listen."

"You're lucky he didn't say anything to his dad. Dude was sittin' right out there. Coulda been a serious shitstorm, man."

"He could have been hurt." Ben was yelling. He felt like two hands were pressing on the sides of his head. "What was I supposed to do?"

"Fuck's sake, Cornpone. Back the fuck off. That's what you're supposed to do next time you see some kid." Roger's finger was in Ben's face. He was twice Ben's size. Ben knew there'd be nothing he could do against Roger, but it didn't matter at all. At least that didn't matter. "And back the fuck off when you see me, too."

Ben didn't want any more of it. He didn't want to talk, or answer questions. He didn't want to think about what to do, or explain to Tony why he couldn't be in the shop alone. He didn't want anything to be angry about, or worry about, or have to get involved with some other person and whatever they thought. He wanted to work on cars, and he was good at it. He didn't want to always have some new person to deal with, and some new situation.

He went to work on an alignment job. As he worked his mind drifted to Maria. He could feel the way she felt in his dream. He could still feel her next to him. It was always that way when he dreamed of a woman. Even a woman he'd never met, he couldn't get her out of his head the next day. The dream, and the thought of the dream, felt more real than a woman. Better than a woman. Simpler.

The day passed. Tony and Enrique mostly sat around the desk and talked in Spanish. He was left alone to work. And think about Maria. It was better this way. Better than if he had gone in with her. Like this, she belonged to him. Just his Maria.

After a while, Ben heard Vic's voice in the office, and Tony and Enrique stopped talking Spanish. They didn't even talk with accents. Vic was Indian. His voice was out of place trying to joke with the other two. At least Ben thought he was Indian. He knew better than to ask.

It was Thursday, which meant payday. Vic liked to give out the checks himself. He did it most weeks. He talked and joked with Tony and Enrique for a while longer, and then Ben heard the door from the office and the sound of hard-sole shoes on the concrete floor of the shop. Ben kept his head under the car, pretending not to hear.

"'Ello, Ben." Ben came out from under the car. Vic had a hand extended, but Ben showed him the oil on his hands. "You know I have some-ting for you?"

"Thursday already?"

Vic pulled an envelope from his pocket. "I'm sure you earn it."

Ben folded the envelope and slid it into the pocket of his coveralls. "Thanks." Ben didn't feel like he should have to thank him. Not like this. Like it was a present. He was just working, like he was supposed to. But Roger had told him he should always thank Vic. That it was an important part of working there. That it was expected. So he did it.

"You are very welcome. I am sure you earn it." Vic half-bowed to him and turned on his heel to walk back out through the door.

Ben wiped his hands and opened the check, just like he did every week. There was no reason why. It was always the same. He knew the other guys got overtime if they were asked to work extra. Ben was there most days, even Saturdays, and worked nine or ten hours a day. He was there as long as there was someone in the shop. His check stub read forty hours, base pay. Just like it always did.

Ben followed Tony and Enrique to the carry-out for lunch. He was hungry. He hadn't eaten breakfast. They brought Chinese back to the shop and sat around the desk eating. Tony and Enrique had been talking in Spanish off and on. Ben wished they would keep talking in Spanish, or that he could go eat by the cars. But there was no way to ask for those things, so he sat and listened.

"Hey you guys hear about that *cholo* prick over in Edgewood?" Enrique asked. "Man, dude, like, kill't his whole family. Wife. Two kids. Some black dude. I heard about that shit yesterday, but I didn't even want to bring it up with Roger around."

"Who, Roger? You know he don't care. It won't bother him."

"I don't know shit about what will bother him if it's talkin' about some mass murder. That's liable to make anybody get crazy." He took too much chicken and rice in his mouth. He chewed over the bowl and pushed rice back into his mouth with his fingers. "I mean, I'm not even gonna say nothing about how it was some kinda black thing or nothing, but it still could make anybody crazy to talk about."

Ben didn't want to listen to them. He wanted to think about something else, or about Maria, or about nothing. But he knew he had to listen to this. He knew it was important to pay attention. To pay attention to how they looked, and how they looked at him. The food in his mouth felt like something he shouldn't eat. That was dangerous to eat. But he knew it wasn't really because of the food, so he made himself keep eating.

"The point is, this ain't some racial shit, anyway. It's one thing to go kill some dude to take a drug corner, or break a guy's legs when he owes you money. Even runnin' around crazy like these bangers do, trying to make a rep. That all has a reason. This crazy dude ain't have no reason. And it don't matter if you black or white or Latin or whatever. If you lose your shit like that, it could happen to anybody."

"Come on, man. I ain't gonna lose it like that." Tony shook his head. "That don't happen to just anybody, you know? It's only gonna happen to some dude who has something deep down wrong with him. Right from day one. The kinda dudes that do that shit are wrong from the start. There's nothing they can do about it. They can't even help themselfs."

"What? So you let him go?"

"Whattaya mean, let 'em go? Who said I'm letting 'em go?" Tony stabbed his fork into his rice. Ben watched his hands to make sure they weren't shaking. He wanted them to shut up. The way they were talking was a threat. Like an animal you couldn't turn your back on.

"Well, if they've got it so bad, if they're wrong right from the start? If they can't help it? If they can't help it, how are you gonna punish them? If you put me in a trance or mind control or some shit and I go out and rob you, you can't come and convict me now, right?"

"Why I'm gonna put a trance on you to make you rob me?"

"You know what I'm saying."

"The fuck if I do. I thought it was about black guys." Tony winked at Ben.

"Fuck you, man. You know what I'm saying. If a guy can't control hisself, how can you punish him when he does something wrong?"

"Shit. If he's that messed up. If he can't help it? That's even worse, right? That's worse than someone who thinks it out and tries to do something wrong. That's someone who's just basically evil. Like a snake. Like not knowing any better than to just destroy everything, just for kicks."

Ben knew it wasn't their fault. Ben knew they didn't mean to threaten him. To push him. He knew they were stupid. They couldn't help it.

"So what do you do with him? Give him a shrink?"

"If that will really fix him. Or a pill or something. But how's a pill gonna fix a guy who's been a natural-born killer since he was like two years old?"

"So what are you gonna do with him?"

"Shit, man. Give that dude the chair. If that's all he is, is some natural-born killer, I don't care if he can help it or not. He's not even a person. He's like some rabid dog. Even PETA don't want them around."

"What the hell PETA got to do with this?"

"You know, man."

"Shit." Enrique ate for a moment in silence. "So this guy's worse than some dude who thinks it through? Who maybe wasn't so bad but then decides one day he's gonna up and kill his family, like this *vato*?"

"I didn't say I liked none of those dudes better. Why don't you be their friends if you're so worried about it?"

"I'm just askin' you which is worse? The crazy dude or some guy who's got it all planned from the start? What if they do the exact same thing? The same crime? Which is worse?"

Ben didn't want to look at them. He wanted to close his eyes. To throw up the food that was dead and heavy in his stomach. Tony leaned back in his chair, looking off at the ceiling of the shop. "Well in that case, it depends."

"Depends on what?"

"On who their lawyer is." Tony laughed hard at his own joke. Ben stood too quickly from the table, and he could see them watching him. The food smell in the room was like rotting.

The phone rang on the wall behind where Tony was sitting. The sound of it was like an alarm and Ben turned to go back into the shop. It would be better if he left. Better if he could go back to work. "*Ay.* For you, man." Ben turned back in the door, thinking they must be making fun of him.

Tony held out the receiver. The cord was short so Ben stood by the desk and put it to his ear. He could feel them watching him. "Yeah?"

"Ben?" A woman's voice.

"Yeah?"

"I can't believe it." It wasn't a telemarketer. He knew what it was. "I can't believe I found you." He'd imagined this a hundred times. A thousand. It was what he'd been afraid of. "I'm so glad I found you." Dizzy fear, like falling and falling in a dream. It was what could never happen.

Ben put the receiver down as gently as he could. Tony and Enrique were quiet, watching him. Not pretending they weren't. He walked out of the office and into the street. He wanted so badly to run.

CHAPTER THREE

The bell rang at the end of class and the boy pushed out into the hall as quickly as he could and ran to his locker. He never liked the crowd of students and the pushing and yelling and laughing but today it was worse. Today it made his skin burn all over and it made him afraid like running from something that was closer and closer.

When he got to his locker he leaned into it like he was looking for a book, but he was happy where it was dark and he was alone. He was breathing hard and he knew he had to breathe more slowly or it would get worse and worse. He knew if he closed his eyes that everything would feel like an electric shock. He leaned in the dark and he took long slow breaths and he pretended he was alone in a room with no windows and no doors and even though the walls were thin and he could hear everyone around him, they couldn't see him and they would never find him.

"What are you looking for?" A girl's voice. He stood up straight and looked and it was her. She was looking at him and smiling. She was standing alone and the others weren't with her and she wasn't acting like one of them. It was just her and she was nice and perfect and kind.

"I found it."

She saw there was nothing in his hand and she smiled and shrugged. "Okay. Are you okay?"

"Yes."

She looked around the hall, but she didn't move. "You've got Mr. Jensen for English too, right? Isn't he stupid?"

The boy didn't want to talk. He would rather listen to her for hours and hours than say anything at all. "Yeah. He's fucking stupid."

It sounded different when he was talking to her. After a second she laughed. "Geez. You're funny. Are you trying out for drama club?"

"No."

"You should. You'd be really good at it. Being funny is really helpful."

The boy tried to think of how he was going to be heroic with her. To save her from something terrible. That would be better than talking. But he couldn't imagine anything or think about anything with her standing there. There was just her, and nothing was happening. "Maybe."

The boy could see the other kids she always hung around with coming down the hall. She saw them, too, and she stopped looking at him. "Hey guys." *She smiled a real smile when she saw them. She was always different when she was talking to them.*

"Who's that?" *One of them pointed at the boy. He was tall and wore a school jacket all the time, even inside like now when it was too warm.* "He looks like a retard. What are you looking at, retard?"

"God. Stop it, you guys." *She laughed at them like a mother would laugh and shook her head.* "Leave him alone." *She didn't push them but she walked away and they followed her. The boys said a few more things as they walked away, but it didn't matter.*

The boy turned back to his locker and waited until they were all gone and there was no way they could see him. He closed the locker without taking anything out and walked into the bathroom. It was empty in the bathroom. He went into one of the stalls and he heard the bell ring. He stood alone in the stall and he heard the noise in the hallways drain away to nothing. It made him happy but he knew there was something passing him by.

With the flat of his hand he slapped the side of the stall. The sound of it, like a bell, amazed him. But there was no other sound and no one paying attention. He slapped it again, and again. Again and again until his hand started to sting, then go numb. Again and again and again.

‡

Ben was still wearing his coveralls when he got to the bar. It was earlier than usual. There were only a few people there, and he didn't recognize them. He walked into the bathroom without stopping at the bar. He took the check out of the pocket of his coveralls. He took off the coveralls and stuffed them into a trash can. He'd worked four days that he wouldn't be paid for, which was more than the cost of the coveralls.

There was a drink in front of his usual seat when he came out of the bathroom. Ben took it like a shot as he pulled out his wallet. The bartender poured again and Ben laid a twenty on the bar.

He couldn't go back to the job. He knew that. He wasn't sure if he could go home, or if he could even stay here. He didn't know how far away the voice on the phone was. If it was from a pay phone across the street, then there was nothing left to do. It probably wasn't. You couldn't tell anymore, like you used to be able to, if someone was calling from far away. It all sounded the same, and it was no help to him.

Ben had moved apartments a few years ago because the one he'd been living in was condemned. He'd never given his work the new address. He didn't need to because they gave him everything in person. It was good they wouldn't have it on file. He'd finished his drink again and mostly the bar was quiet and still.

Someone knew what city he lived in. He knew he should leave, but he had to tell has case manager if he was moving. He could move; he just had to let them know. The woman couldn't have found Ben through his case manager. He had called there after he first got out pretending to be someone else asking to find Ben. They wouldn't give him any information. They told him he could leave a message. He never got the message.

Ben didn't want to leave. He could change apartments if he had to, and he could find another job. He would call his case manager, and he could help Ben find a job. He didn't know what he'd say to explain losing this one. He could think of that later. He'd tried to drink more slowly, but his glass was empty. His heart still shook his rib cage. He thought maybe he'd have a heart attack, which would be simple. But his dad had lived a lot longer than this. And his mother would have, too, if she'd been stronger. It wasn't going to be simple like that.

"Mr. President. It is a relief to see you back amongst us." Ben signaled the bartender to bring them both a round. "We've been worried about you, sir. Thought perhaps they went and took you to a secure location, some shit like that."

Ben tried to smile. "No. Just busy." Ben held up his glass to Black Jacket's but didn't look at him.

Cities were better. Easier to get lost in. This city was better. No one knew anything about anyone. No one had his right address. He didn't have a phone number. No one would come to this neighborhood looking for him.

"Listen, man... that bitch piss you off or something?"

"You talked to her?"

"No, man. Well, not about you. I mean I talked to her when she came in here." Black Jacket drank. "Shit, man, don't look like that. We talked because that's what people do. Most people talk to each other." He laughed. Low and growling. "Hardest thing to teach a man is what he should already know."

"She still come in here?"

"Naw, man. Shit. She gave that up after a week or so. What'd she do, anyhow? Get up in your shit about something?"

"No. It wasn't anything. I told you I was busy." Ben had finished his drink. He signaled the bartender.

"Yeah. Working on them Oval Office memoirs, I suppose?" Black Jacket pinched his drink at the stem and swirled the red liquid. He looked at Ben's empty glass. "For your information, since I don't imagine you have too much experience one way or the other, if you want to fuck a bitch and leave her behind, you can save yourself some hassle by tellin' her she got left."

Ben paid for his drink.

"Thirsty tonight, Mr. Taft? Anyway, ain't you gonna tell me what she did? Wasn't she no good? Hell, I'd'a thought you'd be grateful for most anything. Huh. No offense."

"She didn't do anything." Ben wanted to leave, but there was nowhere to go but home. He didn't want to be home.

"Yeah, okay."

Ben held his glass up to the light from behind the bar and tried to get back the feeling he'd had that morning. It was gone now. Distant. Thinking of Maria was like watching her walk away. Too much else was wrong.

He had to stay here. There was nowhere else to go. He'd rather fight to stay here than leave. But no one would find him.

Who was it? How had she sounded?

Not angry. It didn't sound like a reporter, like when he'd first gone inside.

Scared. She sounded scared.

Ben's dad would go away, sometimes. Not just for work, but for months at a time. His mother could never find him. No one at work would say. No one around town knew, or else they wouldn't say either. Ben wished he knew how to do that.

"Don't suppose you're gonna tell me how she was or nothin'?" Black Jacket ordered another round for them and put it on his tab. His drinks were coming out red tonight. "Not a kiss an' tell kinda fella?" He chuckled another low growl. "I respect that." He took a long sip from his drink. "Mmm. Yeah. I do respect that. I guess I just think, as a matter of parliamentary procedure an' shit, that whole sentiment is a little out of date for men our age. Shit, your highness. There's a number in the sky, for both of us. One number for you, and one number for me. You know what that number is?"

"No."

"That number is how much tail we've got still comin' to us. No telling how small it's getting to be. Could be as low as a thousand, in my case. But the point is, there's a number now, where there didn't used to be one. And when you hit that number, that's it. No more tail." He shook his head. "So you get what I'm tellin' you, here, don't you, Mr. President?"

Ben shrugged.

"Huh. I should know better than usin' a parable with the likes of you. My point, you dumb fuckin' hillbilly, is that with finite tail on our respective horizons, we can at least optimize it by reflecting over drinks. Meaning you ought to tell me about that ass."

"It was fine. She was." Ben thought of her, the feeling of her body, and the way she'd been that night. The real night. "There wasn't anything wrong with her."

"Yeah. Well. One for the record books then, huh?" Black Jacket shook his head. "It's my own fault, I suppose. Trying to make civilized conversation with the likes of you. Or any conversation at all, for that matter."

"I suppose." He would stay. It felt right to stay. He would find another job, but that could wait. He had money saved, even after not getting any overtime, and the fees from the check cashing joint. It was better to stay here. This was a better place for him, and it was better than trying to start from nothing. He had money from when his father passed. Enough money for a few months, anyway. Long enough to find a new job. And he didn't need to think about that tonight. There was nothing else to think about. He could still feel the sound of that voice on the phone. He couldn't make that go away. But there was nothing he could do about it. Nothing else he needed to think about. It felt good. Like finishing a job. He drank off his glass in a long swallow.

"What's the matter with talking, anyhow?" He'd forgotten Black Jacket was there.

"What?"

"What's the matter with talking? Or what's the matter with you? I met plenty-a guys who kept quiet, but you're something different. Most any guy will eventually go on about something, if you give him time and booze. But not a word from you."

"I don't like talking."

"Yeah. Okay." Black Jacket ordered two more drinks, but Ben put money on the bar.

Ben's father would get angry. He had a temper. That's what his mother always called it. His temper. He would come home late sometimes. He would yell. He would break things. All the stupid crap around the house they didn't need anyway. If he was really drunk it would be worse. She would blame Ben's father for the worst of his anger. Like it was something he'd planned. But Ben knew it wasn't like that. He'd known it even when he was young, in the way that boys know things and understand things because they've always been that way. Ben had always known what his mother was too stupid to understand. With all her bitching and crying and even when his father would hit him, Ben knew better. Ben didn't blame his father for being angry. For doing what he did. Ben knew that it wasn't his father's fault. It wasn't his father at all. Even when everything was as bad as it could be. When Ben would be so scared. When he would hide but it wouldn't do any good because his father was like an animal that would find him if he wanted to find him, and when the fear was always worse than the hurt when it finally came. In those times, that wasn't his father at all. He was something else. A spirit. A demon that made his father do things he never wanted to do, that he would always feel bad about later.

Ben's father would cry, and Ben would wish there was a way to help him. A way to make him feel better. Ben had always known it wasn't his father's fault. Ben knew. It had always been the same for him. "My father told me talking is for people who can't control themselves. Talking about your problems, talking about what you're afraid of. Talking about what you think. You only do that if you can't get by." Ben signaled for another drink.

"Well. A life lesson from the man and his father. Them bitches over at Hallmark better look out now." He laughed and shook his head. "If you don't mind me sayin', that's some pretty grim shit there, Mr. President."

"You can say what you want. It is what it is."

Black Jacket looked down at his drink, spinning it in the glass, watching the light in the curve of the clear glass and the red liquor. "I suppose that's true."

When it was quiet, Ben could almost imagine her. The whiskey was helping. It didn't feel good. But it was easier to concentrate. To find that simple feeling again, of her with him. Of no words, and no people. Not really her, not really him. Just a good moment. Something good to think about.

Black Jacket sipped at his drink. Ben was finished with his, and signaled the bartender for another. "You know, my dad used to tell me I should smoke. No shit. Told me all real men smoked." Ben didn't want to hear this. He didn't want to hear anything. "I smoked for fifteen years, until cancer got him. Not a day goes by I still don't want a cigarette." As close as she'd been, she was gone again. The bar was swaying. Stuttering. It had been still and quiet when she was there, but now it wasn't. He couldn't think. No one would let him think. "You dig what I'm tellin' you, Mr. President?"

Ben stood from the bar and the room drifted off to one side. He had to get out. He had to get clear. "I don't give a shit about your father." Ben walked through the bar, supporting himself against the wall. It was crowded.

Outside it was dark. Colder than he expected, but it was good. The streets didn't sway; didn't reel the way things had inside.

He walked down the street like pushing against wind, his body bent forward. The whiskey washed over him in waves, and he shook it off like he was trying to stay awake. Missing her felt like homesickness. Like being drawn to where he knew he ought to be. He wanted the thought of her back, the feel of her. The home she made for him, sweetly, with the edges of her body. He wanted it back, but nothing would stay still. No one would stay quiet. There was nothing else to do but this.

He walked down the street until it became unfamiliar. He backtracked when it felt like he'd gone wrong. He found the street they'd turned down. He was almost sure. It felt right when he walked down it. His father had always told him that you never got lost if you trusted your instincts. This street felt right. He was sure this was the right thing to do.

She had wanted him. He knew that. He was sure of it. She had really wanted him, the man, to come to her home. This was right. It was the right thing to do.

He found the building. *Everyone Needs A Ruff Over Their Head*. He walked up the outside stairs. To a row of buzzers. He didn't know her last name. He didn't press a buzzer, but tried the door instead and it opened easily. He thought that he would try to remember to tell Maria, because it was dangerous to have it open like that in this neighborhood.

He knew from the poster that hers was the first apartment on the ground floor. He stopped at her door. Something was about to happen. He knew that. He was sure that it was right, but it wasn't what usually happened. He didn't know if it was supposed to happen. Inside she was waiting for him. She'd brought him here. She'd come back to the bar. He was sure that was right. It had to be. She had been waiting for him. She'd wanted him. And now this was going to happen. It was right, now. Now he would make it all right.

He knocked loud on the door. No response. He knocked again. He realized anyone could hear him. Anyone could see him. He didn't want to be out here, where people could see him. It wasn't what he expected. Why wouldn't she let him in? He was about to knock on the door again when he heard footsteps from inside.

The door opened with the chain bolt still secure. There was her face. Through the narrow opening, there were her eyes and lips. She wasn't wearing makeup. She looked pale and older, and he thought she must have been sleeping. But he didn't mind.

"What are you doing here?" She was whispering. Her voice didn't sound like it was supposed to, like it had when he imagined it.

"I wanted to..." His voice was thick with whiskey and he couldn't talk low. He knew he was being too loud and the look on her face was turning wrong. And anyone could hear him or see him.

Unthinking, in one motion he threw the butt of his hand at the door where the chain was attached. As it sprang open, the door struck Maria and she fell back. He hadn't thought about it hitting her, and he hadn't meant for that to happen. She made a noise, but she was quiet.

He felt strong pushing through the door. He knew it didn't matter how he looked. He knew he was strong. She fell back away from the door holding one hand over her eye. He came through the door and locked it behind him. He saw her realizing that it had come true. That they were together now. She was wearing a sweatshirt. Old and worn at the cuffs. He thought it must be her favorite. No pants and no skirt. He could see the edge of her black panties under the hem of the sweatshirt. Her legs were perfect and for a moment he stopped, imagining the feel of them. The feel of touching them one inch at a time. Alone, with no one to see him, no one to talk. Just holding her flesh one inch at a time.

"What are you doing here?" She was confused, he could see. Scared. She didn't understand. It was dim in the apartment, and all the light was behind her.

"I came for you. Came here for you. Like you wanted."

"You're drunk. What are you doing?" She was whispering. He didn't know why, and he didn't know why she was talking so much. There was nothing he could say. Nothing he could say if she was going to talk and talk. He was trapped. Tricked. She had tricked him. Or maybe it wasn't her, but something else. Someone had tricked them both. When he tried to speak he slurred. He was senseless. He didn't want to talk. He hadn't come here to talk.

He moved quickly to her and put an arm around her. Around her waist and his hand ran across the top of her panties. Across the curve of her and he couldn't believe he could imagine this so many times and now it was his. To really have. Not just a dream but finally, really his. He put his other hand on the back of her neck, curling his fingers in her hair. He pulled her hair back and she cried out like the noises he'd imagined her making and her mouth was open and her face was looking up at him like it had in the street. "No no no no no," she whispered and she shook her head and he saw in her eyes that she couldn't believe it was happening. He kissed her like he had, and he pressed her against himself, and all that she was saying became a whimper in her throat. He felt her arms pushing at his sides, but he was strong. He would be strong for her. He had been strong, and come back to her.

He ran his hand up and down her back. He held her high under her sweatshirt. He stopped kissing her and let her stand back from him, but only a few inches.

"Wait wait wait wait wait."

He pulled the sweatshirt up over her head and off her and when he let go of her to pull it off she backed up quickly to the edge of the couch that was facing the front hall at an angle.

She stood there for him wearing almost nothing. She didn't turn her back on him. She didn't run away. "Wait wait wait wait." She put her hand on his chest.

He gripped the back of her neck and he ran a hand up and down her flesh. He put his lips on her breasts, and ran them up her chest and across her neck.

"Wait wait wait wait wait." Still whispering.

He ran his hands along her legs, her back and then her stomach while he held her head back and he kissed her neck and he would make this his dream. Their dream.

"Please. Please wait."

Holding her neck, he pulled open the snap buttons on his shirt and pulled it away from his chest. He pulled her close to him and could feel her flesh against his and when he kissed her again he couldn't hear her words but he felt them in her chest. In their body. He held her cheek to his chest.

She was shorter than him. Shorter than he remembered in bare feet. Whispering, "Please please please."

He thought he could stand forever with her like this. Just quietly, softly standing. When they got tired they could lie together. And sleep, or lie awake. But that wasn't what was supposed to happen. Not yet. Not now. He pulled her back and he could see she was crying.

"No no no no no."

He pushed her down on the couch and he tore her panties as he took them off. He undid his belt and pushed his pants down as he held a hand on her chest.

"*Wait.*"

He stopped, still, and waited. Everything was still.

"My daughter is sleeping. She can't see this. I don't want her to see this. It has to be quiet."

He didn't understand. He didn't move, and he didn't know what had gone wrong.

She took his hand and held it over her mouth and she pushed it against her so he was holding her tight. He could feel the breath from her nose, fast and warm across the back of his hand. She turned away with his hand held tight over her mouth and looked away, at nothing. The rest of her was limp. She wasn't fighting any more. This was what was happening. Now they both knew it.

With his free arm he held one of her legs up and he pushed himself inside of her. It wasn't easy. She screamed into his hand. Her body arched and writhed and her face was red and veins stood out in her neck but he held her mouth tightly and held her head against the cushion of the couch. Her eyes stayed shut, and he moved slowly until it was easier. She held her legs up without him having to hold them. With his hand free, he ran it along her chest, her neck, her legs. He cupped her breasts and ran his finger through her hair. He moved faster and faster and he held her by her shoulder and pulled her to him. He was strong, and she shook with the force of him. She held his hand over her mouth tighter and tighter, and put her other hand on his arm and his shoulder and the side of his face. He got closer and he could feel her hands holding him tighter and tighter and her legs wrapped around his waist. He could hear himself grunting. Animal noises, but he knew he had to be quiet and he held her mouth shut tight and he pulled her

closer and closer and closer and closer. Her eyes were open and she
looked at him and he remembered why he'd come here and what
he wanted and what he was looking for and what she could mean
to him and the home she could be with her body and her hands
and the feel of her skin and the whisper of her voice in his ear that
everything would be okay and nothing could hurt him or find him
and that they were alone and together and he could hold her and
hold her and hold her and nothing would take her away and when
he felt all of himself raging and screaming into her it echoed back
through her body and in the sound of her voice that he could feel
in his hand and in his chest and they screamed like that together
without making a sound until he thought they would snap or break
and then suddenly, as suddenly as everything always happened—
suddenly it was over. He let her go. He let himself go. He lay on
top of her, the sound and the rhythm of their breathing, together,
like an irregular poem.

   Slowly, and only once, she ran her fingers lightly through his
hair. "Get up. *Get up.*" She was pushing him with her hands and
with her legs and trying to move her body out from under him.
"You have to move. It's okay. Just move."

   He pushed himself up and sat on the floor away from her.
Obeying like a child. She sat on the edge of the couch with her
legs open wide like a man and took the sweatshirt he'd left in
a pile next to the couch and pressed it between her legs. She
winced when she held it to herself, and Ben could see a welt
over her eye from the door. She held her legs together and put
her head down on her knees and he could see her trembling. She
was breathing hard. Rasping. He didn't think she was crying.
But she wasn't his anymore.

   Ben watched her, half-lying on the side of the couch. Her face
hidden. Trembling. Silent. The shine of her beauty was gone. She

wasn't like the person he'd been imagining. Now should have been the good time. The time when they would lie together, and she would hold him, and everything would fall into place.

Ben stood from the floor and buttoned his shirt and his pants. "Are you okay?" he asked.

She didn't answer. He put his hand on her waist and she didn't respond at all. He straightened up and fell back a step, still uncertain on his feet. The place was nice. Shelves along the wall with pictures and figurines and candles in wine bottles all over the room. The coffee table was pushed away at an angle and an empty bottle and a glass had fallen to the carpet. He must have done that and not realized. He reached to pick them up but almost fell over and thought it was better if he left them. There was a large, thin television on the wall opposite the couch, next to the hallway leading to the door. One of the new flat screens. He walked over to it and ran his hands along the edges and touched the screen. He touched it lightly, worried it might break or fall off the wall. He touched it again, just to feel his hand on it.

After a while Maria hadn't moved and there was nothing left to look at. He stood over her and put his hand on her again. "Good night," he said. He stood for a moment over her and turned to leave.

"Where are you going?" She looked up as he walked toward the door. "Are you leaving?"

"I should go."

"No. Stay."

"I should go." He had decided to go. It was the right thing.

"No." Her voice was like ice. Like rock. Ben could feel it and he stopped moving at all. Maria was across the room in an instant. She didn't stand so much as crawl across the floor and when she came to him she was still on her knees. "No. No no. You can't come here like this and then leave. You have to stay." Her voice was panic and urgency. Her eyes were wild and weak. Pleading and threatening. "You have to stay. Please stay." She pressed his hand against her cheek. "Please please please."

Ben tried to pull away. To leave, because that was what he had decided to do. To leave because she scared him, and it made him scared to think what had happened. She was on her feet, his shirt gripped in the balls of her fists. "Stay. Stay. You have to." Her bare breasts pressed against his chest. "If you leave, I'll call the cops. I'll tell them what you did."

He was still. Trying to understand. Trying to think it through. But he couldn't. "How do you know? Did they talk to you?" He turned from the door. "How do you know?"

He stood and he watched her. "Talk to who?" She didn't know. She really didn't know. He watched her soften. He watched the wildness drain out of her. With one hand gripping his shirt, she ran the other down his cheek. "Talk to who, sweetie? I only want to talk to you." She let go of his shirt and rested her head against his chest. "You just have to stay. Nothing will be wrong if you stay."

She took his hand and led him across the room. She picked up the sweatshirt and her panties as she walked past, and pulled the coffee table back into place. She didn't let go of his hand. They walked past the couch and down a hallway. There was a bathroom, a closed door and an open door that she was walking toward. On the closed door hung a piece of construction paper. *#1 Daughter Loves Her Mom! Happy Mother's Day!* was written in crayon around a picture of a girl. He stopped to look at it. She wore glasses and a long black ponytail.

"That's Sophia's room," she whispered. "My daughter." She squeezed his hand and smiled. The tip of her tongue just poking through her teeth. "You'll meet her."

She pulled him into her bedroom and closed the door. A king bed took up most of the room, except for a chair and a small table at the foot of the bed. There were closets on the wall opposite the bed, with mirrored sliding doors. The bed was unmade and the closet doors were open. One lamp was on, placed on a shelf that was part of the bed frame.

"Good thing she's a heavy sleeper, huh?" She laughed and they had a private joke. "We should have come in here, but I was so surprised to see you." She stood before him, still holding his hand. He felt like everything was wrong. He felt like nothing was real, but it was too still to be a dream. He touched her shoulder. Her arm. It was strange that she was real. She smiled when he touched her. She wasn't going to cry or yell or call the cops. She didn't know anything about him. She couldn't know. He'd broken her door, but he would fix it in the morning. He touched her hip. Her breast. She didn't stop him. She smiled. "I like the way you smile," she said. "Just like a little boy."

She undid the buttons on his shirt one at a time. He was facing the mirrored doors. He could see her, and see himself. It didn't look real to see her. To see her smaller body touching his. His chest still looked sunken. Sickly. She pushed his shirt off over his shoulders. She ran her hands across his chest and down his arms. She made him feel strong. Not the way he looked. She made him feel different from what he was. What he knew himself to be. She undid his belt and his pants and slid them down his legs. She rested her head on his leg and she pressed herself lightly to him as she stood. She put her hands on him, and he could feel soft electricity all through his body. She put her hands around his neck and pulled him down to kiss her. He could feel the length of her body against his.

She pulled him on to the bed, over her. "Wait just one sec." She bent around underneath him, brushing him with her hips, and reached into the drawer of the night stand. She had a tube like a toothpaste tube from the drawer and she opened it out of his sight, underneath him. She breathed in as she put it on herself, and smiled when he was surprised by the cool feel of it on himself. "Sorry, baby. I'm just a little sore." She held onto him, and wrapped her legs around him. She brought him to her and she winced, but only for a second. "I know you didn't mean it. I know you didn't mean to hurt me." She spoke like she was casting a spell. Ben closed his eyes and the sound of her voice ran up and down his skin like fingertips. "I know you didn't mean it. I know you'll never do it again." And she smiled even though he couldn't see it. She put her hands on his face and slowly they made love. "You didn't mean it." Finishing was like falling, and falling, and waking. "You'll never do it again."

He slept with the sound of her breathing and her voice in his ear.

CHAPTER FOUR

Ben woke as the bedroom door closed behind Maria. He stood up quickly, all at once. His clothes were not on the floor. They were folded on the chair at the foot of the bed. He dressed by a nightlight. A clock over the bedframe read 5:33 AM. He didn't feel sick. He felt hollow and his throat and his skin burned all over and he tried to move quickly to keep from thinking.

He stood still, waiting. He wanted to leave, but he didn't want to walk through the apartment. He didn't want to be wrong, or to make anyone angry. He didn't know how he should act in this house in the morning, or what he should do.

At 5:57 the door to the bedroom opened and Maria came back. "Hey, you," she said. She wore a long robe and had a towel wrapped around her head. "There's coffee made in the kitchen. I don't have a spare toothbrush, but I left toothpaste out on the sink in the bathroom. You can use your finger if you want." Before he could back away she hugged him and rested her face on his chest. He could feel the damp of the towel through his shirt. He put his hands lightly on her at the base of her shoulder blades. "Not a morning guy, huh?" She laughed and nestled her head closer into his chest. "I'm not usually, either. Why don't you go get some toothpaste and I'll make you a cup?" She kissed him lightly on the cheek. "It's probably better if you're gone before Sophia wakes up. I want you to meet her, but it would be strange for her that I was alone when she went to sleep."

When he came out of the bathroom and walked to the kitchen, she was there with two cups of coffee in floral mugs. The only light was from a vent manifold over the stove. The light rested softly on her body but left her face in darkness. The kitchen was open, with the sink on a fixed island that separated the kitchen from the living room and the dining room. He could see the hallway to the front door on the far side of the room, past the TV and the dining room table. She handed him a mug. "I didn't know how you liked it. It's just black now but there's that raw sugar they make a big deal out of, and there's two percent. We don't keep half and half or cream. I hope that's okay."

"Just black is fine."

"Really? If you like it any other way, just let me know and I'll get it next time I'm at the store."

"Black is how I take it."

"Okay, sweetie." She put her hand on his chest and smiled. "You don't need to rush. She's never up before seven. She's going through that lazy time. She probably will be for years. She just turned twelve. She's still a little girl, but you can see she's figuring things out." She sipped at her coffee. She looked up at him but looked away quickly. "Figuring out adults, and how they act, and figuring out she's got to start acting that way, too. She's a really good kid. I can't wait for you to meet her. You aren't upset I'm asking you to leave, are you?"

"No."

"Just quiet in the morning? I know. We were up late last night." She ran her hand down his arm and took his hand. "Do you want to meet her this weekend? We could all do something on Saturday…"

"I'm working on Saturday."

"Oh. Well, okay. She's going up to her grandparents for a week before school starts. Do you have to work Sunday, too? We could get dinner, just you and me?"

"Yeah."

"You mean yeah you can, or yeah you've gotta work?"

"I can see you on Sunday."

"That would be great, sweetie. Do you want to wait to meet her for a little bit? We can wait for a little bit if you want. Do you have kids?"

"No."

"Okay, sweetie. So if it's weird for you we can wait to have you meet her. I bomb ahead and I don't always think. You can just tell me if I'm being too pushy."

It was quiet for a while. "Okay," Ben said. "It's okay."

"So I have to drop her off at Union for the train in the afternoon but I can be back here by five if you want to pick me up. We can go to dinner somewhere. Do you know any good places?"

"No."

"I know a couple places that aren't too steep but are still nice. Do you like Italian food?"

"Yeah. It's good."

"There's a place over on U Street that isn't bad. Or some Chinese places. I've never tried Ethiopian, and there's a lot of places that are supposed to be good. But Soph always said she wanted to try it with me so let's wait on that."

"It's fine. I don't mind." He brought the cup up to his lips, but it was already empty. It was 6:20. He put the cup down. "Do you have a screwdriver? Phillips-head?"

"Yeah, baby. What's wrong?" She dug into a drawer by the sink that was a jumble of tools, manuals, receipts and small dishes of screws and nails. She handed him a long screwdriver with a yellow handle and a paint stain on the end.

He walked to the front door, trying to be quiet. The chain lock had broken at its base, on the door frame. The screws were less than a half inch long. The wood was cracked and the paint was uneven around the screw holes, but the screws were short so they'd come out cleanly. With the backing plate in place it would cover up any damage to the paint. In the drawer with the tools there was a bottle of wood glue that was still soft, and he dug through a shallow plastic tub and found two screws that were thicker at the shank and more than an inch long.

Maria watched him. She held her coffee in both hands at the top of her chest.

He walked back to the door and put wood glue on the tip of each screw before he sunk them in the holes that were there. They were both hard to finish but he got them in and the plate was where it had been before. With the lock in place and being as quiet as he could he pulled the chain taut and tried to pull it loose. The lock held. Ben was happy to finish a job and he was happy the problem was fixed. He walked back to the kitchen and put the glue and the screwdriver back in the drawer.

"Thank you, sweetie. One more cup?" She poured him out another cup from an electric coffee maker. Ben didn't like it as much as his percolator, but it would be rude to say anything. And he would be home soon and he could have the kind of coffee he liked. "You sure you don't want anything in it? You don't want just a little sugar?" She smiled when she said it and moved up close to him so that he could feel the press of her beneath the fabric of her robe.

"No. Thank you."

She handed him the coffee and kissed him. "My handy man. Thank you for doing that. Watching over us."

It was 6:50. "I should probably go."

She sighed and held him closer. "I know. I'm sorry, sweetie." She pushed herself against him. "I wish we had more time, too."

He drank off the rest of the coffee in one swallow so that he wouldn't be rude. She walked him to the door and she kissed him again and he wondered how it had ever happened, and if it was good, or bad, or if he should leave her before she got hurt, or if everything was already too late.

"Remember," she said. "Five o'clock on Sunday."

"Okay."

‡

Even after so many years, when he slept Ben would still see the girl. Not every night. Not always. And it wouldn't scare him like it used to. He wouldn't always wake in a sweat, he wouldn't always feel sick. Sometimes the dream would just pass away. Sometimes he wouldn't wake. But he always remembered them, and he always remembered seeing her. And he always missed her and had the feel of her in him and around him for the rest of the day.

This time she was in a field, at the edge of the woods. It had begun to feel like a routine. Even in the dream he could know and feel that it had happened before. There was snow on the ground but he didn't feel cold and they both wore t-shirts and she was dressed brightly, with the old kind of jeans that came high up over her waist and her stomach. Her hair was big and curled and wild at the edges. Her glasses which were still new were thick square frames and she hated them because she told him they made her look like a freak but her mother wouldn't buy her contacts. And she smiled when she saw him and Ben couldn't remember why he wished she wouldn't smile at him. Wouldn't wave at him or welcome him or wish he would talk to her.

She held her arm up over her head and waved like they were miles apart. He could see the yellow fabric of her t-shirt pull against the first hint of her breasts. She wasn't a woman. She was a girl. Women would come later, and they would be one thing, but she was a girl. As he ran along the edge of the woods he could feel in his body, in his speed, that he was a boy. They were young together, and she would wave to him and this was how it always was.

They ran. She ran ahead of him, and ran into the corn that was taller than both of them. It was summer and the stalks and the leaves were green and he felt lost as he followed her into the corn. She was gone, but he could hear her. She called to him but everything, everywhere was the green of the cornstalks and the leaves. He ran toward the sound of her voice. He couldn't find her, and his heart leapt and sank like he was really afraid. But it was all okay. This wasn't wrong. This was just a game. Playing with fear. Because they were just kids and that's what they could do. And when he ran in one direction, and then another, and then another, the leaves of the stalks made a hollow slap against his legs and his arms. He would push through them but never break a stalk because it was food that someone needed and you should never ruin food.

On the far side of the corn field was a river, and he knew there wasn't really, but it was there now and he ran toward it because that was where she would be. He heard her in the water and he saw her through the thick weeds at the edge of the river and before he could stop his shoes were off and he was in the river with her.

She laughed and splashed him with water and laughed at him for getting in the river with his jeans on. He was always too shy to take them off. He knew she'd taken hers off, and he thought he could remember her white panties, but now she was in the deep part of the river and it was only her head above water. Where the water touched it her hair hung heavy and straight in slick black clumps under the wildness of her dry curls. She splashed him again and he splashed her and she screamed, "My hair, you asshole!" even though she was just a kid and her hair was mostly wet anyway. But she smiled and she didn't mind how close he was to her or that she wasn't wearing all of her clothes.

They were laughing, together, and splashing and she called him an asshole when the water hit her but she kept laughing and laughing. They played, like children, close to each other, pushing and splashing, and he could feel her leg brush against his. And when she stubbed her toe and started to cry, it was still just a little girl crying. A young girl who cried, but crying came and went. And Ben took her hand and she didn't stop him and she looked at him and thanked him, silently without saying anything. And he held her hand tight and she smiled at him and it was only river water on her cheek and the water was deep but they could swim and tread water and hold hands and feel the ripple of their legs beneath the surface. Holding her hand was everything. It was a perfect thing. He had a memory that it wasn't right: a memory like a feeling. He shouldn't touch her. But it wasn't true. He held her hand, tighter and tighter, and she smiled, and it was the right thing, just like he wanted it to be. And the water moved faster around them like the rush of joy and happiness that everything was right, and what he'd thought was good was really good, and she was happy and he was happy and the rush of the water was like excitement because he didn't move but let it all rush faster and faster around him.

Faster and faster as the water flowed and it wasn't summer any more, but it felt like fall and the smell of wood stoves and dead damp leaves on the air and the water was cold and rushing faster. But he wasn't cold, and he didn't move. He stood on the river bottom. Still, and holding her hand. But she felt the river rushing and the water's chill and he saw the fear in her eyes. The real fear when she knew the water was fast and cold and she couldn't stand still like he could. He held her hand, tighter and tighter, and he could hold her but she didn't know he could. The water like a floodgate or an emergency rushed by him and she was crying and screaming but he couldn't hear it, and he couldn't feel it, but he could only stand still and try to hold on to her. She was crying, trying to pull away from him. Trying to get loose of his grip. She couldn't see that it was him that was holding her. That he could keep her safe and save her if she would let him. She only saw his hand and felt the strength of his grip, like an animal in a trap. With her free hand she pulled at his fingers, one after another. He could already see her drifting away. She was already distant. Further and further in the flood. He hadn't let go but he could barely see her. He needed to hold her. To hold on to her. He couldn't let her go. She'd be gone forever, like she had always been. He couldn't let her go.

Her hand grew colder and colder and he saw her drifting further. She cried because he was hurting her and suddenly everything was wrong but he was only trying to keep her with him but he couldn't speak to tell her. She was drifting away even though he hadn't let her go and he saw her face. For an instant. A last moment, a last look over the water and the cold and force of everything taking her away. A last moment to see him, and to see, truly, what he was. A last moment to leave him with the truth of her and them and him. A last moment to look at him, to see him, and to feel nothing but simple, perfect fear.

‡

In his dreams the boy was nowhere and nothing, and then he'd done something very wrong. He couldn't remember what, but he knew it had been very bad. Everything blamed him. The voices in the air accused him and hated him and yelled and yelled until he cried out. He was doing something stupid. He was acting up in school and he'd made a mistake on the car when he was supposed to be helping his father. And everyone and everything was wrong and hated him and blamed him and the yelling seemed to come from everywhere.

The boy woke in his bed but the yelling didn't stop. It was his father. His father hadn't been home when he'd gone to sleep. The boy had wanted to see him. To see him before he slept, but his mother had said no. He wasn't home. But now he was. "...Fucking raggin' on me..." They were in the kitchen, he could hear pieces of what they were saying. "...Another one of your sluts..." She wouldn't stop going on and on. "Was it another whore?"

Why was she yelling when he'd just gotten home? When he'd been out working? "...Stupid bitch..." The yelling went on and on and the boy knew he should sleep but he couldn't. He didn't want to. "...Fucking lie to me..." He didn't know what was wrong, but he wanted it to be over. He wanted to see his father and for everything to be all right.

The yelling got worse and worse. They were each yelling now at the same time. Yelling over each other. Louder and louder. And then it stopped. When his father got too angry and the boy could hear his mother fall to the floor he knew that then it would be over like it always was and everything would be fine. The boy held his breath because the breathing sounded too loud. Everything seemed like the beginning of a sound, but nothing was. And everything was quiet. Until he heard his mother crying. His father was quiet. He was letting it go, but his mother was crying. And talking. They were at the bottom of the stairs, and the boy could hear it all. "I shouldn't be here. I shouldn't have ever come here. I shouldn't put up with this shit." Louder and louder and frantic, like the girls in school who cry so hard they can't control themselves and the boy would hate to be near them when they cried because it was like they'd been changed. Like a demon or an animal or something had changed them. "I should take him and go." Louder and louder and her words breaking apart at the edges, drifting into sobbing and screeching. "I should take him and go." It was the last thing he understood.

The rest was just wildness. Senselessness. Shrieking like a witch or an animal in a trap and then the hard cracking slap again and again, but now there was no quiet. And his father told her again and again to shut the fuck up shut the fuck up but she wouldn't listen and she was crying and shrieking and there wasn't any sense or human voice or softness in it and no matter how many times he hit her she wouldn't stop. She wouldn't just stop.

This time it didn't stop. It faded. It slowed. She didn't have the voice to scream. The boy could still hear her crying. His father stopped. The boy could hear the creaking in the floor as he walked away. Let it go. But his mother was still crying, and she kept crying for a while.

When it had been quiet for a long time, or at least the boy thought it was a long time even though he couldn't see the clock on his wall in the dark and he knew it would be bad to turn on the light, he heard someone coming up the stairs. Heavy. Not trying to be soft. It was his father on the stairs. His father outside of his door, and opening the door. And in the light from the hallway the boy could see the shadow of his father and the curl of his hair and the bigness of him. The bigness of his arms and his chest. His father walked into the room, and sat next to him on the bed and the boy tried to seem like he was just waking up and he could smell the whiskey on his father's breath but he was gentle as he put his hand on the boy's head. Brushed his hair back. His father's weight bent the mattress and the boy rolled over on his side and curled around his father who didn't say anything. It was quiet now and it was silent, and there was nothing wrong. Whatever had been wrong was fixed, now. The boy got to see his father before he slept.

‡

Ben was at Maria's apartment at five on Sunday, like he was supposed to be. He pressed the button for her door. She buzzed him in and
met him in the hallway. She smiled nervously and he tried to smile,
too. She hugged him awkwardly. There was a small bandage over her
right eye and it was fading purple and yellow around the edges.

"I called the place. They don't make reservations for two, but
they said we should be fine if we got there by six."

"Good," he said. He tugged at the cuffs of his jacket. It was the
only jacket he had. It was black, for occasions. And he had a white
shirt, and khakis. They fit fine because he never changed sizes, but
they felt wrong to wear.

"Next time, you should be doing that, you know." She smiled
with a nervous edge in her voice. "The man is supposed to arrange
all that stuff."

"Right. I'm sorry."

"I'm just teasing you, honey. You look very nice."

He felt like everything was gears that wouldn't catch.
"Thank you."

She held the cuff of his jacket in two fingers and he kept his
hands in his pockets. "Don't I look nice, too?"

She did. He knew she did. He looked when she was turned away,
locking the door of her apartment. A black skirt and white blouse. It
made him think about the night they'd been together. But it wasn't
right to think about that when she was looking at him.

"You do look nice. You're very pretty." He looked down at her
shoes as he spoke. He wanted to go, but he didn't know where the
restaurant was.

"You're sweet." She slid an arm under one of his. "Come on.
Let's go."

The restaurant looked nice on the outside. It wasn't too crowded
when they arrived. It was mostly young people there. The kind who

always seemed to have everything under control. The kind who'd probably already made it and looked like they never had to worry. Ben stood a step behind Maria at the host's podium. "Two for dinner. It's under Ben." She spoke confidently to the host, who picked up three menus and took them to their table. "This place looks nice, huh?"

"Yes," he said.

"You've never been here before, you said, right?"

"No. I don't come to this neighborhood too much."

The host pulled out a chair for Maria and Ben waited to seat himself. The restaurant was dark, and only half full. Music played softly in the background. Like opera, but with only a woman's voice and a piano. It was still too early. Ben knew that it was a sign of class to want to eat later. His father had always told him that, but he'd never told him why. Maria looked like she belonged here.

"I never came here. Sometimes my ex would take me out to places like this, but this place is new." She took a drink of water from the glass they'd poured in front of her. "I'm sorry. I shouldn't be talking about my ex on our first date." Candlelight from the table cast shadows across her face. It made her look older. Older than she usually did when she had makeup on. But Ben didn't mind. He thought it looked nice, and he knew better than to say anything about it.

The host came back and asked Ben if they wanted any drinks to start. Ben hadn't looked at the menu. He looked at Maria. He didn't like to look at the host. Maria smiled at the edge of her mouth. "What kind of bourbon do you have? Eagle Rare?"

"Yes, miss. Two glasses?"

"Miss. Yeah, right. But yes, please, for the whiskey. Neat, in tumblers."

"Of course."

"We'll tell you which wine when you come back." The host nodded and Maria picked up the one of the three menus. "Do you want any kind of wine in particular?"

At first Ben didn't realize she was talking to him. "I don't know. I think red is better with Italian food, right?"

"How about Chianti? Or they have a Valpolicella. Those are usually wonderful." She looked up from the menu. "Do you like wine?"

"I don't know as much about it."

"There's nothing to know, really. Just what you like. You'll get used to it... all you have to do is try it." She put her hand out across the table. The palm up and facing Ben. After a second he understood and put his hand out as well. "You really are very kind, aren't you?"

The host brought the bourbon and Maria ordered a bottle of wine. The host didn't look at Ben at all.

"I think you'll like this. I like it even better than Maker's but no one ever has it." Ben started to put the glass up to his lips, but Maria held her glass out toward him. "To a wonderful evening."

"To you," he said. It was what his father would always say anytime he toasted a woman. He saw Maria smile.

"You said you're a mechanic?"

"Yeah."

"Do you work on newer cars? Like upper-end cars, that kind of thing?"

"No. I mean, I can, but mostly we see older cars in our shop. I like those better."

"Like classic cars? That must be fun. Those cars are so sexy." She took another drink from her glass. "Do you like this?"

"Yes." It was good. It had a different flavor from Maker's. It was probably better, but all he knew was that it was different.

"Are you like the manager over there? The owner?"

"No. I just work there."

"You. You are all about the false modesty. I can tell. You'll be running the place in no time. And you said you didn't have kids?"

"No."

"But you must regret that so much. I guess it's better if you don't find the right person, but you're going to be so happy when you meet Sophia. You're going to get along with her so well."

The waiter came and described the specials from memory. One of them was something about beef. Ben looked at the menu, but only long enough to see the prices. They were high, but it didn't matter. He had brought five hundred dollars in cash. He'd taken it from the old shoebox in the bottom drawer, next to where he kept his father's knife. The waiter started out asking Maria all the questions. They must have it worked out so the host talked to the waiter, Ben thought. Or maybe this guy could just tell. It didn't matter. It was better this way. "We'll have the artichoke hearts appetizers, and I'll have the osso bucco."

The waiter looked at Ben.

"The beef. The special you were talking about?"

"Bistecca alla Fiorentina?" He looked at Ben and waited for him to nod. "Excellent choice. Shall I bring the wine now, or would you rather wait for your appetizers?"

"Bring it with the appetizers. And two more glasses of this, please." She held up her glass, which was almost empty, and the waiter nodded.

"Certainly. Right away." The waiter turned crisply on his heel and walked toward another large table that had already been served. He asked the oldest man at the table if everyone liked their food.

Maria smiled again. She finished the bourbon in her glass and Ben did the same. The whiskey was like a warm blanket. It made him comfortable and happy, and it was like protection from this place. "She's going to love you, Sophia. She wants a good man in our life so much, you know. She's at that age where she wants a father to adore." She smiled and looked at him from behind her glass. "I guess maybe I am, too."

A different waiter, one Ben hadn't seen yet, brought the bourbon and took the empty glasses. Ben tasted it and it was the same as the last glass.

"I've never spent a lot of time with kids."

"Men never do. Not if you don't have kids of your own, or nieces and nephews. But it's easier for men. Being a father is more natural. Being a mother confuses the shit out of me most of the time, but being a father is just about being yourself. You'll see." She took a quick drink from her glass. "I'm doing it again. I don't mean to pressure you. I don't have expectations. I just mean it isn't something you should worry about. You'll see when you meet her. I bet you'll fall right in love."

The waiter, the one who took their order, brought pale green vegetables in a shallow dish of oil. Ben didn't know what they were. They smelled sour but good. The waiter set two small plates down, one in front of each of them, and a basket of bread at the center of the table. "Can we get a small bottle of olive oil, in case what's in the artichokes runs out?" The waiter nodded and showed Maria a bottle of wine. She nodded, and he opened it with a small tool he'd kept in his apron. He put the cork down in front of Maria, who picked it up and sniffed the side that was red from being in the wine. The waiter's movements looked martial. Military, like a marine drill ceremony with an old rifle. He poured a splash of wine into Maria's glass and stood back. She drank the wine and washed it around in her mouth. She smiled and nodded and put her glass back. The waiter filled her glass, and Ben's.

"Enjoy." The waiter walked back toward the kitchen.

"You're going to love these. Have you ever had artichoke hearts before?" Ben shook his head, but Maria seemed to know already. "You're going to love them. So good. Here." She stabbed her fork into one of the artichokes and reached it across the table for Ben. Oil dripped off the fork and onto the table. Ben reached out to take the fork. "Oh stop, just take it." She held it up closer to him, and Ben ate the vegetable off the fork. It fell apart on his tongue without his even chewing it and there was a flavor like butter, but more rich, all through his mouth. It really was good. Ben took his napkin off the table and dabbed at where the oil had spilled on the tablecloth. "Oh, stop that. For the bail we're going to pay to get out of here tonight, they can worry about the linen. Now, let's finish these off so you can try the wine. I bet you'll love it." She drank off her bourbon in one swallow, and Ben did the same, though his glass was almost full.

She held up her glass, and he held up his. He sipped his wine slowly, trying to watch what she did. She held it in her mouth for a moment, and so did he. "Isn't that wonderful? See? You'll get to like wine in no time."

"It is good."

"Here, try this." She broke off a piece of the bread and daubed it in the oil until the bread was soaked on every side. She held it up to him and it dripped more across the table, but she was probably right about the tablecloth. They must be used to it. He ate the bread from the tips of her fingers and she ran a finger over his bottom lip and coated it in oil. The bread was still warm and the oil on its own was good and rich, but bright like the taste of fruit. "Isn't that wonderful?" She broke off another chunk of bread in the oil and ate it herself. She followed it quickly with a sip of wine. "I love the way the flavors combine. I'll tell you what we should do. We should go over to the wine shop on Dupont, near where I work. We can get a few different bottles and try them together. It's so much fun to talk about all the different flavors. My daddy used to give me a case of wine every year for Christmas and my birthday. I would always go through the case too quickly because I like to open up a few bottles at a time." She took an artichoke and followed it quickly with a swallow of wine. "I never wasted any of it though. I didn't let it sit out and turn to vinegar. I would always finish it all. I think the only sin Italians really care about is wasting wine."

He ate another artichoke on its own. It was good. It felt strange, somehow, to eat food like this. It wasn't normal. It wasn't what he had ever done. It didn't feel like eating to be fed. Everything made him more hungry.

"Look at you. You are such a sweetheart. You never come to restaurants like this, do you?"

"No. Not much."

"Well, don't be nervous. I'm not gonna drag you to places like this every time. It's too much to go here all the time. We'd break the bank. I just thought it would be fun, this once."

"It's very nice." The place was getting louder. Most of the tables were filled and they'd turned up the music. When Maria had sopped up the last of the oil from the dish, the waiter came and took it away. He tried to take the small dishes, but Maria kept hers and put it to the side and poured olive oil out onto it and shook salt on top of that. She used it with the bread the same way she used the oil from the vegetables.

"I know I'm biased, but Italian cooking is the best in the world. And the best thing about it is bread and oil." She broke off another piece of the bread and covered it in the oil on the plate. "Don't worry, I won't lose my appetite. I never do. I guess I'm lucky to be so thin."

The waiter brought their main course. Maria's was a large piece of meat around a bone, like a roast, over what looked like grits, with a thin sauce all around. Ben's was slices of beef in a thick sauce with the grits on the side and string beans.

"Doesn't this look wonderful?" Maria held her hands together at the base of her chin. "I don't even know where to start."

Ben cut a piece of the beef and dipped it in the sauce. It was rich, but simple. Basic. It was like what his mother would have made for a special dinner, except it had flavors he hadn't ever tasted. The grits were thick with cheese and Ben had to wipe strings of it off his mouth. He washed it down with wine. "It's good," he said. "I like the food together with the wine, like you said. It's good with the grits."

Maria laughed at him. "It's called polenta. We've got a lot to teach you about Italian cooking."

"I'm sorry. We never made it in my house."

"Oh, sweetie. I'm just teasing you." She put down her wine and reached across the table to put a hand on his. "They're almost the same thing, anyway. Grits and polenta. The Italians just call it a different word."

He tried the green beans. "That's good, too," he said, pointing at the beans.

"They're just called green beans." She smiled and took a sip of wine. "Don't you worry. I can teach you all about Italian cooking. I'll make us all dinner some night." Her voice and the way she moved her hands in the air were getting bigger. Happier. "It's the only way I can get my daughter to eat anything, is to cook Italian food. It's either that or hot dogs."

"My mom would make spaghetti sometimes." Ben remembered the spaghetti sauce from a store-brand jar. His mother would tear open a little red, white and green packet with spices and let it cook for ten minutes. It was so salty that some nights he'd have a headache until he slept.

"Well, no offense to your mother, but I'll go on a cook-off any time. Just you wait and see. Where does your mother live?"

"She's dead. She and my father."

"Oh, sweetie. I'm sorry." Maria looked down at her plate for a moment, then crossed herself and took a sip of the wine. "It's so sad. Where did they live?"

"Upstate New York. It's where I grew up."

"Oh, right. I think you told me. Country boy, huh? Did you like it?"

"I guess. It's good to be where it's quiet, sometimes."

"Oh, I know. Believe me. I love to go to the country. My dad would always take us—my mom and my brothers and I—he'd always take us down the shore, to the beach. It isn't the same, but it still felt good to be closer to nature and away from the city." Maria cut a piece of her meat and reached it across the table for Ben. "I know I don't take Sophia out to the country as often as I should. My parents take her places sometimes, but they're getting old. I need to be better about taking her places. Maybe we can all go on a trip?"

Ben looked down at his food and nodded.

"You'd be wonderful to travel with." She smiled and sipped her wine. "Where did you go to college?" she asked.

"I didn't go. Just trade school, for a certificate."

"That's probably better. Especially when you know what you want to do with your career. I mean, I went to college, but it probably didn't help me in my career. I just work at Supercuts, anyway. I thought maybe I'd go into business, but instead I spent most of my time there at parties. God. That was such a long time ago. And I met my ex-husband, which I thought was a good thing at the time. But mostly it was just a good time. It's probably different for someone like you. When you always know what you're going to do and you approach it like that. Like a career, right from the start. I guess I just had to learn the hard way."

Ben finished his dinner and put his silverware down on the plate.

"Was that good?" she asked.

"Yeah. I'm sorry. I should have given you some."

"No no no. It's fine. I like when a man has an appetite." She smiled and took a sip of her wine. She finished the rest of her meal and pushed the plate away. Another waiter that Ben hadn't seen came to take the plates, and to scrape the crumbs off the table.

After a minute, the main waiter came back. "How was everything? Did we leave room for dessert?" He poured the last of the wine into their glasses.

"I think we did, yes." The waiter handed them menus and left again. Maria asked about a few of the desserts, and Ben said anything was fine. She ordered something to share and he ordered himself a cup of coffee. He wasn't used to wine.

The waiter put the dish in the middle of the table. It looked like cake, with layers. "Tiramisu," Maria said. "This is my favorite. I make this too, but I'd rather have it while I'm out and not have to think about all the work it takes." She took a forkful and held it across the table. "Do you like it?"

"It's good. I usually don't have dessert." Sometimes his mother would make cookies, but they'd get burned or dried out. He never bought sweets for himself.

"Have you ever had it before?"

"Not this. It's good." He took a bite for himself and let it sit on his tongue. He never knew how many different flavors there were.

"I'll make it for you some time. Sophia loves the kind I make. The little brat. She insists mine is the best so I always have to make it for her. Every special occasion. Birthday, good grades, whatever. It's always tiramisu." She smiled and rolled the last of her wine in the glass. "She's such a good kid, though."

Maria talked for a while longer and then signaled for the check. The waiter brought it, but hesitated, and left it in the middle of the table. Ben took it while Maria reached for her purse. "I can pay my share you know. I never go on a date without enough to cover my share." It was more than Ben had expected, but the wine was in his head and he didn't want to care about the numbers one way or the other. In a class he had once it said eighteen percent was the right number for tips, and he added more than that so he wouldn't need to ask for change and put the cash in the black folio the waiter had left.

"Do we have to take it up?"

"No, sweetie. They just come get it. We can leave it, actually, if you want to go?"

They stood, and walked out into the street. It was cooler, but still warm. Ben didn't know what time it was, but it was starting to get darker. He'd thought it would be dark when they came out, but he forgot how early they'd gone in.

"Come on. I know a great place for a nightcap." She took his hand and led him down the sidewalk. It seemed more alive now that the sun was mostly down. Lights were on outside bars and restaurants. Each place was like a world of its own. The glow and the sound drifted out from inside as they walked past. The streets were busy and the people were young and white and happy and sometimes he would have to walk behind her, with Maria leading them through the crowds. It was wrong of him to do, but he liked to look at her while she walked ahead of him. He thought of reaching out and taking hold of her and a surge ran through his body, but he didn't know if it was right. He didn't know if he was supposed to do that once, or again, or if he had to wait, or if it shouldn't happen at all.

"Here it is." They had climbed an incline for a block or two, and now when they turned they could look down over the tops of low buildings. He'd never known there were hills like this in the city. "Isn't it beautiful?" she asked. She looked at him with her face up toward his. She almost smiled and it seemed like she was waiting for something.

"This place?" Ben asked.

She dropped her face down and looked toward the door. "There's a balcony where you can sit upstairs." He walked toward the door and she followed him. There was no bouncer at the door.

She led him through the door and another on the inside, and up a flight of stairs. It was loud downstairs, and everyone was young. Crowded around the bar. It was loud upstairs, but there weren't as many people. There were people on the balcony, but it wasn't full. "We have to order drinks at the bar and take them out. They have to give us plastic cups, but it's still nice to sit outside." She had to almost yell into his ear, and he felt her breath on his neck. The place was all wood inside, and it looked unfinished in the dim light. They went to the bar and he almost ordered two Maker's, but he asked her if there was anything better. She leaned against him as she scanned the bottles behind the bar. "Oh my goodness, that one. Tell him Black Maple Hill."

"Two glasses of Black Maple Hill, neat."

"We want to take them outside. Please."

Ben put a twenty on the bar, but it wasn't enough, so he took out another and left a couple dollars of the change. He carried the drinks and they sat at a small table on the corner of the balcony. It wasn't as loud outside. Ben could see up and down the length of the street, with all its lights and people and all its noise and it was almost dark.

"There was a place like this near the campus of U of M, up in College Park." She sat close to him at the table. Even though it was quiet outside, she still leaned in close to talk. "All the girls and me would go out a lot. There was a balcony just like this, but it was just in College Park. You shoulda seen how we dressed back then. You probably woulda thought we were whores."

Ben smiled. He knew she was kidding. "No." He held up his whiskey. "To you."

"To us." They both drank the whiskey, and it tasted dark and rich. The people at the next table were young and loud, and as they spoke to each other they had their cell phones in their hands. Ben never had a cell phone, but now he saw that everyone had them. Always pushing at them and looking at them even if they weren't talking on them. He could see the screen of the one closest to him and it was like a computer. Better than that. Like a movie the way the colors and the pictures moved around.

"So how long have you lived here?" she asked. "In the city, I mean?"

"About five years. I guess maybe six."

"You move here right from Upstate?"

"No. I moved around a while before that."

"Like where?" She leaned in closer.

Everything went cold in him, all at once. She was already too close. "Just around. Different places." He looked at her legs. She ran her fingers through his hair.

"You don't want to tell me? What, were you married? Are you married now?"

"No. No, I wasn't married. It just isn't interesting."

"It's interesting to me," she said. "Why don't you want to tell me?"

Ben hunched down in his chair, almost turning away from her.

"It's okay if you don't want to talk, but you really can tell me, sweetie. It doesn't matter. We've all got things we don't want to talk about." She put her hand on his back, and it weighed on him. He could feel the damp of her hand like something cold and sick. "Don't you trust me? Don't you want to tell me?"

Thinking of what he could say made his throat feel closed and tight. He couldn't talk. He shouldn't. He squeezed his eyes shut but it didn't feel like he was alone.

"You know you can trust me. What'll make you feel better?"

Her voice sounded like she was talking to a little boy. A scared boy.

"How about I start? Will that help?" She took a drink of whiskey and sat back in her chair. "I told you about my ex, right? Sophie's father? Don't get angry or weird about it if I tell you this, but I think we should be able to talk to each other.

"We met when I was real young. And I was just stupid then. Not like now. I couldn't see who he really was. Anyway, we dated for a long time off and on. I was drinking a lot, then, and I guess we weren't very careful sometimes. I had a couple scares. I even got pregnant once, when I was like twenty-three, but I got rid of it. I'm sorry; that doesn't bother you, does it?"

"No." He couldn't look at her, but everything in her voice sounded wrong. He didn't know why this was happening.

"Italian guys, sometimes they freak out about that. Anyway, we dated on and off for a long time, and I knew he would cheat on me, and he was gone a lot. He's a salesman for a drug company, so he travels all over the place. Sometimes he would even move to other cities for a month, or three months, or however long to build a new account. I guess he was good at it, too. He made so much money. And it was great whenever he was around and things were good, because we could do whatever we wanted. He would take me on vacations. Down to Florida. The Bahamas. Wherever. He would tell me about how he wanted to marry me if I was unhappy, but then it would never happen. And I saw other guys sometimes, but he would always come back and tell me he wanted me, and he was gonna marry me, or he'd kill those guys, or whatever."

None of it mattered, but Ben knew he had to listen. He had to keep it from going wrong. He had to know what would go wrong. Ben didn't care about the other man. It would be easier if she went back to him.

"So when I got pregnant the one time, when I got rid of it, I didn't tell him. He's like I was saying. One of these Italian guys.

He'll fuck anything that moves, but abortion is a sin, right? Anyway, when I was almost thirty, I got pregnant again. And I didn't want to have an abortion again, and I didn't want to risk it if I couldn't have kids again. I really wanted to have kids. I thought maybe I'd have a big family, but I always knew I had to have at least one kid.

"So this time I told him about it. About how I was pregnant. And of course he told me he loved me, and he wanted to marry me, and we'd raise the kid together. And I wanted to believe him, so I did. Which was stupid, but it was like it was my only choice. Either I get him to marry me, or I'd be alone. When I look back, I can see he was really good at making me think that."

Ben didn't know why she would say any of this, even to herself.

"So we got married, quickly, so I wouldn't be showing too much. And for a while it was great. I thought that with how he changed once I got pregnant that maybe it would be different. Different for real, for a long time. He was there every night, and he cooked. He didn't cook a lot of different things, but what he did cook was good. Lots of fried stuff. I told him, 'Geez, baby, I'm already gonna have a hard enough time with the weight.' But he was good and he took care of me. He was even that way after the baby came. After Soph came. I have all these pictures of her as a little baby, and he's there in almost all of them. Holding her. Playing with her. All the time.

"So it goes on like this for a while, and I was trying really hard to lose the weight. You know, after the pregnancy. I didn't get real big like some girls do. I've always been thin, but I wanted to get rid of it. And he knew how hard I was trying. But for as good as he was with Soph in those days, we were never sleeping together."

Ben took a drink of his whiskey. He watched the way it settled and stilled in the cup.

"I'm sorry to talk about this. He barely touched me after like the seventh month, and then not at all after Soph came. And I guess I knew that he must have been going somewhere else for it, 'cause that was just how he was. But, I don't know. I guess I thought it would be okay if I could get the weight off. I don't know.

"So one night he comes home late, and it was like three months, or four after Soph was born. And I didn't have all the weight off, but I looked pretty good. You know, considering. So I waited up for him one night after Sophia went to sleep, and when he came in I poured him a drink, even though I could smell on his breath he'd already been drinking. And I kinda went up close to him when I gave him the drink. I mean...you know. Anyway, he just took the drink and pushed me away, and he started to walk away from me. And, I don't know, I guess I'd had a little to drink that night, too. And you know how you can't drink when you're pregnant, or even while you're breastfeeding? So I was probably a real lightweight. But I went after him, and I was yelling at him, which I shouldn't have done, and asking him what was wrong with me, and was he with some whore and all this other stuff. So I was probably way over the line, and I was pulling on his arm while he was walking toward the bedroom, and he pushed me up against he wall. Real hard, you know? And it knocked the wind out of me. And he kept going to the bedroom, which was where we kept Soph's crib then.

"So by now Sophia is crying. I don't know why but when he pushed me it just made me angrier. It didn't make me scared. I mean it wasn't like he'd never hit me before. Pushed me, mostly. But hit me a couple times. But now he was in the bedroom and he went over to Sophia's crib, and...I don't know, it was like I couldn't let him anywhere near her. It had been going so good, and he was so good with her, but maybe I was drunk, or maybe I was actually being smarter than usual about him, but I just couldn't stand to see him near her. So I pushed him away from the crib as hard as I could, and I musta been on adrenaline or something because he fell right back against the wall.

"So then I turned back to Sophie's crib, right, 'cause that's all I was thinking about. Like I just needed to get him away from there and everything would be fine. But I didn't realize how mad he was, or how drunk or whatever, 'cause he got up and hit me in the back of the head. It knocked me out cold. I didn't wake up for like an hour after that, and I'd fallen over Sophie's crib when he hit me. I don't know how she wasn't hurt but she fell out of the crib and was lying on her back crying when I woke up. I couldn't move at first, but I could reach out one arm and pull her up close to me and see that she was all right and I just held her there like that for I don't know how long. It was like I realized everything while I was lying there with her. Realized I couldn't let him anywhere near my daughter." She was wiping tears from her eyes. She'd been crying for a while and her drink was gone. "I'm sorry," she said.

"It's okay. Here." He took the cup and went up to the bar and got two more drinks. As he walked back from the bar he thought again and again and again that he could go and she would never find him.

She took a long drink. "Thank you. You're so sweet, and with me going on like this."

"It's okay." Ben knew it would be easier if she left. Went back to the other man. Ben thought it would be different if he was able to protect her. It would be better. But Ben couldn't protect her. He could never save anyone. "Is he still around?"

She wiped her eyes again. "No. Not mostly. I called the cops after that, of course, and got a restraining order. It turns out he left town that night. It took forever to get the divorce, and for the longest time he would call me from pay phones from all over. At night, when he was drunk. But mostly he lives away from here. He was back here once for like a month. I think it was last year, or maybe two years ago. He would sit in a car across the street and watch us come and go. He even grabbed me once while I was on my way into the apartment at night. But Sophia never caught on, I don't think. I just told her that her dad had moved away and we would never see him again. She asks about him sometimes. I probably should have said he was dead. But that seemed wrong, and she was so young at the time and I don't think she thinks about it that much any more." She wiped her eyes again, and she saw mascara on the napkin. "Oh, my God. I must look like a raccoon. I'll be right back."

She walked away and Ben watched her, and then he watched the people in the street and the other people on the balcony. They hadn't noticed her crying. He thought they would be looking at him. To see what he'd done. But they were laughing. Drunk and loud. He didn't mean anything to them, and the sound of their voices and their laughing and all of it disappeared into the open night. He went in and got two more drinks and was waiting with them when Maria got back.

"Oh, thank you, sweetie. You're so kind." She leaned over and kissed him on the cheek and he could feel her face was warm from crying. "Are you angry at me for what I told you?"

"Angry at you?"

"You know. Is it weird or whatever? Did you not want to hear all that?"

"No. It's fine."

"Thank you. I knew I could trust you." She leaned in next to him and held his face close to hers. So close that he couldn't see her. "Now why don't you tell me?" Her cheeks were warm and wet from crying and it felt like she was sick.

He knew he should never, never say. It burned and screamed and roiled inside him, like being sick or trying not to scream or come. Never never never. He should never, never tell.

"You can tell me, sweetie. It's okay."

Never, never.

"I told you all of that. It's only fair."

He was falling, again. He felt like he was falling. He felt like he was torn open and everyone, everyone was standing in a line. All of them watching him.

"I was in prison. For a lot of years." He didn't realize he was speaking at all until he felt her hold him tighter. Closer. "Since I was young. Prison and some other kind of place, just to watch me and see how I was." He felt cold all over. There was more to say, but that was too much. That was enough. Enough to end this. To get her to leave. To get her to leave. To have this all be over. And he wouldn't need to speak to her. He wouldn't have to wonder if he could touch her or kiss her or what was right or wrong or when to lie or not. Everything would be simple again.

"Oh, sweetie. It must have been so hard for you." She held him closer and closer, until she was up out of her chair and leaning over him. She spoke into his ear. "You're so kind and so good. It must have been so hard for you." She held him and held him and when she let him go she still sat close to him. "I'm so sorry, sweetie. Thank you for telling me." She picked up his whiskey from where he'd put it on the table. "Here." They drank together and it all felt right. He was glad she was there, and he was glad it was loud and he was glad she was close. She kissed him, and he knew she was his. Always his, any time. He put his hand on her leg and she smiled. They were just like everyone here. Happy. Drinking. Carefree. She smiled when he touched her and he touched her and touched her and he could feel the whiskey, now, and the night and the city and the feel of living a life he was never supposed to have. And he was happy and so was she and everything was going to be all right, and better, and better. He hadn't lied to her. Everything was fine. He would never have to tell.

CHAPTER FIVE

Ben thought of taking time off before he looked for another job.
But when he was home alone during the day he couldn't concentrate
or think about anything clearly. He read in the morning, but couldn't
keep his mind with the words on the page. He went walking to look
at the monuments and the neighborhoods, and to try to go where
he had never been before, but it was hot and he felt bad and even
when he was walking he couldn't think about anything but Maria.
He liked to think about her. It was like always having something to
hope for, but it made him restless.

Ben went to the library, and he felt like a kid out of school
to be there in the middle of the day. The building was squat, ugly
concrete and it felt like a warehouse or a hospital inside. But Ben
didn't mind, and it made him feel happy and simple just to be
around all of the books. To have them there on every side of him.
He went to the history section and found the book that he wanted
to take out. The first book of Shelby Foote's Civil War trilogy.
He took it down off the shelf and he liked how it felt heavy, and
he liked the smell of the pages and the dust when he held it up to
look at one page, and then another. He took the other two volumes
down off the shelf. He carried them to an old fake-leather cushioned chair, with the white stuffing of the seat exposed and brown-
ing. He sat in the chair and sank too low and he held the books on
his lap and he felt the weight of them. He stacked them one on top
of the other on the table in front of the chair and he knew that he
had read all of them, and he looked at the stack and thought about
what it meant to have read them all. He thought that he wanted

to read them all again, right now, and to hear all the stories in his head and to know them all again, just like he was expecting. But he knew that he couldn't. So he sat and he looked at the three of them, stacked one on top of the other. And he felt the good feeling of the books all around him, and the quiet, and the hidden feeling of sitting in the chair at the end of the row where no one ever came and where even if they came and found him and talked to him at least they would have to be quiet. He sat there until it didn't feel the same, and he took the first of the three books to check out. It would be wasteful to check out all three at once.

He called his case manager from a pay phone on Tuesday. He'd heard about everything at the shop. Or at least he'd heard that Ben had walked off. Vic had talked to him, angry about the coveralls. Ben told his case manager he had worked four days he wouldn't get paid for. That was thirty-two hours, which was enough to buy a new pair of coveralls. There were all the other hours, too, but Ben knew that was part of the arrangement.

He made an appointment to come in and sit down later that week. He was going to see Maria again that night, before her daughter got home the next day. She knew he was nervous about meeting the girl, so she'd mostly dropped it, but she'd probably bring it up again soon. And maybe it would be all right. Ben didn't want to think about it yet.

Ben's father had been good with kids. He always knew how to talk to them, and make them laugh and keep them happy. Sometimes his mother would be all right. He remembered she could be fun, and warm, and kind. But she got worse and worse as Ben stopped being little and got close to being a teenager. Usually she was emotional. She'd be angry a lot, or just crying. He had to be nervous and careful around her all the time. Mornings and days when nothing could possibly be okay. When she was never soft

and when she never smiled like Maria would smile at him. Ben
didn't know how anyone could hurt a woman like Maria.

They'd stayed out late the night they'd gone out. Ben spent
almost all of the money he'd taken out. It was fine, but he knew
he had to be careful. It was good to be out, though. Maybe they'd
gotten a little crazy, but it didn't feel bad like it usually did when
he was alone. They were getting close and pretty physical toward
closing time, and she would laugh and Ben knew that other people
were watching them. But he didn't care like he normally would
have, and Maria didn't care at all. The next morning he slept in and
said he didn't need to be to the shop until ten, and she'd made him
breakfast and coffee. He couldn't think about whether he deserved
it, or how it had happened. He knew he didn't deserve it, and maybe
it would all go away. But for right now he had it and it was his.

Ben had said he would bring wine for the dinner she was
making, and she'd mentioned the nice store by Dupont Circle.
There wasn't good wine like she liked in the stores he usually
went to. He walked there one afternoon, and when he got to the
store there were hundreds of bottles. Some of them were sorted
by place, and some of them by the kind of wine. She'd only ordered red wine, so he looked at those. He tried to look around
for a while but nothing made any sense. There were wines from
Italy, and he knew she would like that. He couldn't remember the
kind she'd said at dinner. After a while a salesman came over and
picked out ones he said were good. The salesman asked some
questions but Ben didn't know, aside from that they were having
Italian food, so he just picked some out. Ben didn't know how
much to get, but they'd had two bottles at dinner, so he got two,
and then got a third just to be sure. He saw they had different
bourbons, and he saw the kind they had at the bar that she liked.
Black Maple Hill. He got a bottle of that, and a bottle of Maker's

for his apartment. It was all expensive, but he still had money. He never spent money at all, so he had it to spend, and it felt good. It was a long walk back to the apartment, and the bags got heavier as he walked.

Since they were staying in, Ben only wore jeans and a plaid shirt to dinner. Maybe he should have tried to dress up, but he only had the one set of nice clothes.

When he arrived the front door of her building was still loose, and he would mention it to Maria and get her to call to have it fixed. There were probably laws about that kind of door. For safety. She buzzed him in when he rang, and the door to her apartment was wide open. He knocked as he came in. He saw Maria in the kitchen, stirring a pot and talking on the portable phone.

"No. No, I don't think so. No, I told you. Listen, wait a minute." She held her hand over the mouthpiece and whispered to Ben, "I have to take this. Stove's down so you don't need to touch it." She opened the cupboard and took out two glasses. "Make us both a drink?" She tried to smile, but it made her look unhappy. She went into the bedroom and closed the door. He could hear her talking, but not what she said.

He took the wine out of the bags and put it on the counter. He took the whiskey out and found a knife to cut the wax seal on the bottle. It had a pull tab like the Maker's bottles always do, but those never worked and his fingers were too big to get a hold of it. He made a mess with the wax, but he pushed it all into his hand over the counter and dumped it in the trash can under the sink. He poured a finger of whiskey in each tumbler. He wanted to take a drink as soon as it was poured, but he knew she liked to toast first and he liked it, too. He let the whiskey sit and he waited for her. He could hear her on the phone, yelling sometimes, but it wasn't his business.

The sauce smelled good when he took the pot lid off to look at it. He didn't think it would hurt it to look, but he didn't touch it. There was nothing to do, so he went into the living room and sat on the couch. He thought about turning on the television, but he didn't know if it was rude, and there were too many remote controls and he didn't understand them. There were magazines about clothes that women wore and magazines about cooking on a bottom shelf of the coffee table, and he took out one about cooking. He didn't really care about cooking, but he felt strange just sitting there.

The couch was comfortable. He was nervous, but he liked being in Maria's apartment. It was nice, but not too nice to where he felt like he had to be careful with everything, or where he would get everything dirty. It felt open, and the kitchen and the living room and dining room were all one big room. He liked that you could stand and talk to someone in the kitchen but you wouldn't have to be in the way. You couldn't do that in Ben's apartment, but it didn't matter because no one was ever there.

Something started beeping in the kitchen. Ben thought it was better just to leave it. The door to the bedroom opened and Maria came out. "Wait a minute. No. Wait. Wait. Just wait." She put the phone down on the counter and put on an oven mitt. She took bread out of the oven and put it on the stove. She took another dish out of the oven, covered in tin foil. She took off the tin foil and put it back in the oven. She turned a knob on the stove, she looked at Ben and mouthed, "Sorry," and picked the phone back up. "Hello. No. I'm making dinner. I told you." She walked back into the bedroom and closed the door.

She was gone for another ten minutes and he could hear her yelling sometimes. He tried to read the cooking magazine, which was about ingredients he didn't even know aside from chicken and asparagus. But the pictures looked good. It was probably the kind of thing Maria would like. He thought about showing it to her, but it was her magazine and he didn't know anything about it anyway.

After a while Maria came out of the bedroom without the phone. She walked into the kitchen and opened the oven and stirred the pots on the stove. She turned on the heat under a pot of water. She saw the drinks Ben had poured sitting on the side of the counter. "Oh, thank God." She picked up one of the two glasses and took a long drink. Ben stood and walked around the island into the kitchen. He picked up his glass.

"Oh, sweetie, were you waiting for me? I'm sorry, baby." She drank the rest of the glass and re-filled it from the bottle Ben had brought. "Now it's a new glass and we can do it right." She held up her glass. "To cooking for my handsome man." They touched glasses and drank and she put her hand behind his head and moved up close to him and she kissed him hard, and then harder, pushing Ben back against the wall. She stopped and rested her head on his chest. "I saw what you got me." She held up her glass. "Thank you for the present. Where did you find it?"

"Where I got the wine. The place you told me about."

"Oh, you went there? Isn't it great?" She took another drink. "You go sit. Dinner will be ready in ten minutes. Do you want to watch TV?"

"I don't know how to use it."

"Here, I'll show you." He tried to follow what buttons she pushed to turn it on, but he didn't think he'd remember. She showed him how to make it say what programs there were to watch, and to find one and select it, and she turned it on to a sports show to start with. He just used the channel up and down buttons, and there wasn't really anything he wanted to watch, but he couldn't believe all the channels there were. There was tennis, and golf, and one where they showed a real person's house, and another where they showed a real mechanic's garage where they worked on bikes. He watched that for a while, but there wasn't anything about the bikes, just the mechanics yelling at each other. There were channels in Spanish and channels where you could call the TV station and buy something from them that he remembered from when he was a kid. After a while he found a western—a Clint Eastwood movie his dad had liked—and he left it on to watch it. His dad would always watch it when it came on TV, but they only got two stations where he grew up. When you have to shoot, shoot. Don't talk.

"What are you watching? Oh God, my dad loves that one. I think it was that one. Anyway, dinner's ready. Do you remember how to shut it off? Here, sweetie." She pressed one button on the control that he was using, and everything went off. "Don't you use these guys, or do you use a different company for TV?"

"I don't have it."

"Oh, God. That must be great. I would get rid of it in a second but Sophie loves it. She doesn't watch too much, but after she does her homework she likes it, and she deserves something fun. There are worse things, anyway, God knows."

On the table there was a pot of red sauce, a dish of noodles and a plate with chicken cutlets cooked with melted cheese over them. Maria brought bread on a cutting board and put it on the table. "I hope you like chicken parm. I thought it would be better if we just put everything out on the table and we wouldn't have to get up again and again for seconds." She poured out the wine in two glasses and left the bottle on the table on a small dish that kept it from dripping on the tablecloth.

She dished the chicken and pasta with sauce onto a plate and put it in front of him. He waited for her to serve herself, and held up his glass. They toasted without speaking.

"This is good, sweetie." She held up her wine glass. "Thank you."

He cut into the chicken. It was moist and the cheese was brown.

"Try it with the pasta and sauce, all together." The sauce was spicy, and rich with flavors. Maria broke off chunks of bread and dipped each in the sauce and in a dish of oil as she ate, like she had in the restaurant.

"It's very good. Thank you," he said.

"It's simple, but it's always been one of my favorites. Sophie, too. She can't get enough of this. I probably should've made a vegetable, but I thought maybe the sauce would do. I don't know. I guess I was just lazy."

"It's good. The sauce is good."

"I told you Sophie gets home tomorrow night, right?"

"I think so. Yeah."

"She wanted a few nights at home before school starts. It's already time for her to go back to school. Can you believe that? We're heading into fall already?"

Ben chewed the food in his mouth. The pasta and the chicken all at once was a lot. He washed it down with a sip of the wine. "I kinda like it. Fall, I mean. And winter. I always liked it."

"It's 'cause you're from up north. People up there always like the cold." She took a sip of wine and squeezed his forearm. "Ugh. I get chilly just thinking about it. Good thing I have someone to keep me warm."

She smiled, and he looked down at his food. He cut another piece of chicken and tried to roll it in the noodles like Maria did.

"So, I was thinking. Maybe did you want to come over this weekend and meet Sophie?" She'd put her fork down and was brushing her fingers against the stem of her wine glass. "I mean I kinda hinted about you before she went up to see my folks. Maybe I should have checked that with you first, but I think you're really going to like her. And I know she'll like you. She might be shy at first. But I know she will."

"Yeah. That's okay." Ben nodded, still looking down at his plate. "Whichever day is fine."

"That's great, sweetie. Let's do Saturday night so we're not having to fuss around thinking about school on Monday. And you can come right here if you want. I'll just make dinner. Lasagna is Sophie's favorite if that's okay with you."

"Yeah."

"That's great. Thank you, sweetie."

They ate in silence. Maria would look at Ben and smile. Ben would try to smile but looked down at his plate.

"So how was work today? Are you tired?"

"No. I mean yeah, some. But it was okay. It was the same as ever."

‡

The boy would sit near Satch at lunch every day. A few seats from each other. They would swear and the boy would laugh. It was different from everything else and it was better than everything else and when it was over the boy would feel sick and embarrassed. He could never remember what they had talked about. The boy would be quiet and look away when the other kids walked by.

The boy would stand and leave before Satch did. He didn't want to walk down the hall with him. Satch would always sit there as late as he could and not leave the cafeteria. The boy didn't want to be there when the cafeteria was empty and there was no reason for him to be sitting with Satch.

"Mrs. Watkins is a stupid bitch," the boy said, and he smiled and he could feel the nervous burning in his throat that made him want to laugh. But he didn't.

"Fuckher," Satch said and it was even harder for the boy not to laugh, but he didn't. His father never laughed when he swore. He might yell but he would never laugh. It was like holding on to something hot but not dropping it or crying out. It was what men did, no matter how much it scared them.

‡

Ben's case manager had an office in the municipal government building in the northeast quadrant of the city. Ben would never go there if he didn't have to. It probably wasn't any worse than his part of town. It was only fifteen blocks away, but he didn't know it like he knew his neighborhood. He didn't know how to tell if something was really wrong, or if it was just noise and threat. Ben took the bus to the stop in front of the building. There were people gathered around out front smoking. It made the building look bad. Dirty from the outside. But it was actually pretty nice inside. Like any other office building, except the people were different.

Ben told the receptionist he had an appointment. She was a big, older black lady and Ben felt comfortable with her. She punched numbers into the phone with the receiver in her ear. "Mr. Haney? Your eleven o'clock is here." She told Ben he was ten minutes early so he had to wait. The way she talked sounded like she was disappointed in him.

His case manager came out twenty minutes later. He looked younger every time Ben saw him, and he dressed nice. He said something to the receptionist. The receptionist smiled and laughed the way that Ben liked so much, the way only big black women do. "Benjamin. Long time no see. I guess you finally started missing me?"

"Yeah."

"Come on back to my office; we'll talk." Ben followed him back behind the reception desk and down a hall to an empty room. There was a phone on the desk, but nothing else, and nothing on the walls. There was a chair on rollers and two simple chairs on either side of the desk. His case manager sat in the rolling chair and leaned back. "They fucked us out of our offices when we moved. Got me in a cubical now, except when I need to talk privately, then I get my own office. By the hour. Like a fleabag motel, and I'm just a whore. Know what I'm saying, Ben?"

"Yeah."

"Yeah. I bet you do." He put his feet up on the table. His shoes were deep brown leather under a blue suit. The shoes almost shined, except for a scuff on the right toe. "So it's been a long time since you came around here, Ben. I thought maybe we were done with you. You were gonna be my big success story. What happened? Not a sweet enough gig? Looking for something better? Movin' up the career ladder? Thought maybe you could leverage that prison GED into something in the pharmaceutical field? It's hot right now. Always is."

"It was fine over there. I just couldn't stay any more." Ben tried not to think about how Haney spoke to him. He told himself over and over that being here had to end some time.

"Couldn't stay any more? Why not?"

"I just couldn't." Ben heard the woman on the phone and he started to feel sick. Dizzy. He hadn't thought about the voice at all until now. "I can't go back there."

"Right." He took a pack of American Spirits out of his coat pocket, and a cigarette out of the pack. "I see a lot of fuck-ups, Ben. What I do for a living? Getting ex-cons into honest work? Most of these guys are back here every month or two looking for some new gig. A fight with the boss. Got caught stealing. Whatever. Back here again and again. The only thing that gets them off my plate is when they finally fuck up bad enough to go back inside. Which is probably what they wanted all along, anyway." He tapped his cigarette on the desk, filter down. "You actually had me thinking you were a different bird, Ben. A different beast. I thought maybe you meant it when you told me you didn't want trouble, and you didn't want to go back inside. Why the change of heart?"

"No change of heart. I'm still the same. I can't go back."

"Yeah? This isn't the first of many? You're not gonna burn another of my contacts, like you burned that dothead prick? What'd you do with his uniform? His coveralls or whatever?"

"They're gone. I told you. I worked four days without pay at the end. That's more money than the coveralls."

"Yeah, right. Glad you got the math under control." He leaned forward in the chair. He was up higher than Ben, and he leaned over the desk. "You know they do studies on this, right? You believe that? Bunch of university types thinking about shitstains like you? Chances are fifty to one against someone staying out of jail for good after they did as much time as you. From as young as you were? There's only one thing that ever works for guys like you." He looked at Ben like he might know the answer, and almost laughed before he continued. "A routine. A nice simple routine. Get you set up like those retards that clean the government buildings. Same thing every day. Day in, day out. That's why I told you it's good to work so much. Stay out of trouble. Like therapy. And after all the hard work I did, and my good contacts in the business community, I had you set up in a routine. And we had it working good for... what? How many years? And you go and fuck it up.

"So now I have to wonder when I talk to you. How long's it gonna be before you fuck up the next one? Before you're back inside? If that's what you're gonna do, how 'bout you just do it and get it over with? Save me the time and burning another contact. Steal a computer out of the resource room across the hall. Better yet, how 'bout you assault a woman or something? There's a new girl that works the welfare program. Good looking. Little tiny thing. No match for you. Right outta school, I think. You could drag her into the janitor's closet. How about that? I'll even let you finish up before I call the cops."

It was quiet for a while. Ben knew he was supposed to talk. "No."

"You sure? You haven't even seen her yet. Shit, I might do her myself."

"I'm not going back."

"Right. Well, statistics say different. Someone oughta find a way to bet on this shit. I'd be rich by now." He put the cigarette in his mouth and stood from the desk. "But if you're going to deny the inevitable, I think I might have something for you. Let's talk about it outside."

They walked out of the bare office and farther down the hall to an emergency exit door. Outside was a parking lot with a sign: *For Staff Only*. There were two milk crates up against the wall. Haney used one of them to prop the door open and sat on the other.

"You can stand." He lit his cigarette. "So like I told you there's a lot going on in pharma these days. You mighta seen the construction off Rhode Island? Whole new office park goin' in, and they just broke ground. I can talk to a guy to get you on over there. You'll be doing a shift on the books five days a week, and half a shift off the books. You'll see eight hours a day, up to like seventeen, eighteen an hour once you're past the probationary period. The half shift you don't see. Good news for you is these union guys never work weekends, so you've got that to yourself. They've got a program through the union for ex-cons. Like an apprentice kinda thing. If you do good at it they might even get you into the union. For now, the half shift will cover your dues."

He took a last drag on his cigarette and flicked it onto the hood of the nearest car. "My boss's car. That prick. Cocksucker never heard of employee engagement." He stood up from the crate and brushed off the seat of his pants. He turned his back to Ben. "Am I good, or what? My pants?"

"They're fine."

"I'll give you the address when we get back inside, and the guy to ask for. Make sure you ask for him, or else it could get all fucked up."

They went back inside and he wrote a name and the address on the bottom of a piece of notebook paper and tore it off for Ben to take. Ben waited in the reception area while he made the call, and then walked him out the front door.

"It's all set. Good gig, and they're looking forward to meeting you." He lit another cigarette once they were outside. "Christ, I hate smoking with the welfare cases." He took a long drag from the smoke and walked Ben toward the far end of the parking lot, near the bus stop. "Listen, I'm sorry I talk all this shit to you. But the only way I ever get through to you knuckleheads is to be clear about the realities. Chances are you're fucked, and you're gonna fuck me up in the process. One slip, one bump in the road, a few days with nothing to occupy yourself, and down the drain you go. And probably that's what we're looking at here. But who knows? Stick with it, think before you act, and we'll see what happens. And if you need any more motivation, don't bother calling me again if you can't make it six months at this place."

The bus pulled up as Haney finished speaking. Ben got on so that no one could watch him walk away.

‡

The boy's father had been away longer than usual. The boy thought it was longer, but he couldn't keep track. His father would leave sometimes for work and the boy never knew how long it would be before he got back. The boy missed him and thought every day when he got home from school or woke up in the morning or was sitting eating dinner that it might be the time his father would come home.

The boy would get sick of his mother and the way she acted. He would get sick of the way everything was a big deal, and he had to come home and do his homework and never eat in front of the TV. When his dad was there anything could happen. Maybe they would go out driving, or they would stay up late, or his father would have had enough of his mother's shit and finally tell her off. Sometimes it was scary, and sometimes it was exciting. The boy knew that if he were a man he wouldn't be scared, and there were things he had to get used to. It was better, because he was becoming a man. But with only his mother everything was always the same, and there was no way to learn to be a man.

She would be there when he got home from school. She worked sometimes, but never when they were alone together and he was getting home from school. He would get off the bus at the end of their road that went behind the church and then turned to dirt when it went around the side of the lumber yard. It was where they would drop off all the kids that lived on their road and a few who lived right there on Main Street. The boy would try to walk away and not say anything because he didn't like any of those kids and the older ones that lived on the same dirt road would scare him and push him if they noticed him.

When he got home from school and it was just his mother it would always be quiet in the house. He liked that. When he just got home and the thought of everything from the day and all of the kids being close and yelling and laughing was like something pushing him from all sides, he liked that it was quiet in the house.

His mother would say hello to him and ask about his day and he would put his backpack at the bottom of the stairs so he could take it up later. His mother would talk and ask him questions but her voice was light and soft and he never had to answer her. She just asked and talked and it wasn't bad. He would sit at the table and she would make him a snack. He could choose what kind. Cereal if he was very hungry. Or toast with butter and cinnamon and sugar. Or potato chips in a bowl. And milk or juice or sometimes soda, but only once or maybe twice a week.

While he sat there his mother would be starting dinner, or maybe cleaning something, or doing the dishes, or she would just sit there with him. It was cleaner when it was just the two of them, because that's the kind of thing his mother liked to do when it was just her and there was nothing better to do. Even when it was clean their house didn't look like other kids' houses. The boy had seen other houses and he knew this one was different. The floor under the rug in the living room was just plywood that his father had put down when there was a hole in the floor because it was old and something had fallen through. The stairs were steep and there were no walls or railings on the side of them. The kitchen wall was mostly drywall except for one side where his mother had painted. In the winter the oven would be open just a crack to keep the kitchen warm if the heat from the wood stove wasn't enough.

When his snack was over he would do his homework. He always had to do his homework before dinner and show it to her and show her everything he'd done. He could sit at the kitchen table if he needed help or go upstairs to his room and lie on his bed and do it there. And sometimes it would make him angry because it was all so stupid and no one ever explained it right and he would punch his book again and again if he was alone, but just sit there quietly and feel like he was burning if he was downstairs and his mother could see him. When he asked for help she would look at it and always know the answer and she would tell him slowly and it would have been easier if someone would have just told him like that at first, or if the book and the teachers and everything wasn't so fucking stupid. Sometimes she would know he needed help without him saying anything and come to help him when he was sitting at the table, or if he was upstairs he would leave things blank that he couldn't do and she would see them and help him later. When homework was over he would still be angry for a while, but then he was allowed to be alone until dinner time and it would make him feel better.

When it was just the two of them they never ate in front of the TV or skipped vegetables. They would sit and eat whatever she had made and he wouldn't mind talking as much as when he'd first gotten home so he would talk about his day, or something he'd seen on TV, or something he'd just imagined. And she would sit and listen and smile and ask him questions and he could talk on and on and he never worried about whether what he was saying was right or wrong. He would talk about his dad and about what they would do together when he was home, and how they would work on a car, or go driving or stay up late. The boy would talk about how much he missed him and something he said or did or something the boy had just made up but that felt real and sometimes he would forget he'd made it up. When he talked about his father he would feel happy and excited and almost as good as if his father was really there.

After dinner he could watch TV, and he would watch shows while his mother did the dishes. It would piss him off to miss the beginning of a show because he had to sit at the table until after it started, but he could usually figure out what was going on, or maybe it would be one he had seen before. He liked to watch everything and he liked to stop being himself and thinking about everything and being in his house and with his mother and no matter what was on it was like he was somewhere else. It didn't matter what show it was or if it was good or stupid or if he liked it or not. When the TV was on everything was different.

When his mother was there he always had to go to bed at 9:30, or maybe 10:00 if there was something really, really good to watch, or it was an hour and he wanted to see how it turned out. Whenever he would have to stop watching he knew that what he was missing would be even better than what he'd already seen. There would always be something even better. And if his father had been there sometimes he could stay up late and watch the television that was only for grownups and that kids were never supposed to watch. The shows that came on late and he and his father would watch them together and even if he felt tired he would be a man and stay awake and watch them and always laugh when his father did even if it didn't make sense.

But with his mother he would have to go to bed whether he was tired or not and no matter what he wanted to watch or do. And she would wait outside of his door for him to get changed and get under the covers and be completely covered up and almost hiding under the blankets before she would come in and sit on the side of the bed. He would always lie facing away from her and he hated how stupid it was that she wanted to treat him like a baby even though he was almost a man, but she would run her nails through his hair and it was like magic that would make him feel warm and safe and good under the blankets. And he could never tell how long she sat there because he couldn't keep track of anything and when she stopped it always felt like she had just

started. When she stood up from the bed it wouldn't be as warm.
He would pull the blankets tighter and before she turned and
walked out and pulled the door almost shut behind her she would
lean down close to him and say so softly that he could barely
hear her, "Good night, sweet prince."

‡

Ben was going to Maria's for dinner at five. They were going
to eat at six, but Maria wanted him to meet her daughter, and for
them all to have some time to talk before dinner. Ben had gone
back to the store for another bottle of wine. He got the one he
remembered Maria liking most from the last time. But he only
bought one. He didn't think he should bring two bottles when her
daughter was going to be there.

Before he went to their apartment he walked and walked for
hours. He walked down to the National Mall. He walked as far as
the Lincoln Memorial, and back to the Capitol past the World War
II Memorial and the Washington Monument. There was construction and everything was torn up near the monument, but he looked
up and saw the two different shades of rock. He'd read how they'd
started working on it but had to stop for twenty years because of
the Civil War, and because there was no more money, and how
when they started again they couldn't use the same kind of rock,
and you could still see the two different kinds of rock when you
saw it in person.

He walked past the Smithsonian, and it felt like it belonged
somewhere else, in some different foreign city. He walked through
the Botanic Garden, and up into the high walkways where he never saw anyone go, and down into the primeval forests. He would
stop and lean against the railing and close his eyes and breathe in

the wet, heavy air and feel all the confusion and the tension seep out of him. He shouldn't be nervous about a little girl, but he was. He wished they had animals—like monkeys or maybe just wild birds—to live in the Botanic Garden so it would be even more real. Even more wild. He knew they could never do that, but he liked to think about it.

The last place he walked was in front of the Capitol, by the reflecting pool. He'd read that they built the city to make it seem scary to foreigners who would come to visit, to show how power-ful America was. He could feel that when he looked at the Capitol. He didn't like to think about what would go on inside with politics and the government because it all seemed bad. He didn't watch the news or read newspapers. He would rather read history. In history everyone seemed better. More noble. Even though everything was probably always the same. Always bad. But it didn't seem that way when he looked at the buildings.

It was hot, and he was sweaty and worn out from walking, so he took a shower before dinner. He wore jeans, but he felt like he should wear his button-down shirt. He thought about bringing some-thing for the girl, the way he was bringing wine for Maria. They had fake champagne that was just sparkling juice at the store, so he'd gotten a bottle of that. His hands shook while he did the buttons on his shirt.

He walked over and got to their apartment early, so he walked twice around the block. He rang the bell, and the buzzer released the door.

Maria was standing at the door to the apartment. She was wearing jeans, too, and a simple purple blouse. He thought she could wear anything and look good. Beautiful, but he didn't know how to say that. He saw Sophia at the far end of the apart-ment, walking out of the bathroom and into her room. "She's just finishing getting ready. She's nervous, too. Just like you." She smiled the way she did when her tongue would show between her teeth and she kissed him on the cheek and leaned against his arm. "Come in and have a drink."

He stepped inside.

"She's just on the edge of teenagerdom. I can feel it coming any minute. But for now she's just shy and nervous, not angry twenty-four seven. Let's thank God for small favors while we can."

He gave her the wine and she poured them both a glass of whiskey from what was left of the bourbon. "I've been saving this for your visits. Believe me, that makes you pretty special." The whiskey tasted good, and Ben put it down on the counter after he took two quick sips.

Maria chopped vegetables for a salad and Ben watched her, leaning against the island counter. He tapped his fingers on the ceramic and then held his glass when it seemed like he was being too loud. He took another sip of the whiskey and it felt like being at home, alone, or working on a car without anyone talking. He heard a door open in the back hallway and he stood up quickly but didn't know what to do next.

The girl came into the kitchen with her back to Ben. She was almost as tall as her mother, and she crowded against her at the stove to ask a question that was meant to be private. Ben turned away and pretended he couldn't see them. The girl started to walk away.

"Sophia!" Her mother's voice was gently chiding. "Say hello to our guest. Ben, this is Sophia. Sophia, this is Ben."

The girl turned and held her hand across the island. She was a beautiful girl, with her hair down and falling to her shoulders and half a smile on her face when she couldn't bring herself to look Ben in the eye.

"How do you do?" She held her hand out like she was putting on a show, but she couldn't make herself look up from the floor.

Ben took her hand and he smiled without realizing. "It's nice to meet you."

She retreated back against the stove, pressed tight against her mother. "Ugh. You little leech; can't you see I'm cooking?" Maria laughed and smiled and put her hands on Sophia's face and pressed on her cheeks. "Why don't you go finish getting ready and then we can do something before dinner. It's gonna be like forty-five minutes."

Sophia rolled her eyes as she pushed her mother's hands away and walked back toward her room.

"She's afraid of me." He'd waited to speak until he was sure the child's bedroom door was closed.

"What? She's what?"

"She's afraid of me. Kids usually are."

"The two of you, I swear." Maria finished chopping a piece of celery and wiped her hands on a towel on the counter. She walked around the counter and held Ben's cheeks the way she'd held Sophia's. "She's a shy, almost-teenage girl who doesn't know how to talk to anyone, much less her mother's boyfriend. I had to tell her the same thing before you came over. You're both afraid of each other." She squeezed his cheeks and made him make a face. She laughed at him and kissed him. He knew he should laugh or at least smile. "Are you okay?" He nodded, and she let him go and kissed him on the cheek. "I have to finish the salad. Here." She filled their glasses with whiskey, a finger higher than it had been at first.

Sophia came back after a few minutes and crowded into the kitchen next to her mother. "What are we going to do?"

"What you are going to do is show Mr. Ben your Xbox. Whatever that stupid game is. Mr. Ben doesn't have a TV. He just reads books. You remember how they told you about books in school? You know, in the same class when you learned about the steam engine and the cotton gin?" The girl rolled her eyes and turned her head to hide a smile. "Well, now you can show him how the other half lives. Go." She swung her hips to bump her daughter away, and Sophia walked with her head down into the living room.

"You can sit there." She pointed to the couch facing the television. She opened a drawer and pulled out a handful of thin plastic cases. "Do you know what game you want to play?"

"I don't know them."

Sophia flipped through one after the other. "Well, my mom says you're a mechanic, so this game has cars, and we can play at the same time." She put a small plastic disc into one of the machines on the shelf and turned on the television and pressed another button to change the screen. "It's just starting up. This is just a racing game, so you use this." Sophia handed him a plastic controller and pointed at the buttons. "Use this one to steer, and this one to accelerate, and this one to brake. This one is for nitro boost if you get the power up, but you won't always have it. You'll see on the screen." She kept her eyes lowered as she spoke.

The screen looked almost like a cartoon, like they had when Ben was a kid. But sharper. Deeper. He didn't know how they could have drawn it all this way. Sophia pressed a button again and again to change the screen. The screen turned to a split screen, with the same line of cars on the top and on the bottom.

"Yours is the car with the red ball over it. Mine is green. Your screen is the top one. Are you ready?"

The screen gave a countdown from five and then everything was in motion. The cartoon cars roared away, except for the car with the red ball, which stayed still.

"That's the brake. You have to press the green button."

Ben pressed it and the car moved forward, and he let it go.

"Hold it down."

He did, and the car surged forward, but crashed into a wall.

"You have to steer! Steer with the knob in the middle."

The car lurched to the right and crashed into another wall. Sophia laughed at him but he didn't mind.

"No! Everyone's going to lap you!"

Ben turned the car the other way and it was smashed from behind by the other cars coming around the track. Sophia screamed; she was smiling and laughing.

"No! No no no! You're going to make me crash!"

Ben was laughing and he hated the way it sounded and he hated the way he couldn't control himself but he looked and he saw the girl watching him and laughing harder, and he knew it wasn't bad. The car with the green ball over it flew by and another car crashed into his and knocked it around in a circle.

"Oh, my God! You have to concentrate. I'll reset it."

She pushed another button and the cars were all back like they were to start, but now there was only one screen, and one car with a red ball over it.

"Now you do this one alone, and I'll show you what to press."

Sophia sat next to him, showing him the buttons to press and when, and he did a little better. But he still crashed, and after a while the cars came around the track and crashed into him and no matter what he pressed the car wouldn't move without being hit. Her arm was pressed against his and she screamed every time he crashed, and they both laughed and laughed.

Maria was standing behind them. "It sounds like you two are having fun." Ben thought that no time at all had passed since they started playing. "It's time for dinner, Speed Racers." She asked Sophia to set the table, and Ben to pour the wine and the sparking juice he'd gotten for Sophia. They sat, and Maria asked Sophia to pray.

"Dear Heavenly Father, we thank You for the food we are about to eat, and our family and our company. In Jesus's name we pray. Amen." She and Maria crossed themselves.

Maria had served thick slices of lasagna before they sat, and there was a spinach salad in the middle of the table. Maria held up her glass. "To my family." Ben and Sophia touched her glass and each other's in turn and Ben thought that everything might change, all at once, like in a dream. Sophia took a drink of the sparking juice and set it to the side.

"Did you tell Mr. Ben about going to the eighth grade this year?"

Sophia looked down at her plate. "No."

"Are you going to?"

"I'm going to be in eighth grade this year when school starts. On Monday."

"And can you tell him about the classes you're going to take?"

"I don't know."

"What about world history?" Maria looked at Ben and rolled her eyes. "Normally it's all I can do to shut her up."

"World History. Like Europe and Africa and Asia. South America too, I guess."

"Do they do it chronologically or by country?" Ben asked. He thought it was a good thing to ask.

"I think by country for Ancient History, and then next year we have Modern World History, which is like since America started, and that will be… everything in the order it happened."

"Do you like history?"

"Yeah." Sophia shrugged. "It's cool."

"Most of what I read is history, but I don't remember the classes I took. I wish I did. It would probably make things easier to understand."

"Yeah. I guess."

It was quiet while they ate.

"Aren't you shy all of a sudden?" Maria finished her wine and poured herself another glass before Ben could reach the bottle. "Normally it's talk-talk-talk about this stuff and I don't understand it at all." Ben wished he could think of something to say, but it was quiet again. "I made tiramisu for dessert."

"Yes!" Sophia pumped her fist.

"I never had anything like that before," Ben said. "Like any of this, really. My mom would try to cook Italian sometimes, and we'd have spaghetti and meatballs sometimes, but it never tasted like this."

"I make lasagna a little different. You see a lot of the Italian recipes have more pasta and just sauce, with less cheese and meat. Sophia and I like lots of cheese and everything else. That's why it falls apart a little. It won't do that as much once it cools and forms up, but I like it fresh like this, too." Maria took a sip of her wine. "I'm Sophia's favorite cook. Sometimes my Italian food is the only thing she'll eat." Sophia looked down at her plate. "She won't say it now, of course, but it's true."

"It's very good. Thank you for making dinner."

"You're welcome, sweetie. I'm glad you came. I'm glad to have my two best people together at last!"

"Did you have a nice time at your grandparents'?" Ben asked. "I think that's where you went?" Ben took a long drink of his wine.

"Yeah. It was cool."

"Where do they live?"

"Up near Baltimore."

Maria added, "Not right in the city, though. They used to live in the Italian neighborhood when they were young, but they moved out to the county before it got so you couldn't live in the city."

"Is that like in the country?" Ben asked. He'd never been to Baltimore.

"More like suburbs," Sophia said.

"Sophia!"

"What? They live in the suburbs, don't they? It's nice though. It's like, old, so it's nicer. What did I say?"

"Nothing." Maria poured another glass of wine for Ben, and finished the bottle into her own glass. "Not everyone likes the suburbs, though, and you don't want to give a bad impression. You like it up at your grandparents' house, don't you?"

"Yes. I said."

They ate in silence for a while. Everyone finished their first helping and Maria served seconds for everyone. A large piece for Ben and a piece half the size for herself and Maria. Ben wasn't as hungry, but it was easier just to eat.

"I don't know how I'm going to stay skinny eating seconds," Sophia said.

"You'll stay skinny. You've got my genes. I stay thin no matter what. I even got skinny right after I had you. Anyway, you shouldn't be worried about being skinny yet."

"Yeah, right. All the girls at school ever talk about is who's fat or how a girl's hair looks or what they do on the weekends."

Maria shook her head. "This is why I'm glad they give you uniforms. That way at least you don't have to worry about how you dress and have these little bitches talking about it." Maria took another drink of her wine and set it down hard on the table. She heard the heavy clang it made, and she picked it back up and set it down more gently. She leaned closer to Ben to whisper in his ear, but she wasn't quiet. "You know I still have my old uniform from high school somewhere."

"Mom!"

"What?" Maria picked her wine glass up again but stopped before she drank the last of it. "What? I was just telling Mr. Ben a joke. For grown-ups. You don't need to worry about it. I don't think you even need to…"

"What do you do for a job, Mr. Ben?" Sophia looked down at he plate while she spoke. Ben knew they'd talked about it already, but he didn't say that.

"Well, I was a mechanic, but I'm starting a new job on Monday. I'm going to be working on the new office complex out on Rhode Island Avenue. Construction."

Maria put her glass down, heavily, again, but she didn't notice. "When did this happen?"

"I talked to a guy on Thursday."

"You never told me about this. We had dinner on Wednesday night. Did you not even know you were going to change careers a day before it happened that you couldn't tell me?" She picked up her wine and drained the glass. She reached toward the bottle but stopped when she saw that it was empty.

"I only talked to him on Thursday."

"But you didn't have any idea before then that you might be changing jobs?"

Ben looked down at his food. He'd started on his second helping but now it made him feel sick to look at it. "I wasn't sure. I didn't know anything for sure. It wasn't worth talking about."

"Well, good. At least I know why you sit like a mute half the time. It isn't 'cause there's nothing going on, it's just 'cause it isn't worth telling me."

It was quiet for a while and no one would eat. Sophia and Ben looked down at their plates and Maria stared off at the wall. After a few minutes she stood up quickly. "Well, since no one is going to finish I guess I'll clear the table."

Ben stood with his plate and started to gather his silverware.

Maria grabbed the edge of the plate. "I've got it."

"Let me help you. You did…"

"I said I've got it." She put the plate on top of hers and it balanced unevenly with the food on each plate. She put some of the silverware between the plates, but a fork dropped onto the floor. "Fuck." She started to bend down to reach it, but stopped and walked toward the kitchen. "Sophia, bring your plate into the kitchen, please."

Sophia took her plate and silverware and the fork from the floor and followed her mother into the kitchen. Ben could hear Maria talking to Sophia in the kitchen, but she whispered low and he couldn't hear what she said. Sophia came back to the table with two plates of dessert and put one in front of Ben. Maria followed her with two tumblers and a bottle of Maker's Mark.

"Would you like some of this? The Black Maple Hill is out."

"No. Thank you."

"Coffee?"

"No, thank you. I'm fine."

"Are you sure? You had coffee the other night. It's no trouble, you just need to say."

"Actually, that would be good. Coffee would be good."

"Fine. Now at least I don't have to drink alone." She put the tumblers down on the table and poured out two fingers of whiskey. "I'll make the coffee. You two go ahead. Eat."

"Don't you want any?" Ben asked.

"No. I'm not hungry. I'll get some later." She finished the coffee and sat down at the end of the table, but faced away from it, with her side against the back of the chair. Sophia ate mechanically. Methodically; each bite took the same amount of time. Ben took a bite and he could tell it was good, but he didn't want to eat.

"It's very good," he said. "Thank you."

"Yeah. Thanks, mom."

"You really like it?" she asked Ben. "You don't have to eat it if you don't think it's good."

"No. It is good."

"You don't need to convince me."

"I'm just not that hungry," he said.

"Then don't eat, for Chrissakes."

Ben took another bite, and then another, but it didn't taste like anything at all.

"Can I go finish my homework?" Sophia asked.

"How do you have homework already? School starts Monday."

"These are the summer reports, on the books we got for Literature and Composition."

"On a Saturday night? You want to do homework now?"

"In case we have to go shopping tomorrow."

"All right. Go." She took another long draw from her glass. Sophia took her plate into the kitchen and put it by the sink. Ben stood from the table as well. "Where are you going?"

"I'll do the dishes."

"Don't worry about it."

"I should do something."

"Leave them. I'll take care of it later. I have a dishwasher."

Ben sat back down. His plate was clear. Maria was staring forward at the wall. He stood again. "I have to use the bathroom."

At the bathroom sink he splashed water over his face. He tried not to look at the mirror. He stood there long enough for it to make sense that he'd gotten up, and to clear his head. Put his thoughts in order. He dried his hands and ran the towel over his face.

At the dining room table Maria was still sitting. Her drink was full again. Ben didn't sit. "I think I should probably get going."

"You're leaving? Now?" The softness was back in her voice. The warmth he thought belonged there.

"I should. With Sophia here."

"That's okay. She understands."

"I think it's better if I go."

"But you still haven't had your coffee." She was standing now. "I made it for you so we could sit for a minute." Her face and her eyes danced between anger, warmth and sadness. "I spent all night on dinner. Don't you want a cup of coffee? Or a drink?"

"I don't know."

"Please just sit and have a cup of coffee. Sit and talk to me."

"Okay." Ben sat.

She poured him a cup of coffee and brought it to him at the table. Her drink was half full, but she pushed it away. "I didn't mean to upset you. I'm sorry if I seem tired. I just worked so hard on dinner. While you two were playing that video game. I just got tired."

"It's okay." The coffee tasted burnt.

"I've been waiting and waiting for you to meet her. You know how important it was to me. You know because I told you." She looked at him and Ben didn't know what to say, and he couldn't look back at her. "And having you here, with her. I was happy. I was so happy you came. But I was worried, and I worried so much about what you would think and she would think and about dinner and if it would be okay. All I was doing was thinking about you, and you couldn't even tell me that you changed jobs? You didn't even think to tell me that? It's like you don't think about me at all."

Ben sat and looked down at the floor, and from the floor to the wall, and from one wall to the next. Not knowing what to do or to say. Knowing he should have expected this. Knowing he should always know better. She was crying, or keeping herself from crying. He wished he knew how to change all of this. He wished he knew about women, and he wished he knew how to change her back.

"Are you sure you don't want another drink? There's the bourbon, or I can open another bottle of wine?"

Ben thought that maybe a drink would make everything the way it was again. Maybe it was that simple. "No. Thank you. I've had enough." He drank his coffee and Maria looked down at her hands and toyed with the rings on her fingers. She looked like she wanted to say something, to ask him something, but she didn't. Ben finished his coffee and stood from the table.

"You're still leaving?"

"I really should. With Sophia here. We're both tired."

"Right. Are you going to say goodbye to Sophie, at least?"

"Sure. Yes, I'd like to."

"Just go knock on her door." She picked up the coffee cup off the table and walked into the kitchen. Ben could hear the noise of the dishes as he walked down the hall. He knocked on the door with the poster on it.

"Come in."

Ben didn't touch the handle of the door. "It's Ben. I wanted to say good night."

"You can come in." Ben heard movement and footsteps in the room. The door opened.

"I just wanted to say good night. Thank you for showing me the game."

"You're welcome. Are you coming back for dinner again soon?"

"I think so."

"You should." She shifted from one foot to another. "I think my mom isn't feeling good tonight." The noise was loud from the kitchen. The water and the dishes. "But I think she'd like you to come back again."

"Okay. Thank you again for the game."

"Good night."

Ben walked back down the hall. Maria was at the sink. She was doing the dishes by hand and piling them in the drying rack. "Can I help with those?"

"No. I've got it." She put a pot in the sink and scrubbed it hard with the sponge. "You said you had to go."

Ben put his hand on her shoulder but immediately took it back. She didn't look at him. Ben thought of pulling her away from the sink and kissing her. Pushing her up against the counter. But he knew he never would. "I'll call you later this week."

"I thought you didn't have a phone."

"There's a pay phone near my apartment."

"Right. Okay."

"Good night."

"Yeah. You too." She didn't look up from the sink.

Ben walked out the door and closed it behind him. He heard the chain lock fall into place.

CHAPTER SIX

Ben got to the work site at seven, like he was told. He asked around for Hardgrave, and was pointed to a trailer behind the main construction. Everything was steel frame and concrete and piles of scrap on the edges of the building. He knocked on the door of the trailer. No one answered, but he could hear voices inside. Two men walked past him into the trailer without knocking and he followed them. They punched timecards in a machine by the door and left without speaking. A large man was sitting at the desk and another on the couch across from him. Both were reading the paper.

"Mr. Hardgrave?" Ben hated that his voice sounded nervous.

"Yeah?" The man on the couch lowered his paper.

"I was told to report here at seven this morning. Ben."

The man didn't pay attention. "Who? Oh, you're that one that Haney was sending over? You steal anything yet?"

The man behind the desk laughed without looking up.

"No."

"Good for you."

"Not another of Haney's dipshits. How're we gonna run this thing?" The man behind the desk didn't look at Ben, but talked only to Hardgrave. Hardgrave was repulsively fat. Looking at him made Ben think of how he must smell.

"We'll run it fine. If Whatshisname here can keep himself straight. He'll do fine. He's gonna make a show of his commitment. Over and above. Aren't you?"

"Yeah."

"What kinda construction you worked?"

"Not much. Some carpentry. I'm trained and certified in HVAC. I was a mechanic before this."

"Good. Perfect for hauling scrap." Hardgrave picked up a walkie-talkie from the cushion next to him on the couch. "Ramirez? Get down to the office. I got a new one for you." He threw the walkie back on the couch cushion. "Time cards are there. Fill one out with your name and address and punch in. Come back to the office at three and punch out. Jackson'll be here by then, and you'll be his problem. Until then, Ramirez'll take you around. You report to him for day crew."

"Thanks."

"Yeah. Wait outside after you get the card filled out. And make sure you get it right, 'cause that's what the girl will use for your permanents. And for your union card app, if you get that far."

Ben took a blank card off a stack on the table by the door and filled it out with his old address. It was the same one he had on his driver's license, so it was fine.

Ramirez opened the door of the trailer. He was average height and only a little overweight. "Come on. Over here."

He walked Ben across the site. He picked up a hard hat from a pile and handed it to Ben. "All the time," he said, and pointed to the hat. As they walked he pointed to various piles of loose scrap, bent metal and broken concrete. "That's all the shit that's too small to bother with the front loader." Ramirez led them to a set of dumpsters with a large wheelbarrow leaned against them. "Go through each of those piles and clear them out. Don't worry about dirt or small stone, just the pieces you can lift without a shovel. Pile it all up here, in front of the dumpsters. We'll load it all into the dumpsters with the front-end loader at the end of the day, unless you're certified with one and you can load it. Lunch is a half hour while you're on proba-tion, but punch out for an hour. He tell you about punchin' out at the end of the day?"

"Yeah."

"Good. I'm around if you get finished, but this should keep you for the day." Ramirez walked off, and Ben took the wheelbarrow to the most distant pile he'd seen. He put on a pair of gloves that he'd brought from home and piled the wheelbarrow full. The work was simple and there was no one to talk to and he didn't mind it. After an hour he felt it in his arms and his back, but it didn't bother him.

No one noticed him as he walked over the site. Maybe it was because they'd been told about him, or maybe it was just that there were so many people it didn't matter who anyone was. His mind would drift in the easy rhythm of the work. He thought about Maria and her body, or sometimes just her smile or how she would look at him. But he was angry. And nervous. Angry to think of how she talked to him, and how she betrayed him by acting that way. But wanting her. Remembering her like he thought she was. Like maybe she really was. Wondering if it would go back to being like it should be. It couldn't be over, or maybe it had never been like that. Not really. Maybe she'd pretended to be better. Maybe she'd pretended to be good, and to care for him. Maybe he'd done something he shouldn't have done. His father would have known, and known never to do the wrong thing, or known that it was her fault all along.

It was like his mother had been. That look on her face. The wild look, like she was an open wound you couldn't touch without it hurting. The look when Ben knew there was nothing he could do. The look that was a trap. No matter what you did. It was why he shouldn't ever be around women. They all had something wrong with them.

It was hot in the middle of the day, and Ben sweat through his shirt and he had to wipe his brow on the back of his gloves. It felt like real work, and he knew he would feel the strength in his body, and it wouldn't matter how much he'd had to drink the night before. People left him alone, and the day went quickly. He punched out for lunch and went to the food truck they had near the entrance. He had to wait in line, but he would remember, for the next day, to come earlier or later so he wouldn't have to.

He thought about calling Maria the next day. He wanted so much to tell her he was sorry, but he didn't know for what. It was a trick she was playing on him. Some kind of trick women probably always played. To make you think everything was your fault. He knew he should call her and tell her off. Tell her good. Show her how she ought to act. How she ought to treat him. And then maybe everything would be fine again, and she would know to go back to being simple and sweet and treating him sweetly.

Ben felt like he did when he was a kid and he would break something he cared about. The picture on the wall of a football player that everyone said was the best one. Ben had gotten the poster for Christmas when he was eleven, and it was signed and it was in a frame with glass. And when he'd gotten angry and he wasn't thinking he brought the heel of his hand down hard on the football player's face. He couldn't remember why. Maybe he'd never known why, but his mother had pissed him off, and in his room where he didn't have to pretend to be anything and where he could look as angry as he wanted to he got angrier and angrier until he hit the picture of the football player. The glass had broken and it cut his hand, but only a little. Ben had to take the glass out of the frame, and there was a scratch all along the middle of the poster, and it creased where he'd hit it. The poster stayed in the border of the frame without the glass, but Ben could always see the crease and the scratch. It was the first thing he saw when he looked at the poster. The poster never looked the same, and it only looked broken and ruined and he didn't like to look at it or to have it. It made it even worse to think about what it had been, and how much he'd liked it, and that now it was gone and it would never, never look good again or be something he could be proud to have.

He could feel how Maria had been, before it had gone wrong. Before it had broken and changed. He could feel it in his skin. He could feel it without trying to. Without even wanting to. But maybe all of that was gone now, and maybe it would only be bad to remember how it had felt.

No one seemed to work too hard. They walked slow, and they spent a lot of time prepping jobs, or talking about them, or on smoke breaks. Ben didn't mind. It was good. He could work harder and never complain, and they would leave him be.

It didn't take long for the end of his first shift, and he thought it would be fine. He was tired all over, but even when he moved slow no one minded. He hadn't seen Ramirez again all day, and the work would take him another two days at least, and by then there would be more.

He stood with a line of guys waiting to sign out. Some of them talked to each other. But mostly they were quiet. No one talked to him. Inside the trailer Hardgrave was still on the couch, but the other guy was gone from behind the desk. Ben put his card in the machine to sign off and then went and stood in front of Hardgrave.

"Made it, huh? How does working feel?"

"Good. I like it."

"Yeah. Wait outside till Jackson gets here. Son of a bitch shoulda been here fifteen minutes ago. I'll send him out to you once he signs in."

Ben waited outside as a line of workers filed in and out. The first shift leaving, the second shift signing on. He stood for about fifteen minutes before a young black guy stood in front of him and held out his hand.

"Jackson. You're Ben, right?'

"Yeah."

"Long shift today?"

"Yeah. Probably every day."

"That's what I heard. You get dinner yet?"

"No."

"Go over to the truck and get yourself something. If you don't mind, get me a sandwich. Whatever. And a water." He held out a ten. "By the time you get back to the trailer, these fat fucks should probably be on their way and we can talk."

Ben took the money and got two sandwiches. There was a short line with new guys coming on, getting coffee or water or soda, but it was faster than the lunch line. He got two ham and cheese hoagies and two waters and walked back to the trailer.

The crowd of guys checking in and out was mostly gone, so he walked in and handed Jackson his sandwich and the water, and Jackson thanked him. Ben held out the change he'd gotten from just one of the sandwiches. He'd paid for each separately. "No, keep it. My first boss always bought lunch for the new guy on the first day. He was the only guy I ever worked for I didn't wanna punch in the face."

"Thank you."

"No problem. Siddown. Eat. I just want to talk to you about your work history. They never send me résumés or applications or anything for second shift." Ben sat on the couch and opened the sandwich on the coffee table. Ben thought he could smell Hardgrave on the couch. Jackson sat at the desk. "So what were you doing before this?"

"Mechanic. A garage in the city."

"Old cars? New? What?"

"All kinds, but I liked old ones better."

"I hear that. Nothing like really getting into one of the old machines. Nothing you can do with a computer." He was trying to make friends. There was something eager and needy in his voice. Ben wished he could eat alone. "What else've you done?"

"Nothing much. I got trained and certified on HVAC and engines. I've done some carpentry."

"HVAC'll be good to have once we head into winter. We got other jobs inside. A lot of these grunts'll be out on the street by then." Jackson took a bite of his sandwich and talked with his mouth full. "For now, though, let's get you out on engine patrol. We've got two rigs sitting useless 'cause no one around here knows how to fix a real engine. They're diesel, large engines, but usually it's something simple that no one ever takes the time to fix. I'll show you once we're done with dinner and you can see what you can do with them. That sound better than shit patrol?"

"Yeah."

"Listen. I know how they do with guys in your situation. And I've seen a lot of you guys that were just lookin' to fuck up. If that's your game, I'm just as happy to bust you back as anybody. Happier, maybe. But if you want to do some work, and do right by me and the crew, I'll treat you as good as I can."

"Thank you." Ben's mouth was dry. The words sounded rough in his throat. He took a drink of water.

"Let's just see how you do. I know you're coming in here after a day's work already. Couple other guys in here got the same deal. There are no bosses other than me around for evening shift, so I let y'all go a little easier. Do better work, not work as hard. Do right by me and we'll work it out." Ben thought maybe he should thank him again, but he didn't. They finished their sandwiches and Jackson showed him to the downed rigs.

‡

It was hard to wake up. The boy's mother had to come into his room three times, and finally his father stood in the door and yelled at him. He got up then. He flew out of bed, like a fire drill. But he was only half awake, standing in the middle of the clutter in his room in nothing but his underwear.

He'd been up late the night before. His father had gotten home from a run and his favorite movie was showing on Channel 2. An old western, and the boy got special permission to stay up late to watch it on a school night, even though it didn't start until after he was supposed to go to bed. His mother said he shouldn't be allowed to stay up, but his father had let him, and they stayed up together to watch it.

At the breakfast table the boy sat in front of a bowl of cereal while his parents got ready for work. His mother was brushing her teeth in the kitchen sink because his father had been in the bathroom for a while. His father would come out and ask where something was that he thought he should have been able to find and the boy could hear him getting angrier and angrier. The boy was too tired to eat and being in the kitchen and everyone getting angry made him wish he could go back to bed and be under the covers with the door closed.

"Where the hell is my belt?" his father asked. "The brown one."

"I don't know," she said.

"I know I left it in the laundry room."

"Then it's there, or I took it upstairs with the laundry."

The boy's father walked into the laundry room. He was walking quickly and the boy could see how his face looked. He could hear him in the laundry room, moving things around. He came out still walking quickly. Bent forward as he walked and he didn't look at the boy at all. It was like he wasn't there, and he wished he really wasn't.

His father went up the stairs and called out to the boy's mother and asked her why the hell she always moved things around, but he still couldn't find the belt. His mother took pills from the aspirin bottle and told the boy to hurry up and finish his cereal. He tried to eat another bite or two. His father came down the stairs and he still didn't have the belt and he went back into the laundry room. "It's still not in here," he said, and the boy heard him moving things around even louder this time.

"Did you look on the coat hooks in there? Did you hang it up?"

"It's not on the coat hook. Why would it be on the fucking coat hook?"

"You hang it there sometimes." His mother was fixing the boy's lunch for school and her hands were shaking as she cut an apple. There were lines in her face that made her look worse. Angrier. Older. She looked at the boy and he tried to eat another bite but he already felt sick and he wished he could leave the table, but she looked at him and looked at him while his father yelled from the laundry room.

"I can't find the fucking thing anywhere. If you'd clean shit up around here maybe I could find something and not be late for work every fucking day."

His mother was still looking at the boy. "I told you five times already to finish your cereal. Now hurry up. You need to eat before school. You can't be hungry until lunch."

His father came back and looked at his mother, then at him. He walked to the table and picked up the cereal bowl and some of the milk and the colored pieces fell out over the side. "If you're not gonna eat, don't fucking eat. See if you like it better being hungry all day." He threw the bowl in the sink and milk and cereal splashed out over the side and onto the clean dishes in the draining sink. "Now get your ass up and go get dressed. And stop fucking looking at me like that if you're not going to do what your mother says."

While he was talking, the boy's mother had gone into the laundry room and came out with the belt. His father took it and he followed the boy up the stairs to finish getting ready. The boy hurried up the stairs and hunched over and put his hands on the steps in front of him so he could go faster and not trip and fall. He could feel his father close behind him.

It felt better with the door to his room closed and taking a few minutes to put his clothes on. He had taken a shower the day before so he didn't need to that day. He put on jeans and a black t-shirt with nothing on the front. He sat on his bed for a minute when he heard his father walking by and walking down the stairs. He heard the sounds of footsteps over the floorboards and the sounds of the front door opening and shutting hard. The house shook, and then it was quiet.

The boy went back downstairs and the bathroom door was closed. He heard the sounds of the faucet running in the tub. And the splash as his mother checked the temperature. There was a low thunk and the water stopped and started again; he heard the thin hiss of the shower head. The boy heard the shower curtain draw to one side and back again and the uniform static of the water turn to broken, random splashing.

The boy knew that the way the shower faced in the bathroom made it hard to see the door with the curtain drawn. He walked as quietly as he could to the bathroom door. He turned the handle very, very slowly so that it wouldn't make a sound, and then pushed the door open just an inch or two and slowly let the handle turn back.

When he was younger he could walk into the bathroom while his mother was there. He was too old for that now. He knew he was too old, and his father had yelled at him for it after he turned ten. With the door open just a crack the boy sat against the wall outside of the bathroom.

The sound of the water made him calm and warm inside. He drew his knees up close to his chest and put his head down, and he felt like he was drifting on the ocean. It was probably what drifting on the ocean was like. He felt weightless. Thoughtless. Carried out of everything and he didn't think of anything or even press his teeth together or always have something on his mind. He didn't feel the nervous feeling that always made it hard to close his eyes. He felt blank. He felt like nothing.

The sound of the water was like dissolving at the edges. Most of the time there was the boy, and there was everything else. There was everything he wanted. And there was everything that was wrong, and there was everything that laughed at him and everything that was angry with him and everything that was just angry and everything he had to do and everything he hadn't done. And him. And he was always in the middle of everything else and it was always all around him and pushing him and seeing him and pulling him and making him be different from what he wanted to be or thought he was. Everything was always closing in on him and getting into his mind and making him nervous and making him angry and making him afraid. But now there was only the sound of the water and the feeling like that sound was everything and all around him and all throughout him and he was floating on it and sinking under it and there was nothing else at all. His body was gone. His hands and his eyes and his mouth were gone. What had happened and what would happen were gone. In the sound of the water he drifted and sank and floated and didn't feel anything at all.

The water stopped and the boy was standing up before he realized it was over and everything was back. He walked out to wait for the bus.

‡

Ben was home by seven-thirty. He poured a drink as soon as he walked through the door, then turned on the water in the shower to get it hot. He could feel the ache in his muscles. It was good, and it felt right.

He drank the whiskey in the shower, resting it behind the curtain on the edge of the tub. Everything felt different now. He thought he should call Maria, but thinking about her made him angry. He would forget about her for the night. He would worry about her later. He got out of the shower when the hot water ran out and he'd scrubbed himself twice over. He combed his hair, put on deodorant and a pair of boxers. He walked across the apartment like that because there were barely any windows, and he kept the blinds closed. He poured himself another drink. It was warm in the apartment, still, from the heat of the day, and it felt nice. He thought maybe he would go out. At least for a walk, or maybe for a drink. He hadn't been as good as he should have been at the bar the last time he was there, but maybe it wouldn't matter as much. Maybe he should go over there. He could get something to eat on the way.

Ben sat in his chair to think what to do next and it felt good and simple to be clean in his old chair. He hadn't thought much of it either way since he'd first been with Maria. He'd sat in it plenty of times, but he hadn't just sat like he used to. He put his head back and it was just enough so that it felt right, and he put his feet up on the edge of the coffee table. Ben took a long drink from his whiskey and he knew he could do anything he wanted. He could stay in or go out, or call her or not. He didn't have anything to do until work tomorrow. For just a moment he sat back farther and closed his eyes to think, and to be happy sitting in his chair.

Then he was sitting at a table and it felt good. The girl was sitting across from him. It seemed like her. Long, dark hair, but he couldn't see her face like he usually could. But it had to be her. It was always her.

He sat at the table and he held her hand and everything was fine. Something seemed wrong. Something could go wrong. But he worried all the time, so maybe everything was fine. It felt fine to sit at the table. It felt good, and he didn't know why he wasn't just happy. Everything was the way it was supposed to be. He felt the warmth of her hand in his, and the feel of her skin under his thumb. She was young. Just like she always had been. And so was he. Nothing had changed.

They were sitting at Maria's dining room table and he held her hand while she looked away. Was Maria here? They were all friends. They all knew each other. It had to be that way. Sophia pushed the hair back from her face with her free hand and she couldn't look at Ben because she was shy but she smiled and looked down at the table. Was it her? Was it supposed to be her? It was fine if it was her because he liked her, but wasn't there someone else? Hadn't it always been someone else?

"...But I can love you, too," he tried to say but the words were dead in his throat. He couldn't make any sound. He tried again and again until it felt like choking to try to speak and Sophia wouldn't look up from the table.

"You can," Sophia said, because it could only be Sophia. She looked up and he could see her face and she was crying.

"No, no," he tried to say to make her feel better, but he could never, ever talk. He held her hand and he tried to reach her face but she turned away and he reached and reached but he could never reach her and he sat holding her hand looking at her with her hair falling in front of her face. It was cold. It was colder and colder. Maria didn't like the cold. She would be upset. He could make it warmer if the heat needed to be fixed, or if he could build a fire.

He would make it warmer and she would be fine, but now it just got colder and colder and he held on to Sophia's hand. And it was cold, but he held on tighter and tighter. He pulled her to him but she was limp. Her head fell back, and it was no one at all. It was like a doll or a mannequin. It had dead eyes and the hand he was holding was just wood or wax or plastic but he didn't let it go. She'd come back if he didn't let go. Sophia would come back. He held her hand tighter and tighter, and he pulled at it to make the life come back. He breathed on the hand, trying to make it move and be warm. He wanted to shout, but he didn't have words. The mannequin was looking at him without eyes and without a mouth or a voice or a soul and it asked him, "Why did you let me go?" and he was falling backwards in his chair and a different world crashed in around him all at once.

He'd left a light on, and the windows open. There was a glass of whiskey next to him. It was two in the morning. It wasn't morning but it felt like waking in the morning, and it made him sick but he swallowed the rest of the whiskey. He would get more when he could stand up but he didn't want to. Not yet. He sat for a moment, holding his eyes open, barely letting himself blink. He tried to remember everything that had happened the day before, and he hadn't hurt anyone. Everyone was fine, and he hadn't hurt Sophia or anyone.

‡

The next day was the same. Ben was tired, and still drunk when he'd gotten to work, but no one paid attention to him. No one cared. He punched in when he was supposed to and went back to the work he'd been given the day before. The pile of trash was growing but no one seemed to care. He worked slow, and he started to feel sick.

The day passed like it had before, but there was nothing good in his thoughts. He couldn't clear his head and he couldn't get the dream out. He'd had it before. He'd had dreams like that before, but there was nothing he could do about what had passed. He didn't like to see Sophia in the dream. Maria started all of this. She'd gotten him involved. She was a stupid bitch. What was wrong with any of them that they couldn't just leave him alone?

There was a different truck for lunch, and they had burritos. Ben got one with pork and hot sauce and it took some of the sick out of him. He wanted a nap, but he didn't feel the nervous edge of the whiskey when he went back to work. The food was heavy, and the late summer heat made it feel rotten in his stomach. He punched in a half hour after he started working.

That night, after he punched out, Jackson was already in the trailer. Ben saw him and nodded and walked back out toward the engines that he still hadn't fixed. He thought he could figure it out, if he had just another hour, and then order the parts if they needed any. He liked working on the engines. He was glad Jackson had asked him to do that. He liked thinking through the problem, like he used to, and he liked trying to learn the engine. But he didn't want to talk to him.

He saw Jackson coming across the work site from the trailer. Ben kept working. Jackson leaned on the front fender. "How's it going?"

"Almost done. It might need a part. I have to check one more thing."

"Good, good. Parts are in the supply truck behind the office. Let me know when you know and I'll open it up for you. If we don't have it I'll give you the catalogue and you can order it from the company. Should have it here by tomorrow night from their central supply in Virginia."

"Okay. Then I'll start on the next one."

"You get dinner yet?"

"I had lunch."

"Well, take an hour when you want it. Or just head out early. I thought it'd take you longer with the engines."

"Thanks."

"You bet." Jackson walked away, making a loop around the work site.

The engine needed clean fuel filters, but nothing else. He went to the office. Jackson was there alone. Ben told him the parts they would need to finish the engine.

"We should have those. Here, take the keys. Supply truck is around back. Take a flashlight, too."

Ben unlocked a padlock on the back of a semi trailer and rolled up its gate. There was no order to anything, but he tried to look quickly because he didn't want to be seen going through the truck. He wasn't a thief and he wasn't going to be, but it was easier if he could just get in and out. There was every kind of supply you couldn't leave out in the weather, all in the back of the truck. Even office supplies and an old computer. But he found a pile of parts for the large diesels. He found what he was pretty sure would work and closed the truck and locked the padlock. He went back into the office to return the keys.

"You lock it up?"

"Yeah."

"About how long to replace it?"

"Hour and a half. Maybe two."

"Offer still stands if you want to finish up early. You can leave that until tomorrow. No one gives a shit."

Ben thought about going home. Getting a drink. Maybe going out. Being away. He didn't need to be told when to leave or not. "No. I'll finish up and then I'll head out."

"Don't like to leave a job unfinished, huh?"

"Yeah."

"All right. I guess I'll owe you one."

Ben nodded and walked out of the office.

‡

Ben wanted a drink when he got home, but the thought of it made him feel sick. He took a shower, he changed his clothes, and he poured himself a drink that tasted like medicine. But the medicine worked and the sickness faded.

Ben sat in his chair and he felt good and comfortable and he had another drink. But he wouldn't sleep. Not yet. He sat still and drank his whiskey.

He poured another drink and he put his shoes and socks on. When he finished the drink, he stood quickly from his chair, but he was steady on his feet. He walked three steps and turned on his heel. Still steady.

Ben took a few quarters from a dish of change he had by the door and he walked out of the apartment. The night was cooler than he expected. The sun was down earlier than usual. It was quiet. Normally, this was the time to be out. When it was still hot and stuffy inside, but it had cooled off outside. But already it felt like winter. Almost no one was out on the street. Whoever was out wore coats and stuffed their hands in their pockets.

Ben walked toward her apartment. There was no reason to, but no reason not to. He got to the end of her block and he could see where it was. A light was on in Maria's apartment, but he knew it would be. There wasn't any reason to come here.

He walked back down the street, the way he had come. There was a pay phone out in front of a bodega that was only open during the day. It would be quiet there. He put a quarter in the phone and dialed her number.

The phone rang twice, then a third time. Ben wanted her machine to answer, and thought maybe it would be better just to hang up. He heard the click. He heard a voice. "Hello?"

"This is Ben."

"How do you do? This is Sophia." Ben thought of her holding her hand out and he almost laughed. "Do you want to talk to my mom?"

"Yes, please."

"Hold on. She's just doing the dishes." Ben heard pieces of the conversation in the background. Sophia calling for her mother. Maria telling her to finish her homework. He almost hung up, but he didn't.

"Hello?" Her voice sounded thick, like she'd just woken up.

"Did I wake you up?"

"No. Do I sound like it?"

"I guess not." He wasn't saying what he practiced in his head. "How are you?"

"I'm fine. You?"

"Fine. Is this a good time to call?"

"It's fine. Hold on." Ben could hear her say something to Sophia, but he couldn't hear what it was. "Sorry. I'm back."

"I just wanted to see how you were."

"I'm fine." Water ran in the background, and then it stopped. "How's the new job? You started, right?"

"Yeah. I did. It's fine. I think it's going to be all right."

"Well, you can tell me about it next time you see me."

"Yeah. How is Sophia's school?"

"Fine. You should have asked her. You were just talking to her."

"Yeah." Ben held his breath so it wouldn't sound as bad on the phone in the silence.

"So why did you call?"

"I don't know. I guess I wanted to see if you were free later this week." It didn't sound like it was supposed to. "I thought maybe I could see you."

"Yeah. I am. Actually, Sophie is out at a friend's house for a sleepover on Friday. You could come over for dinner."

"Let's go out. Wherever you want to go."

"Okay. Sure." It was quiet again. There was nothing left to say.

"So I guess I'll pick you up around eight?"

"That would be nice."

"Okay, yeah. It will be nice."

"I'm glad you called. I'm really glad."

"Okay. Yeah. Me too."

"Good night."

‡

The boy was standing at his locker watching the girl. She didn't look at him today, but he didn't mind. It was too hard to try to talk to her. He needed a better way to show her who he was. He needed some way, but it wouldn't happen today. And it was easier just to watch her.

The boy knew that sometimes she was kind. Sometimes she would talk to him and be kind, and simple. He knew that it was the others that would change her. The monster. All of them. All of it, together. Change her and make her be different and hard and loud and never nice to him.

The boy knew she didn't like her glasses. He heard her say it to her friends. He'd heard her say it softly, when she was standing at her locker looking at the small mirror mounted on magnets with a shooting star across the bottom. "These glasses make me look stupid." He'd heard her say it and it was almost like she was talking softly, and only to him. He'd heard her say it when she talked like it was just for him. Just for the two of them. The boy knew that he could save her. The boy knew that he could save her from them.

The boy looked down at the pile at the bottom of his locker. He didn't want to go to class or talk or see anyone else, but just stand there for the rest of the day until he could leave and go home and be in his room and away from everyone. He saw the girl's friends coming and he put his head deeper in the locker and pretended to look for something. A book, or a notebook.

The girl and her friends were laughing together, but they didn't go away like they normally did. The girl was already changed and different because they were here. The boy felt sick and he could feel a cold sweat on his neck and his back. He closed his locker and walked away and it felt like an emergency he had to escape but there wasn't any time.

"Look, it's the retard," one of the boys said and they all laughed. The girl laughed.

"Yeah, retard. Where's your other retard butt-buddy? You faggots sure like to eat lunch together."

The boy's skin was on fire. He closed his locker and he walked away.

"That's right, retard, go get your faggot boyfriend. He'll give you a kiss."

The boy walked away, but there was no way to leave it behind. He heard everyone laughing as he walked. He heard everyone calling him a faggot. Everyone calling him a retard. He felt everyone watching him and laughing and he knew that he had to change it. That he had to save her.

‡

Jackson let Ben off work early on the night he was supposed to meet Maria. Ben didn't want to talk to him, but it was nice to get out early and not have to rush. When he got home Ben had time for a drink. He thought maybe he shouldn't have one, but he did before he showered. He leaned against the kitchen counter under the bright light. It made him feel good and all to himself and it took away the nervous feeling of already knowing how the night would go. He could feel it. Imagine it. Just like his mother. Having to be so careful all the time, and still never doing anything right. It might be different, but it probably wouldn't be. But the whiskey made him feel different. He took a shower and got dressed.

He wore the same thing he always would have. The restaurant he picked didn't look fancy. There was still time after he got dressed, so he sat in his chair and poured another drink. He could sit there all night. Not go out at all. It might be simpler. Easier. She didn't know where he lived. He didn't have a phone. He'd lost her once. But he'd said he would go, and now he was starting to feel good.

The restaurant was one of the ones where you brought your own liquor, so he'd gotten two more bottles of red wine and he put them in a plastic grocery bag and they clanged against each other when he picked them up. He got his keys and his wallet. He put more cash in his wallet but this place wouldn't be as expensive. It was always better to have extra. He took the bag with the bottles and he left.

Maria was waiting for him at her apartment. She looked beautiful. She wore a long dress with a V-neck top that he liked, and a sweater. Ben thought it looked formal, but it still looked right on her. She wore a coat over the dress for the walk.

Ben could tell she was nervous. She didn't talk as they walked to the Metro station, and Ben didn't feel like talking either. It was just as good not to talk, now.

They were only on the Metro for two stops and it was almost empty. Only a few people who looked tired, having to go to work or come from work after eight at night. No one looked at anyone else, and Ben liked it better that way. He liked the bus better than the Metro, because at least you could see outside.

When they came up the escalators from Gallery Place station it was bright and the sidewalks were packed. Everyone was loud and happy. It was like being inside a bar, and Ben had to push through groups of people to move toward the restaurant. He took Maria's hand, and she laughed and wrapped two arms around his and held him as he pushed through the crowds. They walked quickly under the Chinatown Archway where Ben usually liked to stand for a moment and look to try to pick out every different color. Past the Archway the crowds got thinner, but she stayed close to him. It felt good to have her like that, but he didn't look at her.

The restaurant was busy, but there was a table waiting for them. Ben had walked down the night before to make a reservation. The waiter seated them and poured water into their glasses. He came back with a cork tool and two glasses and opened the first bottle of wine. He poured out two glasses, but he didn't ask Maria to taste it first. Ben thought that must be because he brought it himself.

Ben raised his glass without speaking. Everything he could say seemed stupid, so he didn't say anything at all.

"To you," Maria said, and they touched glasses. When he could look at her he saw she was smiling, but she seemed shy, almost scared.

They looked at their menus. Ben wasn't hungry at all. His chest and his stomach felt like one solid object. Like stone or brick or dirt. He drank the wine quickly but he couldn't feel it at all.

"How did you hear about this place?" Maria asked him.

"A guy I work with. A boss for one of the shifts."

"It looks nice. He must have good taste."

"Yeah."

When the waiter came he ordered the kind of chicken he would always get at carry-out. He wanted to see if there was any difference, and it was the easiest thing to order. There were things he didn't recognize, but he couldn't think about anything like that. Maria ordered something he couldn't understand, but she looked happy enough.

They sat in silence and he tried not to drink too quickly. Not faster than her. He still couldn't say anything so he looked around the restaurant. It wasn't like the other place. The walls were bright with intricate decorations. Dragons and Oriental murals. Ben could see the walls were water-stained beneath the ornaments. He could see the age of the carpet, and the cracks at the corner of the ceiling. The lights were bright, like they would be in an office. He wished the lights weren't as bright, but he liked it here. He felt better here.

He felt her hand on his and it startled him. "I want to talk to you," she said, but she wasn't looking at him. "I wanted to apologize. For the other night. I was just so…" She trailed off and stared at his hand. She picked it up in hers and traced her finger along the veins that stood out through his flesh. "I probably had too much to drink. I was just nervous about you and Soph. I know I ruined it."

"No. It's fine."

"It isn't fine. I was so excited that you got to meet her."

"It's okay."

"Are you still angry at me?"

"No. It's fine." It made him angrier to have to lie. He couldn't look at her. She half-smiled and pulled her hand away.

The food came and they picked at it. Maria used chopsticks on a whole fish that they brought with the head still on. She pulled pieces of meat off the body with the chopsticks. Ben forced himself to eat, because he knew that he could even if it made him feel sick. He could see by her face she was hurt but there was nothing he could do about it. It was her fault. He knew he could reach out to her. Put his hand on her arm. He could tell her he loved her, and it might be true. He could tell her it was all right. And everything would be all right, just because he said it. It was like a movie. So simple. But he couldn't. It made him angry to think about. It wouldn't be fair. It would be too easy. For her. It wouldn't be fair to let her off so easy. She deserved this. It was the right thing, even though it made him feel sick.

Ben didn't know how long they'd been sitting there when she stood up from the table. The waiter had walked by, watching them not eating. But he always kept walking. "Come outside for a minute." He looked down at his plate. "Just leave it. Just come outside for a second. Please." Other people were watching them.

He didn't know what this was, but he stood and he followed her through the door. She told one of the waiters that they were just going to smoke, and that they'd be right back. The waiter looked nervous but nodded as they walked past.

It was cool outside. She'd left her coat inside at the table. He could see she was cold and he thought she would hold her arms against herself to keep them warm. She reached out and tried to take his hands, but they were in his pockets. She held his arms in her hands. Gripping him, a few inches at a time, like making sure he was really there. She wouldn't look at him, but only watched her hands. She pulled at him but he wouldn't move so she pulled herself close to him. A hand behind his neck. A hand under his arm and behind his waist. "Please. Please, sweetie."

She tried to pull him down to her height, but he stood straight. She stood high and crushed her lips into his. "Please, please."

He could see she was crying. The damp and the mascara made a shadow on her cheek even in the dark, huddled near the building and away from the lights. "Please."

And she held herself up and held her lips against his and everything about it was like a kiss but the way it felt, and the way he wouldn't bend, and the way they weren't one person, and the way he noticed the damp of her cheek and the taste of her breath and the desperate, childish madness of the low humming moan that came from her. She pulled one of his arms free and took his hand and pulled it around behind her, pressing it up against her ass, running it down her legs. She rubbed her chest on his and crushed herself against him and she kissed him again and again and the longer they stood there the more his anger became like a thought. Like an idea. Like an idea that he'd had that wasn't real. That was a mistake. He cupped his hand around the curve of her leg and at the small of her back. He didn't bend down to meet her but picked her up to his height. He felt his strength. He felt the need in her body and the brief but burning memory in each kiss and he remembered that they weren't two. They weren't separate. They were one. The idea of anger was like a dream he could barely remember. There were fragments. Pieces of memory. But it was gone. Maria was gone. He was gone. The smell of her breath and the sick damp of her cheek and the awful sad and desperate press of flesh and the child's need and all of it was all gone. And now it was them together, and he kissed her and pulled at her and wanted her and had her and he would have thought he'd been a fool but he didn't have to because there was only them, together.

After a while she giggled and tried to speak, muffled under his lips. She pulled away, but it was good, and he could look at her. Right at her. And touch her anywhere. She watched him and laughed again, this time free in the open air. "We should go back in before they throw our food away. And our wine."

"Yeah."

She kissed him again and smiled and held him. She took him by the hand and they walked back into the restaurant.

Inside they didn't speak, but they smiled and he watched her and it all felt good again. He felt free of something he could

barely remember. He felt giddy and foolish and he laughed and
he grabbed at her and she laughed and swatted at his hand. He
was hungry. Hungrier than he'd ever felt. He ate through his dinner and he took bites of her fish that she fed him with rice and
hot red oil with pepper flakes. She smiled at him and laughed
like he was a fool but none of it mattered. They finished dinner
and he paid and she didn't say anything or reach for her purse.
Back out in the night, in the street, there were still crowds and together they pushed through into the bars and they found a corner
to themselves and ordered whiskey and pressed close together
and felt completely alone in the noise. Ben thought he wanted to
leave, to be with her. But she ordered whiskey again and again
and she paid for it and somehow there always seemed to be more
and it was all fine and everything—absolutely everything—was
just the way it should be, and they could drink all night and still
have time and each other and still forget anything that wasn't
right. Anything that didn't fit, or wasn't good, or wasn't them.
They forgot it all but each other, and every line was blurring.

CHAPTER SEVEN

Things were good for a while. For weeks. Ben would work, and most nights go home and read and maybe have a drink. Other nights he would go to Maria's. They would laugh together and she would talk about her day. He would see Sophia and they would play video games together and he got better and better at talking to her. He always felt strange about spending the night, but he would leave for work before Sophia woke up.

Sometimes, while they were playing video games, sitting next to each other, Sophia would lean close to him. Lean against his arm. Once she even laughed so hard at the way he drove the car that she fell over against him. He put his arm around her and she didn't stop him or pull away, but leaned against him while the music of the video game kept on in the background.

Maria would ask why he had to work so late when he got in so early, and he tried not to tell her too much about it. He knew she would think it was wrong, and that it would make her angry. He knew there was nothing to be done about it.

One night when Jackson let him off an hour early he went home to shower then walked to Maria's for dinner. When he got there she was talking on the phone, and she went into her bedroom and closed the door. Sophia was finishing homework in her room and he knew they would not play video games until she was done. He didn't have a book, so he sat back on the couch and sipped his drink and it was more than enough.

He could hear that Maria was upset, again, but it was none of his business. He thought about leaving. He had never left before when she was on the phone, and he thought that maybe she liked to have him there so she could talk when she was done. There was dinner on the stove but everything was set on low, and there was nothing to do. He sat on the couch and thought about the feel of the whiskey as it settled into him.

It had been quiet for a few minutes when the bedroom door opened. Maria's face was pale, and her eyes and her mouth seemed drawn. He knew she'd been crying. She walked into the kitchen and checked on the food and poured herself a drink. After a while, when she didn't speak or come into the living room, Ben stood and walked to the edge of the kitchen where he could lean against the wall and talk to her.

She was nervous. Opening one pot, then closing it, then opening it again. She didn't look at him. He walked closer to her and put his hand on her shoulder and she flinched. She put her hands up over her head. "I've got to finish this. I'll be done in a minute."

Ben sat back on the couch and sipped at his drink. He listened to the pot lids and the faucet running. The low hollow pop of a cork from the bottle and the wash of whiskey in a glass.

After a few minutes Maria sat next to him. She leaned against him, almost lying on him. He put his arm around her. He thought for a moment how it all felt so natural. "I'm sorry about that," she said.

"About what?"

"You know. About the phone call."

"Is everything okay?" He asked that too much.

"Yes. It's my ex. Mark. My ex-husband. He calls sometimes." She took a long drink from her glass and it was almost empty. "He's living back here, now. Living back in D.C. for a while. On and off, while he works on a new contract. I guess he rented one of the short-term apartments, like they have for students and political staff. He said he was going to come over, but I talked him out of it. I know him pretty well. I think I talked him out of it." Her voice was hard, but she wasn't crying. Ben liked that, that she could talk about hard things without crying. It made it easier. He held her closer and she rested her head on his leg and lay there. He knew he should ask a question, but he didn't think there was anything to ask. Either she was right or she was wrong.

When the door to Sophia's room opened she sat up and stood. "I'll get us another round." On her way to the kitchen she put her arm around Sophia's shoulders and pulled her close. Sophia rolled her eyes but leaned into her and they stood like that for a moment. "Dinner's on in fifteen minutes. You want to play that game with Mr. Ben until then?"

"Sure."

"You wanna be nice and let him win?"

"No." Sophia held out her hand to Ben. "How do you do?" She sat on the couch where Maria had been and turned on the television and the racing game. Maria brought him his drink and held his hand for just a second. "You think you can keep your car on the track this time?" Sophia asked him.

"I'm gonna win it this time."

"Yeah, right. How come you barely ever even finish?"

"I've been sharking you," he said. He liked to joke with her.

"What's 'sharking'?"

"Like when I pretend to not be good at something to fool you, and then one day I surprise you and beat you every time." Ben didn't think he should tell her about betting money.

"Yeah, right."

At dinner they ate and talked and Sophia talked about her day and about tryouts for the volleyball team which were coming up. Maria seemed better, and happy, the way she normally was. Everything was very good.

"My teacher said today that it probably wasn't Columbus who discovered America the first time."

"You mean because of the Indians?" Maria said.

"No. Like, the people from Greenland, or Norway."

"Leif Ericson?" Ben asked.

"Yeah. And, anyway, Columbus didn't even really come to America. Just to the Bahamas or something like that."

"You know, Columbus was Italian," Maria said.

"So?"

"So you should be proud of him. We're Italian, too."

"Well, but if he didn't get here first?"

"It was still hard," Ben said. "To do that, then. And he didn't know there'd been anyone else before him. People thought he might just fall off the side of the earth."

"Yeah. I guess."

"You guess?" Maria said, and she pinched Sophia's side the way that always made her laugh. "I have to spend twenty minutes every morning just to get you out of bed and you guess that discovering America was hard?"

"But he didn't discover it."

"Whatever. Coming here on a sailboat." Maria pinched her again and Sophia couldn't help but squeal and laugh. Maria smiled. Whatever had bothered her was gone. Everything was very good.

"Stop it!"

"These are the things they teach you in school now? I oughta take you out of there and make you sew clothes with your little fingers, like those Chinese kids they have."

"I could be in fashion."

"Fashion. Right. More like a sweatshop. Maybe that would teach you to get up in the morning."

"Actually, I think I'd wanna get up even less in that case."

When they were finished Ben took the dishes into the kitchen and washed them. Maria poured out the last of a bottle of wine for them, and, after the whiskey, Ben could feel it like a warmth in his head. But it wasn't too much.

After dinner they played a board game, and Ben was better at that than the video games because it was one that he had played when he was a kid. He still lost and the girls both laughed at him, but the way they laughed made him feel happy and know that nothing was wrong. He did better and was glad to be playing a game where he could do well. They were all doing well, so the game took longer to finish, and they stayed up playing it until after Sophia's bedtime. Ben could see how tired she was when Maria finally put her to bed.

When she was done saying good night to Sophia, she took Ben into her room and they were both tired. But they made love without either of them having chosen. It was better than sleep and they needed it as much, and they needed each other. And it was late when Maria turned off the light and Ben fell asleep and didn't dream at all.

‡

Ben was up early the next morning for work. He would leave Maria's at five-thirty to be sure he had time to go home, shower and get to the site. He would make coffee at home, because he liked that before he had to go to work. He knew Maria would make it for him if he asked, but he didn't like to bother her. It was enough that she got up to walk him to the door.

She was half-asleep as she stood in the hallway to say goodbye. They had been up late. It had been a good night, and he was glad he had stayed, and that he could get up early and leave before he had to see Sophia in the morning. He pulled back the chain lock. "Cover your eyes," he said.

The light was always on in the hallway, and it would hurt her eyes when he opened the door. Sometimes she would laugh and say he was sweet to think of her. This morning she only smiled and kissed him. Before he could open the door she fell against him, still half-asleep like she was falling onto a bed. "I have to go," he said, but he didn't want to. It felt better to be here with Maria, and with Sophia. He turned the bolt lock and brushed her hair back from her forehead. He'd seen that in movies and it felt good to really do it, and to feel her head rest against his hand. "I have to go," he said again, to himself. He turned toward the door and she stood back in the hallway to be out of the glare of the light.

He turned the handle of the door and all at once it rushed in on him, like a living animal. The corner of the door hit him hard over the eye. He fell back against the wall, but he stayed on his feet. The figure in the doorway was a shadow, draining the light from the hallway. Ben couldn't focus. The figure seemed like nothing real, but it was poised to strike like a man. Ben saw it and held his arm up in time to keep the punch from landing over his eye, but the force against his arm knocked him off his feet.

"So this is why I can't come around?"

Ben didn't understand, and he couldn't find his balance to stand up. He could see the man, now, not just the shadow.

"This piece of shit?"

Ben could see his size. There was nothing he could do about him.

"Stand up."

Ben knew what was coming, but there was nothing to do. At least he could be on his feet. He could hear Maria screaming. Or was it screaming? Her voice was quiet, like she was shrieking in a whisper. Ben leaned toward him to get his balance and he waited for the punch while he was low, on his knees, defenseless. It didn't come. He pulled a leg up under himself, and then another. He stood up straight and he saw the man. Bigger than him. All anger, like he was playing a part. Ben stood with his arms down and they watched each other.

The man was big. "You piece of shit. Fucking my wife?" He was wearing a dress shirt. Pants that belonged with a suit. But they were wrinkled and there was a stain like a water stain down the front of his shirt. There was nothing to stop what was coming. He heard Maria, still quietly screaming behind him. There had been times like this before. When he was inside. And when he'd been a kid. There were times that bad things came to you, and there was nothing you could do. It wasn't because of you, or what you'd done. It was a thing that happened, and you couldn't stop it.

Ben put his arms up and the first punch was on him in an instant. He raised an arm to cover his face, but the punch came to his rib cage. He crumpled to one side, but tried to stand straight. The second punch came to his face. It came hard but he didn't feel it. He couldn't see, and he knew he was on the ground. Maria was whispering. Or was she? Was she screaming now? Was there a light on, or the light from the hallway, or was the front door closed? He tried to move but he couldn't. He couldn't breathe. The man was kicking him in the stomach and in the chest. He knew there was pain, like a fact, but he couldn't feel it. It was somewhere else, and he and the man and Maria were somewhere else. Sophia was somewhere else, but he thought he could see her in the living room. Maria was pushing her away and he was glad about that. Sorry she had to see anything at all. He would tell her that things just happened sometimes. That it was no one's fault, and there was nothing to be done about it. She probably didn't know that yet. He would tell her, and he would tell her that it would never happen to her. He would make her a promise. Never to her.

‡

It was light when Ben woke. Natural light, from outside. He pulled his head up off the couch cushion and there was blood and spit where his mouth had been. He didn't know what time it was. He couldn't get his eyes to focus. His ears rang and the shock of pain from his ribs was muffled like a gunshot behind a closed door. Everything was sharp, frantic hurt as he tried to push himself up. He thought Maria might have something to clean the couch cushion. Under the sink, or in the utility closet next to the washing machine.

He sat himself up and he felt around his eye. It was swollen and bleeding. From the door or the punch. Or both. Three of his ribs screamed pain through him like an electric pulse. No longer distant. His vision cleared and he could see by the clock on the wall that it was almost three in the afternoon. Maria had left a note on the coffee table. It hurt to reach for it, but he took it and read it. She'd gone to work because she didn't have any more days off. She'd be home by five. Sophia was going to a friend's house for the afternoon, but would be home later. Ben knew he couldn't stand yet. It wasn't a question of will or pain. He knew he'd fall over if he tried to stand, so he sat still. He should call the job site. He had the phone number on a check stub. But they had caller ID. He'd seen Hardgrave once write down a number off it. He couldn't call from Maria's phone. He would have to wait until he could get up.

He tried to remember the fight. The man. There was nothing but flashes. Maria's ex-husband. It must have been. He could remember her screaming for him to leave. To leave them alone. That she would call the police. Maria left a note and Sophia was at school. He must have left. Maybe she did call the police. He must have left. The man, her ex-husband, was still in town. There was more he had to think about but none of it came clear.

He tried to stand, slowly. It hurt but nothing gave out. He stood for a moment and rocked on his feet to check himself, then he walked slowly into the kitchen. Broken ribs. A bloody eye. His hip was stiff and difficult to move, but he could walk with a limp. He breathed shallow through his stomach, trying not to expand his ribs. He got to the kitchen and it made him dizzy to crouch down to look under the sink, and his legs gave out and he ended up on his hands and knees. He pushed through the spray bottles collected around the drain pipe and found one for fabric and upholstery. It said it worked on stains but was color safe. Ben found a clean rag and slowly got back to his feet, pulling himself up by the counter's edge. He soaked the rag, squeezed it out and walked back to the couch.

He tried to sit down carefully, but as he bent his legs a shock of pain came from his hip and he fell back all at once. He was gasping for breath. He held the spray bottle close to the blood stain and squeezed the trigger. The cleaner came out and collected in a pool around the blood. Ben sprayed over and around the stain and put the bottle down on the coffee table. He let it sit and soak for a few minutes, then he daubed the stain in tight circles, making sure he didn't spread it. He got up as much as he could and he sprayed it again and let it sit. He scrubbed it again and sprayed it again. Twice, then three, then four times. Each time it got lighter, and he made sure it wouldn't spread. He sprayed it a fifth time.

He stood up from the couch. It was easier this time. It hurt, and he could feel everything going stiff. But it was just pain, and nothing wanted to give out the way it had before. He walked into the bathroom and closed the door. He used toilet paper and hot water to clean the blood off his face. He pulled up his shirt and there were dark purple bruises. Except where it hurt the most, where it was still red and pink with dots of purple. Those were the worst. The deepest. The bruises would come up over the next few days and stay for a week or more. He felt where his ribs were broken and they hurt but there was nothing to do about it. He could go to the health clinic and get them taped up and probably be able to work just fine. He could even try to do it himself if he could get the right kind of wrap at the drug store. It needed to be tight enough so it hurt more going on than when it wasn't there before, but after that it would be easier. He wiped the blood from around his eye but it was still bright purple and swollen. It didn't look good, and it was hard to see if he held his other eye closed.

He wrapped ten or twelve sheets of paper towel around ice from the freezer and held it over his eye. It was too late for it to help much, but it felt better. He went back to the couch and sat down next to the stain. He sat more evenly this time. He scrubbed the stain and scrubbed it until it was almost gone. He cleaned with one hand and he held the paper towel and the ice over his eye with the other. When the paper towel was soaked through, he squeezed some of the water out onto the stain and sprayed it again, very lightly. He found a clean spot on the rag and scrubbed again.

He heard the door open and Maria walked into the living room. "What are you doing, sweetie? I'll take care of that." She walked over and looked at the stain. "I should have put a towel down. It's my fault. Leave it. I'll take care of it." She smelled like chemicals and the burnt hair smell of a beauty salon. "How are you?" She ran her fingers through his hair and pulled the towel and the ice away from his eye. "Oh, my God, sweetie. I'm so sorry. Here." She walked away and into the kitchen. Ben heard a bottle open and the splash of whiskey on glass. Maria walked back into the living room and sat next to him on the couch. She handed him a drink. "Guess we both could use this, huh?"

They drank and the whiskey burned a cut on the edge of Ben's lip that he hadn't noticed. It felt good, but it was strange to have it before he'd had coffee. It was five. He'd already missed the morning shift. There wasn't any point in calling, and he didn't want to talk to Jackson anyway. He would go in tomorrow and see if they took him.

"I told him I'd call the cops if he didn't go. He was drunk, or else he wouldn't have come over. I should have known from when I talked to him." She took a long swallow of her drink and sat back on the couch. "Did the door hit you when he opened it?"

"Yeah."

"I thought so. I couldn't remember. I was barely awake. It must have been the door that knocked you down."

"Yeah."

She put a hand on his shoulder. "Does that hurt?"

"No."

She pulled her hand away and took another drink. "Sophia saw it."

"I'm sorry."

"No. I mean, it isn't really your fault. I just hate that she saw that. I hate that she has to think about that. I guess it's good that she didn't know that was her father. I just told her it was about something else. Something that was just about you. But I hate that she had to see that."

"I'm sorry."

"It's not your fault." She took another drink and finished her glass. She stood and brought the bottle back from the kitchen. She poured herself a drink and put the bottle down near him on the coffee table. He drank off the rest of his glass and put it down on the table next to the bottle. "You'll just need to be more careful when you open the door. For a little while. While he's here. Just so he won't surprise you again." She took a long drink and he could see her hands tremble. She gripped the glass tight in two hands. "I know it wasn't your fault. He surprised you and the door knocked you down. Otherwise, it would have been different. You would have kept him out. You would have protected us. I know that. And it all turned out fine anyway because I got him to go and I got Sophia back into her room before he could talk to her." She put her hand on his shoulder again, then took it away. "It's all okay."

They sat for a while. She didn't speak but he could hear her breathing. She looked down into the glass and drank nervously. When the glass was empty she poured herself another. He scrubbed at the stain for a while more and she didn't notice. The stain looked like it was almost gone. He would know for sure when it dried out.

"I'll take the cushion to a dry cleaner if the stain is still there later."

"I'll take care of it." She didn't look at him. They sat for a while longer and he thought about having another drink but there was no point, and he felt light-headed already. "I'm really sorry to ask this, sweetie... but Sophie's gonna be home soon." She paused and she took a long drink from her glass. Almost finishing it again. "She was really scared by what she saw last night. And, you know. The way you look. It would probably be better if I have some time alone with her. To talk to her tonight."

"Yeah. Okay."

"You don't mind?"

Ben stood up from the couch. "No. It's okay." He walked toward the door and Maria followed him. He looked out of the peephole even though he knew there would be no one there. Maria leaned against the wall at the end of the hallway. He undid the chain lock and the bolt and he opened the door and Maria walked back toward the living room.

‡

Ben didn't have any trouble at work. They gave him a hard time and accused him of everything they could think of for how he got hurt. A drug deal. Gangs. Caught stealing. Anything they could think of. After they got bored with it they told him he'd have to work a week without pay and let it go.

After he'd left Maria's he went by the drugstore and got some wrap for his chest. Everything else would be fine, but he needed to wrap his ribs. It would be easier than having to go to the clinic. When he got home he made coffee and a drink and took his shirt off. In the mirror he saw the landscape of bruises already changing. The deeper ones around his stomach starting to show. It was just as well. It was healing.

He took a shower so he wouldn't have to the next morning. The hot water felt good, except on his open cuts. He stood in front of the mirror with a glass of whiskey and curled the wrap around him high on his chest, just under his arms. He went around three times until it started to hold on its own, then he pulled it tighter and tighter and put it around twice more. Pulling it as tight as he could he put it down around his chest, letting it overlap again and again. When it hurt so much that he almost couldn't keep from crying out he would take a drink. When he was done he tied it off. It hurt worse but he knew it was better.

At work it was hard to bend down for anything, and everyone watched him. They saw the purple all around one eye, and the cut on his lip that had puffed up and looked like a gash and that hurt like hell when he drank whiskey. They all looked at him, but they didn't want to talk to him. That was for the best. He worked slower, but no one said anything.

It was different on the evening shift. He went to punch out and Jackson was already there. Jackson thought they were friends now, because he let Ben off early sometimes. When Jackson saw him, he called him over to his desk. "What happened?"

"Nothing. I got jumped. It's no big deal."

"You miss both shifts yesterday?"

"Yeah."

"You work it out with Hardgrave?"

"Yeah."

"I guess I don't wanna know," he said. "You okay to work?"

"I've been working all day."

"All right." Jackson looked at him. Half judgment. Half concern. The kind of privilege he thought he could take. "You gonna tell me what really happened?"

"I got jumped. My neighborhood's not so great."

"Yeah. I saw your address. Did you file a police report?"

"No."

"You should."

"It wouldn't make a difference."

"Yeah, it would. Give them a description to work from, even if you can't remember much."

"They jumped me in the dark. I didn't see anything." He was saying things he'd heard other people say. At the bar or on TV. He was trying to say them the way other people said them. "The cops in the city are useless anyway."

"I'm a cop in the city. That's my day shift. Why don't you tell me what you remember?"

"Sorry."

"Don't worry about it. Just tell me what you remember."

"Three guys. It was late. Over near Shaw, between the Metro and the gas station with the Dunkin' Donuts."

"On Rhode Island? What time?"

"One-thirty. Two, I guess. Late at night."

"You were out?"

"Yeah."

Jackson smiled. "These guys were black, white, Asian, what?"

"I don't know. Probably black or Latin. But I didn't see." Ben thought if he just walked out and never came back it would be better.

"You didn't see at all?"

"I told you."

"Anything else you remember? They take anything?"

"They took my wallet out and took the cash. They left the wallet."

"They didn't just take the wallet?"

"No."

"And you don't know what color these guys were?"

"No."

"That's not much."

"I told you."

"All right. Take it easy. There's nothing else you can think of? Did they say anything?"

"Nothing."

Jackson stared at him and Ben could feel himself in a cold sweat. "All right. You wanna take a look at that Husqvarna again? It starts, but one of the day guys said it's seizing up."

"Yeah."

"Get dinner first if you haven't eaten yet. Skinny guy like you oughta eat more while your body's putting itself back together."

"Yeah. Thanks." He stood there, not sure if he could move.

"Anything else you need?"

"No."

"All right. Go get some food, then."

Ben walked out and behind the work site, not the fastest way to the truck. He went around and behind the dumpsters where no one ever went. His chest shot through with pain while he threw up what he'd eaten for lunch. When he tried to stand up straight he was dizzy and he stumbled backward, but he kept his feet. He stood and he breathed in and out as deeply as he could. It hurt, but the pain was like cold air, and it helped him think straight. He could feel his pulse slow and his head clear and he knew it was all right. There was nothing to worry about. He walked to the truck and got a sandwich, some gum and a bottle of water.

‡

The boy could hear the music coming from his house when he was still down the road, walking from the bus. His father's truck was outside, next to his mother's car. The boy saw his father's truck and ran toward the door.

The music inside shook everything. Even the air. Led Zeppelin. The boy knew that's who it was. It was what his dad liked to listen to the most.

No one saw him when he came through the door. His father was leaning back on the couch and his mother was over him. Close to him, but facing away from the door. There was a whiskey bottle open on the coffee table. There was a pizza box open on the counter, but it was empty and there were dishes in the sink.

His father saw him first, and pushed his mother off to the side. "Hey, boy. When'd you get home? They let you off from school early?" His mother turned away and fixed the buttons on her shirt.

"No."

"Well, look at that. I never even saw the clock." His father wasn't wearing a shirt and he was thin but the boy could see his muscles and he could see that he was strong. Stronger than anyone, even the big bodybuilders who were probably just fake. His father tried to get up off the couch but he fell back. He stood up right the second time.

"Do you have homework?" His mother had turned back around and was lighting a cigarette.

"A little."

"Why don't you go do it now and then you'll be done?"

"No. I can do it later."

His mother walked up to him and her face looked old and mean. "I told you to do it now."

"Oh, lay off him about the homework. He'll do it later." His father poured whiskey in both of the glasses on the table and picked his shirt up off the floor. "Come outside a minute. I'll show you what your daddy got today."

"Don, no."

"Helen. Fuckin', yeah. And that's all there is to say. We'll be back in a minute."

Behind the house was a shed that his dad kept locked. He took the key from under the ledge of the shed roof. He unlocked it with the glass still in his hand, fumbling with the padlock. Behind the house was all a stand of woods along a steep ridge. His father owned some of the land, and then it was all Forest Service land, which meant they could go on it when they wanted to.

The boy's father came out of the shed with a gun in his hand. It wasn't like a gun the boy had seen before. It was a handgun, but the barrel was long, and it looked bigger than most of the guns he'd seen his father with.

"You know what this is?" His father looked at him but he wasn't sure if he was supposed to really know or not. "This is a .44 Magnum. A Smith & Wesson Model 29, just like Clint Eastwood has in Dirty Harry. I got it from a guy at work. You believe that?"

"Yeah!"

"Come on, I'll show it to you."

They walked back into the woods and it didn't take long for the sounds of the music from the house and the cars on the road and the wood mill to disappear. It was still, except for the sound they made *walking, and that sound seemed to crackle through everything. They walked along the base of the hill until they were far enough. His father handed his glass to the boy and took the gun in two hands, pointing it out in front of him.*

The sound of the shot was bigger than anything the boy had ever heard, and he saw his father's arms jerk back behind the force of it. The boy half-heard the snap of the bullet through the leaves and brush. His father held it out again with two hands and sighted along the barrel at a tree that was twenty feet away. When the boy could open his eyes from the sound of the gun and the feel of the shot in the air he looked and saw a gap on the side of the tree and the exposed meat of the wood all new and bright. There were wood chips all over and some were still falling to the ground and it looked like snow.

"Hollow points. The bullets. You see the way it blew out the side of the tree like that? If you shot this same thing into a human, you'd barely even notice the hole in front, but the hole behind them where the bullet came out would be just as big as that."

His father shot the gun four more times and sometimes he hit the tree and sometimes he didn't. He tried to shoot it once with just one hand but the gun flew back and his shot missed.

"Here. Come 'ere." His father took his drink and held the gun out to him and the boy was afraid even to touch it. He'd been hunting with his father before, but with a rifle. A rifle was like a tool. The boy saw the way the gun jumped and he heard it and he saw what it did and he saw that his father didn't care at all and it scared him. "Come on. Come 'ere. Weren't you listening? Six shots already. There's no more left. It can't hurt you."

The boy walked slowly up and took hold of the gun, but held it by the handle the wrong way, like holding a dead bird by its foot. "Go on. Hold it right. I told you there's no bullets. You think I'd give that thing to you with bullets in it? You'd probably kill us both. Or me at least." His father laughed and took a drink and the boy didn't like to think of his father being shot. The boy turned the gun in his hands. He tried to hold it like he was supposed to but it didn't fit. His hands weren't big enough. Even with two hands, he could feel he didn't really have a grip on it. He tried to make it look right and held it out in front of him the way his father had, with his legs in a wide stance and his body leaning forward, in case his father was wrong and somehow the gun went off and the kick came. "Damn, boy. You look even smaller with that gun in your hand." His father took the gun and felt to see if the barrel was still hot and put it in the back of his jeans. "Don't worry. Someday soon you're gonna be a man, and you'll be big enough then."

Inside his mother was lying on the couch. The music had stopped because the record had ended and now it was just the hiss, hiss, hiss of the needle skipping at the end. "Look at this shit. She fell asleep. Go get some water from the faucet and sling it on 'er."

"Do that and you'll be the next one to get a bottle to the head." His mother got up from the couch and turned to the boy. "Now I told you before to go do your homework. Go up now and finish it up and then you can come back down."

"No. Come on. I want to stay down here."

"What did I just tell you? Get upstairs right now."

The boy picked up his backpack and started to walk toward the stairs.

"What the hell are you raggin' on the kid for? Let him stay down here. He'll do it later. We're havin' a good time." He poured whiskey in his glass that he'd finished while they were walking back from the woods. "Tell you what. Let's watch the Betamax of Dirty Harry I told you about. I'll show you it's the exact same gun."

"Don, I just told him. If he doesn't do it now, he won't do it at all."

"Jesus Christ. Do it for him if it's so important." He took his drink and went over to where he kept the videos under the TV. He found the one he wanted and pulled open the plastic case. *"God-damnit. How many times have I gotta tell you to rewind these before you put them back?"*

"Like I ever even watch that movie." The boy's mother lit another cigarette and poured more whiskey in her glass. She was wearing a shirt that was tight on her and she pulled it down over the top of her skirt. The boy could tell from the broken edge of her voice and from the way she threw the match in the sink that she was pissed off. But she was usually pissed off. His father put the tape in the VCR and it made a loud sound but no picture came up.

"We gotta get a rewinder. It's gonna bust the VCR if we keep doin' this." His father was kneeling in front of the TV and the tape stopped. He turned on the TV and hit the play button. *"The power it takes for the engine to rewind is too much for the machine. It's built to go slower, not fast like that."*

The boy's mother didn't say anything, or maybe she wasn't even listening. His father sat down next to him on the couch and got his drink and held it in his lap. The boy didn't know much about the movie, and he didn't really pay attention except when Clint Eastwood had the gun just like his father and he would waste somebody. His father would clap and point and laugh and slap the boy on the leg. They would both lean forward and his dad would cheer and the boy watched him and tried to cheer at the same time. But his father meant it so much and the boy didn't know how to mean it like he did. He would watch the television and watch his father, back and forth and back and forth and try to find the secret of what was so good. He tried to look faster and faster and see from his father's face or from the movie what was happening and what he should do and when he should cheer or laugh, but he could never look fast enough and he was always yelling "Yes!

Yes! Yes!" just a second after his father did. His mother stayed in the kitchen except when she would come in to fill her glass from the bottle on the table. And there was something wrong that made his mother be in the kitchen and them watching TV, even though he could see her and she was just standing there. And he didn't understand that and he didn't understand the movie or why his father was yelling and happy or what he was supposed to do or what he should feel and say to be a man like he was supposed to. And his heart was pounding and pounding and he said "Yes!" and pumped his fist when the gun went off and it wasn't as loud as it had been outside, even on the speakers in the living room that you could hear from down the road. It wasn't big and it wasn't real and when it was on TV it didn't make him want to run.

The movie ended and the credits rolled up the screen and the boy's father poked his elbow into his ribs. "Looks like I pissed off your mom again." He nodded toward the kitchen, and the boy knew she was pissed off and he looked back and forth from his mother to his father and back and forth and back and forth but his father was smiling. "Don't worry. I'll fix it. Watch and learn, kid."

His father stood up from the couch and turned over the record while the music from the movie was still playing. He put down the needle and pushed a button on the stereo. The boy stood up from the couch. He stood up quickly and bounced on his feet. He was hungry. He hadn't realized how hungry he was and he felt like he wanted to run and run, back and forth. His father put the music on loud. Even louder than before. He went over to the boy's mother and he put his arm around her waist and she pushed at him and she held the cigarette in her hand away from them. "You asshole. Stop it." She said 'asshole' to his father and it made the boy afraid. But his father wasn't angry this time, and there was nothing wrong.

"Come on. Come on and dance with me." They were loud because the music was loud and it was the only way they could hear

anything. "Come on and dance with me." He pulled at her waist and pulled her close.

"Yeah, mom. Come on. Dance with him. Come on." The boy jumped up and down and up and down and it felt like something going wild in him. Like it hurt to stand still. "Dance! Dance! Yes! Yes! Yes!" He bounced and yelled and pumped his fist.

"You're such a jerk. Leave me alone." The boy's father pulled her out away from the counter and he was rocking back and forth and it wasn't even in time with the music but he only wanted to dance with her and she just kept pushing and pushing him away.

"Come on, baby. Why won't you dance?"

She didn't say anything and the boy bounced faster and faster and the living room was shaking from the way he bounced on the floor but no one could hear anything. "Dance, dance, dance!" He clapped and clapped his hands to get her to dance with him.

"Jesus. You're such a prick." But she put her arms around his neck and they were dancing. There was nothing wrong and everything was fixed. His father was a hero and he'd really done it and the boy clapped and clapped and his father had fixed everything.

"Yes yes yes!" the boy yelled again and again and he ran up and down, over and over, from the couch to the kitchen and back and forth and back and forth and the house was shaking and he was screaming, "Yes yes yes!" while the music played and his father and his mother danced and danced.

‡

Ben waited before he called Maria. He waited for the bruises around his eye to dull and the cut over his lip to heal. They weren't all the way healed when he called, but it didn't look as bad, and by the time he went there it wouldn't look bad. He wouldn't have to worry about how it would look to Sophia. He was sorry that she had seen it. But there was nothing he could do. He never had a chance. He never would have had a chance. But he was sorry she'd seen it.

He called Maria when he knew they'd be home. Sophia answered and he tried to talk to her but he didn't know what to say. He asked about school and she said it was fine. He asked about volleyball, that he'd remembered she was going to try out for, but the tryouts hadn't happened yet. The silence after she would talk made it hard to think what to say. After a while she handed the phone to her mother.

"Hi."

"How are you?" he asked.

"Fine. Are you feeling better? How's your eye?"

"Fine. You almost can't see it. It will be gone by the weekend."

"Good."

"Did the stain come out of the pillow?"

"Yeah. I used soda water. It was fine."

"I can take it to a dry cleaner."

"No. The stain is out. It's fine."

"I'm sorry about that."

"Don't worry about it. It's not your fault." He could hear a clang of metal against metal. A pot on the stove. "I should have put a towel down."

"Is it a bad time to talk?"

"I'm just making dinner. What are you calling for?"

"To say hi, I guess." He felt stupid saying that. He could hear the sharp sound of something frying. "To see if maybe you wanted to get together over the weekend. Maybe we could all have dinner?"

"Um. Yeah. I guess so. How about Saturday?"

"Yeah. That's good."

"We've both already had a long week, so how about we just stay in? I'll cook, or we can get takeout or something?"

"Yeah. That would be great. Can I bring something?"

"I don't know. You normally bring wine. You know what to get, don't you?"

"Yeah. I can bring wine."

"Hold on." The phone was muffled and he could almost hear Maria calling Sophia for dinner. "I should probably go. Dinner's almost ready."

"Okay. I'll see you on Saturday."

"Yeah. Okay. See you then."

Ben hung the phone up and walked back toward his apartment.

‡

The dreams came more often. He could feel the pain in his side in the dreams, and there was never a moment when they felt good and peaceful. In the dreams, everything was wrong. From the start. Everything was already wrong, and everyone knew it. All he could do was play out the actions. Try to hold on, even though he knew he couldn't.

He tried not to sleep. He tried to stay up, or to only sleep for a few hours. Even when he was exhausted the dreams came. Even when he stayed up and drank coffee he would fall asleep in his chair. He hated to sleep, but he never felt anything but tired.

When Ben got to their apartment, Maria was finishing dinner, and Sophia was playing video games. When Maria opened the door Ben tried to kiss her, and she turned and gave him her cheek. She took the wine and told him dinner would be ready in twenty minutes. He went and sat by Sophia.

"Hey," she said. She wouldn't look at him. He'd checked his face before he came and the bruises were mostly gone.

"How do you do?" he said, and she smiled. She stared forward at her game. It wasn't the one they played together, but a different one, with a guy and a gun. "What're you playing?"

THESE CAN'T BE CHOICES

"It's a World War II game. Do you want to play?"

"No. Thank you."

"Okay." She played the game and he sat and watched. The game showed blood and people reeling in pain, and it was like a violent movie. Ben didn't like to watch it, but there was nothing else to do.

"Do you feel better?"

It took Ben a moment to understand. "Yeah. Yeah, I feel mostly fine." He leaned back and tried to keep from wincing from his ribs. "I'm sorry you had to see some of that."

"Who was that guy?"

"Well… no one. Just a guy who's angry with me."

"Does my mom know him?"

"I don't think so. No. I don't think she does."

Sophia played her game for a while longer.

Maria started setting the table and Ben stood to see if he could help. "I've got it. Thanks." Ben picked up a stack of plates on the counter in the kitchen to put them at the places. "No, wait. Please. I was just going to have us serve ourselves in the kitchen, so I need the plates back here."

"I'm sorry."

"It's okay. But I told you I didn't need help." Ben stood and watched Maria finish the cooking, and watched Sophia play her game. He wished he wasn't there, but there was no way he could leave now. He didn't know what had happened that he needed to wish that. He went and sat down next to Sophia on the couch.

"Finish that up. Dinner is ready in one minute." They served themselves chili and rice at the stove and took it back to the table. There was cornbread out in a basket. Maria had opened the wine and poured some in her glass and in Ben's. "Beer might have been better with this, but this wine should be strong enough."

"How was your week at school?" Ben asked.

"Fine."

"How is the history class?"

"Okay. It's just short sections on all these different countries. It's hard to keep track."

The chili wasn't spicy, but had a sweetness to it, like cinnamon. "What's in the chili?" Ben asked.

"It's a recipe from my cousin in Ohio. It's got cinnamon and chocolate and a few other things. Not what you'd think of for chili, but Soph and I fell in love with it when we went for a visit one time. I'm sorry if you don't like it."

"No. I do. It's good."

Sophia cut a piece of cornbread in half. Steam came off the two pieces and she put butter and honey on each side.

Ben tried it the same way and it was good. Sophia watched him copy her. "I never liked cornbread that much but this is really good," he said.

"I'm sorry if you don't like it. I guess I should have asked."

"I do like it like this. I was saying I never used to like it."

"Okay. Don't get upset," she said.

They ate in silence. Ben wanted to bring his fist down hard, or turn the table over.

"Is everything okay?" he asked Maria.

"Yes. Of course. What's wrong?"

"Nothing. I just…" He looked at Sophia and stopped.

"What?"

"Nothing." He didn't know how to say it, anyway. It was obvious. He could feel it was obvious in every minute he'd been there. "Nothing."

Ben made himself finish his plate. Maria offered him more, but he knew he wouldn't eat it. It bothered her that he said no, but it probably didn't make a difference. When Maria and Sophia were finished, Ben stood up and took the plates into the kitchen. He ran the water until it was hot and plugged the sink to fill it with water and detergent.

"I'll take care of that." Maria almost pushed him out of the way. "Why don't you go sit with Sophia?"

"What's wrong?" Ben said. He tried not to speak loudly and he hoped Sophia was paying more attention to her video game.

"With what?" She had to know. She had to know.

He felt dizzy. "You know. With me. Why are you upset?"

"So you really want to ask what's wrong with me?"

"No. That's not what I mean." Ben didn't have words for what he wanted to say. There shouldn't have to be words. It was obvious. He could put his fist through the wall. He could tear the cupboards down. "I mean what are you upset about? What did I do?"

"I didn't say anything." He could see her up against the wall. He could see her with his hand on her throat. With his hand over her mouth. "Why don't you just go sit with Sophia while I finish up?"

"Do you want me to go?"

"Did I say that? What did I just say?" She wasn't whispering.

He knew Sophia could hear. He walked out of the kitchen and it was like losing something he thought he could hold on to.

He sat next to Sophia, watching her play the game, listening to the computer sounds of gunshots and screaming. They didn't talk. Watching Sophia and sitting close to her and knowing that he was allowed to sit with her and that everything was okay made him feel calm and happy. But something wasn't right and the good feeling came and went and he couldn't hold on to it. He sat like that for a long time, until after the noise in the kitchen had stopped. He turned and saw Maria had gone, and he could hear the water running in the bathroom.

"She's probably taking a bath," Sophia said.

Ben listened to the dim sound of the water running. He heard it stop, and he heard it start again and minute after minute after minute passed and he could have left at any time. He knew he should have left. But he couldn't make himself leave. He sat, and Sophia played the game, and Maria took a bath and he heard the water drain, and he heard the hair dryer. He heard her open the bathroom door and go into the bedroom and close the door behind her.

After another half hour the door to the bedroom opened. Maria called out to Sophia, "You've got fifteen minutes before bed, all right?"

Ben looked at the clock. It was eleven. He should have gotten up to leave. He should do it now, but there wasn't any point. There was nothing to do that could be right.

Sophia got up to go to bed without saying anything to Ben. He heard her door close and she and Maria talked for a few minutes and the door opened again.

"Are you coming in?"

Ben turned and Maria was leaning against the wall at the end of the hallway. She turned and walked back toward her bedroom before he could respond. He stood and followed her.

She closed the door to her room after him. She was wearing a robe that looked like silk. Ben had never seen it before. She put her hair up in a pony tail and took the robe off. She was only wearing panties. She looked at herself in the mirror on the wall and put lotion on her face and on her arms and legs.

Ben walked up behind her. He touched her. Her arm. Her back. He stepped closer to her and put an arm around her waist.

"Wait. Wait, I'm not finished."

He stepped back and she finished putting lotion on her legs. He wanted to watch her but she could see him in the mirror. When she was done she walked past him to the bed and got under the covers. He sat down on the bed and put his hand on the blanket, over the shape of her. "Actually I really don't feel good tonight. Do you mind if we just go to sleep?"

Ben lay down on top of the covers and undid his belt. Maria turned the light off and didn't ask why he hadn't gotten undressed, so he lay there and tried to keep his eyes closed. His heart was beating and he wanted to run as far as he could run, but he was exhausted. His whole body was tired. He lay there for minutes or hours or he didn't know how long. Maria's breathing was steady and normal for a long time. He thought it was a long time. Then it got deeper. Longer. It was dark. Almost perfectly dark and he could barely tell the difference between having his eyes open or closed, but for some reason it scared him to keep his eyes closed. He tried to sleep but he usually couldn't sleep on his back and he didn't want to roll over and he couldn't keep his eyes closed. Everything was like a dream. Where nothing made sense, where nothing was the way it was supposed to be, but it was the way it was and there was nothing he could do about it so he just had to go along. There were no words to say it was wrong. There was no way to say it wasn't real, and to make it right, and real, and normal. Ben wanted to scream. To break through the walls. To show how strong he was and how he ought to be listened to, and how they ought to treat him. But there was nothing he could do but go along.

Ben saw Sophia and he knew it was wrong from the start. He knew it was all wrong. He knew it would only get worse, but that he had to try to stop it. She ran from him. There wasn't one good moment. Not one moment where she looked at him and smiled. Where she let him hold her hand, or got her to stop crying. There wasn't even one moment that was good. She was running down the hallway. Running from him. But it couldn't be him. He would never hurt her. He would protect her. He had to try to tell her. She ran and ran down the hallway and her feet didn't make a sound. His echoed up and down and up and down, but she didn't make a sound. She would turn to look at him. He had said, "It's me, it's me." And she turned to look but now she was so afraid. And she was crying and she didn't make a sound but he heard her say "Please, please," like she wanted him to stop but he couldn't let her go. He couldn't let her get hurt. He needed to protect her. And when he followed her around the corner she was lying on the ground and she was bleeding and she was still scared of him but she couldn't move and he knelt beside her and took her hand and it was only her eyes that were moving with quick, shallow breaths. Her hand was cold but he held it in his and tried to warm it and her body was rising. Rising up and up. But it wasn't her body, it was *her*. It had to be her and he had to hold on to her to keep her and to keep her safe because he was the only one and her body hung before him in the air and it was just barely her and he could still see her behind her eyes that weren't moving, that weren't scared anymore and he wanted to say please please please don't go don't leave I didn't I didn't I didn't mean it don't leave don't leave but he never never had any words so he held her and he held her tighter and tighter even though it was only her body now and she was hanging there before him and the fear was gone, and the breath and the running and anything that he would have ever wanted to hold on to was all gone but he could hear her screaming. Not moving, but screaming. Louder and louder and her body wouldn't move but her hand was jerking and pulling in his and there wasn't anything left to hold on to but he still had to hold on and it was pulling and furious and her face didn't move and she couldn't make a sound but she was screaming louder and louder and everything was suddenly lit as brightly as it could be and the shock of it felt like burning in his eyes.

When the light came on he had one second. An instant to understand. Sophia in her bed. In a t-shirt and sweatpants, trying to pull her hand away as he knelt on her bedroom floor and held her. He could almost understand what had happened. He wanted to explain. He held on to her hand to try to explain, to try to clear his head for just a moment to explain, but she wouldn't stop screaming and all of the lights were on and two hands grabbed his shirt from behind and in one motion he was on his feet and he was up against the frame of the door and it crushed his ribs and he hated the way it sounded when he screamed and he was moving down the hall and through the living room and he could hear Maria's voice but he could barely understand it. Hurt her. Out. Never. Screaming. Crying. Like an animal sound. Like an animal, but worse. He could hear the way the voice broke apart, the way the words wouldn't stay together. He could hear the deep hurt. It was his Maria and he could hear how she hurt and without thinking or knowing or being able to stop from running forward with his feet barely on the ground and it broke his heart to know he'd made them hurt. He was up against the wall by the door and he heard the locks. The chain, the bolt, the door. Then it was light again when the door was open and he tried to stand up straight but he was down, now. Down on the floor in the hallway. And he thought that he would understand it all if he could look back and see what had happened. Just look back one time. To see them. To make sense of it. But all he could hear was the sound of the lock and the chain behind the door.

CHAPTER EIGHT

Ben went to work every day and he worked hard. After everything went bad with Maria he worked harder. He didn't like to talk to anyone, and he didn't like to wear gloves on the job. He would forget, or he wouldn't like the feel of them. He liked the press of the rough edge of concrete. He liked the weight of steel. He liked feeling the thickness of the skin on his hands at the end of the day and he liked it when he got cut or scraped because he knew it would make him stronger.

After Maria had thrown him out he walked home without his shoes on. It didn't bother him. By the time he could get up and walk, he didn't want to stand there or knock on the door or have to hear the sound of her voice just to get his shoes. He could get others, and they weren't even the shoes he needed for work.

While he was walking he saw people in the shadows. Watching him. It was late at night. Three or four in the morning. The worst time when it was cold and there was no good reason for anyone to be out, even on a Saturday. Whoever was out was watching. Always watching everybody. Or they were crazy. Ben knew that the shapes like shadows in the doorways and in the alleys and past the edges of the streetlights were watching him. Trying to figure him out. Trying to see the angle. But when they saw him walking alone and barefoot, they looked away. He looked like nothing at all. Like another animal. Another case. They didn't care about him at all.

When he got home at night after work he would pour a drink and sit. Let his mind and his body settle. Usually he'd take a shower after he'd finished his first drink, or he'd just sit there and go to bed filthy. He always showered in the morning, so it didn't matter.

When the feeling of the first drink would settle over him, after the first burn in his throat and the first high happy sinking feeling, he'd realize he was better off. He wouldn't be angry about it. He wouldn't think about all the bullshit or the things she'd done. He'd realize that it never should have happened in the first place. It wasn't supposed to be part of his life. All the bullshit and the worrying and who the hell knew what would come next. It wasn't simple. It wasn't clear. He couldn't just be himself. Simple. Quiet. He had to be someone else. Always talking and being confused and spilling over at the edges. It wasn't the way he was supposed to be. So he sat in his chair with his drink and he felt entirely his own and it made him feel warm and safe and simple.

Some nights he would call her. A lot of nights. After he'd had a few drinks. He would take a handful of change from the jar by the door. Every night he would leave her one message. He would tell her it was Ben and that she should pick up the phone. That he needed to talk to her. That he still didn't have a number, but that he would call back. The next time he called he would hang up before the machine picked up. And the next time. He knew how many rings it would be and he hung up before the machine could answer.

She only answered once. A few days after she'd thrown him out. She didn't give him a chance to talk. She was angry. "Leave me alone. I don't know what you were doing. I won't have you around Sophia. I won't have you in her life. In my life. I won't have it. Please stop calling here." And she'd hung up. She hadn't given him a chance to say anything, or to tell her what was really happening. He called her back but she didn't answer. Then again, and again.

Some nights when he couldn't stand being at home alone he would go to the bar. He hadn't been there in a long time. The last time had been hard, and he'd gotten angry. But it didn't matter. He wasn't going to look for a new place. He wanted to go to this place.

By the time he would get off work most nights it was already busy. The bouncer was at the door and the bartender was busy. But he always brought Ben a drink, and another when the first was finished, and another after that. Ben saw all the old guys there. Ben saw Black Jacket there, but they never said hello. Maybe it was the way Ben looked. Maybe everyone knew to stay away from him. Or maybe Black Jacket was angry at him from the last time they'd talked. Ben didn't care. He never asked to talk to anyone, and he didn't want to talk to them now.

Once he'd had a few drinks he would realize that he never should have come. That he should have stayed home. Being out at the bar made the thought of her come back. The good thoughts of her. Before everything had gone bad. The thought of her body and the feel of her body and of her smile and her eyes. Of her hands and the soft part of her skin under her neck at the top of her chest. He'd think about how she'd come in one night, and then she was there, and everything worked out. Thinking about her made him hard, and it made him panic, and it made him lonely. He had only come to the bar to keep from feeling lonely at home when he couldn't stand being alone anymore. At the bar it would be worse.

When he felt as bad as he could feel he would sit and try to understand what had happened. What he'd done. He would remember the look on Sophia's face. In the dream. In her bed. Terrified. The thought of it sent a bolt through him and he would have to squeeze his eyes shut. It wasn't him. He knew it wasn't him. He knew he needed to protect her. He knew he needed to hold on to her. To keep her safe. To not let her slip away. To not let her go. That's what he was doing. Keeping her safe. But it had gotten confused. He had been confused, and he didn't know how to tell them. He didn't know how to make them know that he would protect them. He would protect her. He wouldn't fail. He wouldn't let her go. But he couldn't protect her now. He couldn't protect her like this. And he couldn't be with Maria or feel her or be with her like it used to be, when everything was good, and he hadn't known how good it was. He hadn't known that it was perfect for a while, and that he was strong, and she was his, and they were safe. He hadn't known, so he let it go. He'd let them go.

No matter where he was or what he was doing, the sound of Maria's voice would come back to him. Not the way he liked it. Not sweetly. But the way it had sounded that night. Broken down and shot through with hurt. Bubbling up out of the pain he'd caused. Burning like steam off the thought of hurting that girl. The thought that he could ever do that.

Sometimes, later at night, he would go to her apartment. He wouldn't knock on the door. Sophia was sleeping. But he would go and stand. And watch. *Everyone Needs A Ruff Over Their Head.* He would make sure they were okay. Sometimes he would be there while Maria's light was still on. Sometimes he would be there when the lights came on in the morning. And he wouldn't stand in the same place for very long, or night after night in the same place. He knew he had to be safe. That being safe was how to keep them safe, and that is what he had to do.

Sometimes the man would come. Her ex-husband. Usually late at night. After Sophia had gone to bed. Maria's light would always be on when he came. He probably called her first, so she knew he was coming. He would get to the front door and it wouldn't open. Ben was glad she'd had it fixed. Ben could see him pushing the buzzers. He could hear him yell. And she would come up to the front door and talk to him. He was big. Ben had remembered that right. He always dressed well and Ben could see the way his button-down shirt would stretch against the width of his shoulders. The strength in his chest. And he would loom over Maria. Put his hand in her face. But she always knew how to talk to him. To calm him down. To get him to go away. And he would, and he would walk down the street toward the Metro, or try to find a cab. Ben followed him sometimes. As far as he could. Sometimes he would just wander. He would stumble when he walked, but he would just wander the streets. The man would leave, but he would always, always come back.

After the man got in a cab or walked to the Metro station, Ben would walk back to Maria's apartment. Her light would usually be on, just for a few minutes more. Ben could imagine her trying to calm down. Trying to sleep. Trying to feel safe in the dark. He would stand there long enough to see the light go off. Long enough to know that she felt better. Long enough to know she would be safe.

‡

The boy wanted to sit somewhere else at lunch but there was nowhere else to go. Nowhere that wasn't too close to some other kid who would laugh at him and then everyone would laugh and laugh. He had to sit near Satch, but he tried to sit as far away as he could. He sat and looked the other way. Looked off at the wall at nothing.

"Thisfugginshit," Satch said, over a foil wrapper of cold cooked carrots. The boy wanted to laugh, but it made him angry.

*He couldn't talk to him. He couldn't laugh at him. "Howmy sposed
to eat this fugginshit?" Satch said, and turned his fork around in
the cold mush. "I'drather eat ratshit." The boy hated the feeling of
wanting to laugh. It wasn't fair that he had to sit here. It wasn't fair
that he had to listen to this stupid shit. Stupid shit from the fucking
retard. "Guessit's betteren gettinshot." The boy wanted to laugh and
it felt like something he was being forced to do. Satch was making
him feel that way, even though he didn't want to. He was stupid and
he was dirty and he was from out in the country and the boy should
kick his ass. For being such a faggot. He didn't laugh, but he felt
angry, and he felt like something was being taken away from him.*

*"Shut the fuck up." The boy was on his feet and yelling.
"Shut the fuck up you stupid faggot. You fucking retard." The
boy wanted to do something else, but he didn't know what. He
picked up his sandwich and threw it at Satch, but it missed him
and the pieces flew apart on the floor. "No one wants to hear you
fucking talk faggot retard."*

*There were hands on the boy's shoulders. The woman with
the hairnet who walked around the lunch room. She was pushing
him out of the room, but he could see that everyone saw him. That
everyone watched him, and they were all laughing and laughing
and laughing.*

‡

When he was a boy, after Ben had shot the deer, he and
his father had dragged it out of the field to where Ben's father
had parked the pickup. He couldn't have driven it any farther
or it might've gotten bogged down in the wet ground on the
edge of the field. Ben's dad was bigger, so he dragged the deer
by its hind legs, and he and Ben together lifted it up onto the

tailgate and pushed it back across the ridged metal bed of the pickup. The shocks and the chassis squeaked and rattled while they loaded the deer. The rust through the paint soaked up the blood that pooled on the smooth metal. Ben's dad told him to sit in the back, on the wheel well. It was his kill, and people would see him in the back with the gun and know that it was his and that he'd killed it.

The pickup shook and rocked along the rutted jeep trail that led from the field, and along the dirt road that led to the highway. Ben didn't like the way it felt, and he worried that maybe he would fall over and out of the back of the truck. He didn't like how fast they drove, but his dad told him they had to drive fast to get home where they could clean and dress the kill. The longer it waited, the more the heat from the blood and the organs would spoil the meat and ruin the taste.

Ben sat over the wheel well because that's where his father told him to sit, and there were rope ties left over from a secured load that he could hold onto. As the truck rocked back and forth and bounced on the trail, the deer's head would loll to one side or the other. Its tongue hung out and its antlers would scrape across the metal. Ben thought it would look different once it was dead. Like a different creature. But it was the same. The same, but still. Limp. Ben thought it could just come back to life. If it only would start moving, it could come back to life.

When they got back to their house, Ben's father tied the deer's back legs with a heavy rope and hoisted it over the thick limb of a tree. The deer's tongue hung out and its belly was exposed. It looked like it must hurt for it to hang that way.

Ben's father took his knife out of the leather sheath on his belt and handed it to Ben. Because he was still short, Ben's father gave him a stepladder to stand up over the highest point of the deer. Ben had watched this before. Watched the incision from the highest point behind the deer, down along the stomach to its throat. Watched the inside of the deer fall out into a pile. Watched the deer's pelt give way to bare muscle and flesh. He'd never been asked to do it before. Every kill was the hunter's responsibility. This kill was his responsibility.

Before he started to dress and process the dear, Ben's father had him stand next to it, with the rifle in his hand. He took a picture with their Polaroid and they both stood waiting for the picture to show itself. In the picture, Ben was trying to smile, like he always tried when he was having his picture taken. Ben had hoped he would look big, like a man. But he looked smaller than the deer and the gun. The way he smiled made him look afraid.

The knife was old, even then, and the wooden handle was worn and chipped. The wood was stained dark red with blood wherever there was a chip or a fade in the seal. The blade was long and thick. Eight inches of blade. But it was uneven on the sharp side from the number of times his father had sharpened it and sharpened it again.

Standing on the ladder, Ben tried to pierce the pelt of the deer high on its stomach, almost under its tail. He pushed too lightly, worried about the way it must hurt to be stabbed. He knew that was stupid, but he couldn't make himself feel the deer was actually gone. Actually dead. At any moment it might wake. Thrashing. The wild power of an animal in fear for its life. He tried to press against the pelt of the deer and he couldn't make it pierce. He held the knife up a foot over the pelt and brought it down hard. This time it went through. Too deep. He tried to look to see if his father had seen him. He knew it was a mistake, and that it could pierce an organ and contaminate the meat.

Now he could pull the knife down along the pelt and make a seam all along the deer's belly, as far as the throat. He could pull open the cut along the belly and pull out the intestines and the stomach. Now he knew the deer was dead, and it looked dead. He'd killed it. The blood was on his hands and on his knife.

His father helped him open the rib cage and the pelvis with a mallet and an axe, and he pulled out the rest of the organs and cut them where his father said, being careful not to cut in the wrong place and spoil the meat. With his father watching over him, he cut the pelt away from the flesh and the muscle.

His father would do the rest. Process the meat for food, cut the pieces that they could eat on their own, and the others that they would have to cook longer in a stew or a chili. Ben's father took the knife from him. He told Ben that he'd done good work.

One night at the bar, after he'd been going there more and more, Black Jacket sat down next to him. They didn't speak for a while, but Ben bought him a drink. He didn't want to talk with him, but it was the right thing to do. Ben thought he was a pretty good guy, and sometimes he would even think about him and wonder how he was doing. It was easier to buy him a drink.

It was quiet for a while as they both drank, and Black Jacket ordered another round. Then: "Thought maybe we wasn't gonna see you around here no more. Thought maybe that nice lady of yours was treatin' you too good."

"Yeah."

"Yeah. I forgot how engaging you was as a conversationalist." Black Jacket chuckled and sipped at his drink. "Sure have seen a lot of you lately. And somehow even scowlier than you used to be." Black Jacket looked at him. Stared. Ben could feel his eyes on him. Like insects on his skin. He tried to sit still. "You two have irreconcilable differences or something?"

"We're trying to work it out."

"Hmm. Yeah." Black Jacket shook his head and sipped at his drink. He spoke like he always did. Like it was right. Like talking was what he was supposed to do. "There was this old dude I used to know. He was like a cousin or something, I guess. Anyway, he'd been with this lady of his for years. Years and years. Stubborn, this dude was. Real bad. As stubborn as anyone I ever met. That whole time they were together his lady always said, 'You gotta get me some flowers.' For like birthdays, or anniversaries or whatever. You know? But this dude, he's got it in his head since way back that flowers are for suckers. He says you pay all that money, then they dead inside of a week. So he gets her clothes an' jewelry an' shoes an' every other thing she could ever want. All the while she's talkin' about flowers. He can't even hear it. Probably had to put out a new loan on his house for all the shit he bought that woman. And all she could talk about was them flowers.

"Finally, after I don't know how many years—like fifteen or something that they'd been married—he comes home to her on her birthday. All peacock proud and happy. He brought out this little jewelry box, all wrapped up. Inside was like a necklace or a watch or whatever. Gold, diamond, the whole bit. Cost that dumb muthuhfucker a thousand dollars, probly. He give her that box and she don't even open it. Throws it right back at him. Chases him out of the house with a frying pan that was still hot from cookin' dinner. Puts him out on the street, and won't let him back. Won't even answer his calls.

"So it goes on like this for a long time. I don't even know. Like a month he was sleepin' on dudes' couches, staying in hotels. And he'd call her and call her. Show up at her door. Whatever. Didn't make any difference. He even owned the house, but it didn't matter to her. He couldn't even step on the grass before she was out the door with that frying pan.

"So on and on it goes, just like that. Until finally he decides it's time to get her back. Whatever it takes. And he does it, too. Shows up at her door and all of a sudden everything's as good as it can be. They're like newlyweds again. Just like that. So what you think he did to fix it up?"

"I don't know."

"Yeah. You don't know. That's the same reason you sittin' here talking to me when you should be back where you belong. You see, this dude, when he finally figured out there was nothing he could do to reason with her, and after he'd tried every other thing he could think of from pushin' to beggin', finally he just went out and he got her those flowers. Wasn't even the expensive kind. All he had to do was do what she said. Makes everything simple. Every time.

"You dig, Mr. President? Maybe think about just doing what she say, and see if that don't clear everything right up."

Ben bought them both another drink and they sat for a while longer. It was quiet that night, and they were quiet, but Ben was glad he was there.

On his way home Ben walked by a pay phone. He thought to reach for the phone. But he wouldn't call her again. Not for a while.

‡

Ben let his beard grow. It wasn't much of a beard. It never grew in right. It was bare in patches, like his father's had been. He hated the way it looked and he had always stayed clean-shaven. But now he let it grow.

He showered less. Once every other day. Once every third day. Then, once his beard was mostly grown, not at all. No one paid attention at work, except to laugh about how he smelled if they ever got close enough. He would wear the same clothes day after day, and dirt built up on his hands.

He didn't like any of it, even though it was necessary. His beard would itch, and he hated the feel of dirt always on his hands. He couldn't sit in his chair or lie in bed without thinking of the dirt and the filth and the smell of himself. But he got used to it. It came to feel normal. Just like anything else.

He stopped drinking after the night with Black Jacket in the bar. After a few days everything got clear and precise. Too clear. It was harder to sleep, and harder to not remember. But he wouldn't drink. Not for a while.

He would go walking at night, with his beard half-grown and dirt on his clothes and on his body. He wore old thin wool gloves. Everyone passed him by. Everyone looked away. He would go walking when he couldn't sleep. He would go walking without shoes on. It was cold but it didn't matter. He was quiet and anyone who did see him kept away. Looked away.

He would go walking toward Maria's apartment. He would stand and watch. Stand in the shadows. Near a trash can. Hunched over. People saw him, but they didn't. They didn't look. No one knew him, and no one saw him, and no one cared. They left him alone. They would leave him alone to do what he had to do. For her. For both of them.

The two blocks closest to Maria's on the way to the Metro were dark. The streetlights were out, and the houses were empty. Late at night, Ben stood on the second block, and in the darkness he could still see her apartment.

Ben watched the lights in Maria's apartment turn on and shut off. He knew what most of them meant. Dinnertime, with the dining room light in the side window. After dinner, the uneven flash and pulse of the television. Bedtime, when the lights in the

front window would go out, and Maria and Sophia would both
be safe in bed. It was hard for him to sleep, so he stayed and
watched late into the night.

When he would get home from work, before it was dark,
before there was anything to watch for, Ben would sit at home.
He would try to read, or just to sit and to be still. He didn't like
it. It made him want to drink, or go out and watch, even though it
was too early. It made him want to do what he had to do. It made
him want to do something, but there was nothing to do.

‡

One night, like every other night, he sat in his chair waiting to
begin. He scratched himself where he was getting dirtier and he knew
he smelled worse than he smelled to himself.

And there was a knock at the door.

The sound of it pulled at him like a dream, like sound in a dream.
Louder than it was. Louder than it could be. He sat still and listened.
He didn't make a sound and he didn't move at all. He heard the sound
of breath. A sigh outside the door. And a knock again. He stood to
answer it without thinking that he should.

At the door was a woman. An older woman. Ben's age, or maybe
older. She was fat and round. Her face made him want to laugh, but he
knew he couldn't laugh.

"I'm sorry to bother you." She didn't come forward. She pulled
at the strap of her purse like it would tell her what to say. Ben already
knew. He knew what she was. He knew what she wanted. He thought
of running, but there was no way to run.

"You called me," he said.

She nodded. She looked down at his feet and she looked relieved.
Like what was happening here was already over. Like it had already

been done. "Yes. That was me." He walked back from the door and left it standing open. "May I come in?"

Ben nodded and gestured to a chair across from his chair, but he didn't sit down. She walked in slowly and he felt her watching him. Seeing that he was filthy. He could see her trying not to look. Trying to be polite. She walked in and closed the door behind her, twisting the bolt lock secure. She started at the noise as it fell into place.

"I'm sorry to be a bother. But I had to see you." Ben could see she was afraid. Afraid of him, or afraid of all of this. She was stupid to be scared. She had already won. And he had lost. He gestured again for her to sit. "I've never been to a city before. Not like this. It's so different from Upstate." She was waiting for him to sit before she did, but he didn't want to sit. "I guess you must know all about that."

He paced back and forth. He didn't like to pace, but he had to move. He had to stand and move. It almost felt like running.

"It took me a long time to find you. I guess you didn't want me to find you. Or anyone." She spoke slowly, but he could hear that she was scared. Like she was speaking to keep something worse away. She shouldn't have been afraid. "I'm sorry about that." She finally sat, and his old cane-back chair strained against her weight. He never sat in it, and he never had company. "I'm very sorry to intrude." She was settled, now. She was doing what she came to do. "I just felt like I had to see you. Like I had to know."

"Know what?" He knew, already, but there was nothing else to say. It was what he was supposed to say. There was a way to do this, like there was a way to do anything. Or maybe there wasn't. Maybe this was more than anyone could do.

"I know it wasn't really your fault. I know you were just a kid. We were all just kids." She'd said all of this before. Not to anyone. Ben could see her standing in front of a mirror, but it didn't make it matter less. "She was." The woman pulled at the strap of her purse. "I'm not angry. I haven't been angry for a long time. I want you to know that."

Ben knew that this was like the times when he knew he would be hit, but it hadn't happened yet. It would be better after, no matter how much it hurt.

"I just want to know why."

Ben paced back and forth. There was nothing for him to say. If he could give her a reason then this would be over with. But he couldn't give her a reason. He hadn't practiced anything. He couldn't bear to. "I don't know." The words were low and he shook his head as he paced back and forth. "I don't know why it happened."

"You have to know." She said it like a fact. She wasn't simple like she had been. "All I want is an answer. You owe us that."

Ben spoke too quickly. "I don't know why I did it." He stopped pacing and the room flew in circles and he thought he would be sick but he couldn't be. He couldn't be now. Everything inside him and around him and in his stomach felt like falling and falling. But he couldn't fall. This was too important.

Ben steadied himself and he saw her. He looked at the woman sitting in the chair. Quickly. As quickly as he could, but he had to look. She wasn't moving. She wasn't crying. She wanted more from him than anyone ever did. She wanted to know why. Her desperation made her look like half of something.

"You have to know." She looked at him. She kept her eyes on him, like what she wanted was there on his skin. She pulled at the strap of her purse like a garrote. "Who else would know if you don't? Who else would know why?" Her body strained against the chair and against the sudden wash of her anger. Her legs churned like a burrowing animal, and her rage was finally out. Ben was glad it was out. "Why can't you even do one thing for me? After what you took? After everything you destroyed, you can't even make one thing better?" But he didn't feel simple, and saved. He didn't feel like it was over.

It was quiet for a long time and she never stopped looking at him. He thought that if she would look away and let him think, that maybe then he could think of a reason to tell her. But he knew it wasn't true. Maybe the way her eyes felt on him would be enough to give her, but that wasn't true either. She breathed in and out and the sound of her breath was the only sound, and her breathing got slower and slower. She didn't act angry like she had. The anger was seeping back into her. "I remember when they led us out of the school." She'd never said this before. But she knew it exactly. "All of us, everyone, very quickly. We didn't walk in lines. Everyone was running. No one knew what was happening. No one would tell us. Out on the playground, away from the school. My parents were there. And the police were there, and talking to my father. And all the teachers would look at me, then look away. I've remembered it so many times. Even when I didn't want to. Waiting outside, and then going to the hospital and going home. I don't remember that anyone ever told me what was happening. I don't think I even asked. I thought if they didn't tell me there was a reason, and that they probably never would. I kept thinking that I knew she would tell me. As soon as I saw her, she would tell me."

Ben looked down at the floor as she spoke. He breathed in the stink of himself to try to clear the words away.

"And now I finally found you. I came all this way. I've waited all this time. I spent all that time wondering about you. Thinking about you. Your reasons. Who you were, and if I even knew you. Or if she did. Thinking that if she couldn't tell me, that you would have to. That you could. That if I could find you, you would tell me, because you had to do at least that much." It didn't sound like a threat. Or even a complaint. "But there's nothing you can say. You won't tell me anything."

Ben started to pace again. Not because he had to, but because the sound of it was better than the sound of her breathing. There was nothing he could tell her. Nothing that would help her. He was the reason, but there was no way to tell her that. The reason was everything about him, and in him, and everything that he'd done and been and destroyed. The reason was the thought of her, beautiful her, that would always be beautiful her and the look on her face when she knew what he was. The reason was his hands. And the thoughts that made him wrong and disgusting. The memories that made him need to hide and always be careful to never make another mistake. The vision of her in every waking minute and in every dream and every time he closed his eyes and the world would rush in around him and all of it turn into one long and sudden and voiceless scream. The reason was the filth on his skin and the stink of himself. The reason was the last thing he'd ever hoped for. All of his thought and his want and his hope for her and for him and for the different place where they could be together and the different people they would be together and the life that wasn't a life but a child's dream of laughing and hoping and loving. But it was never hope, and he couldn't love. The reason was that nothing he could ever do was good, and when his dreams came true they would always be nightmares.

There was no reason he could tell her. He was the reason, and there was nothing he could do for her. There was only one thing he could do, but it wasn't for her.

"I was wrong. I thought I had to do it." He spoke as clearly as he could. "I thought I was supposed to. I was wrong, and I made everything wrong, and there's nothing I can say that will help you." His throat closed up around his words, but it didn't matter. There was nothing more he could say.

She sat in the chair. Still and trembling. Crying. He was supposed to help her, but he knew he couldn't. Anyone would have known that. It was stupid to think he could. She was stupid to think that he could ever be better, or make anything stop hurting. She stood up from the chair and turned to the door. Maybe she knew, or maybe she just didn't want any more of this.

Ben followed her to the door. Because he'd been her host. Because it was right to do, and it would end this. But it wouldn't ever end this.

She turned back toward him before she stepped through the door. "I'd like to see you again. Would that be all right? I could come down again in about a month. Maybe we could have coffee, in the morning, before you go to work?"

Ben didn't want to see her again, and he didn't know why he should have to. "It's early."

"That's fine. I don't mind." She turned to leave.

"Who are you?" he asked. He hadn't wanted to say anything.

She didn't stop and she didn't turn back. He barely heard her as she walked away. "She was my sister."

‡

The boy got his things and closed his locker as quickly as he could. He didn't want to be near the girl when the others would come and change her. He didn't want to look at her. She was always part of them now. She was never different, and never small and soft and good. She was always one of them, even when she was alone. There was nothing he could do about it. Nothing he could do to save her.

The boy walked into the room where he would have his next class because it would be empty. But it wasn't empty. Satch was

*there, in the space by the teacher's desk between the chalkboard
and the rows of students' chairs with the desks attached. Satch
had been there alone and he looked like he was dancing. He
was turning around and around with his eyes closed. He jumped
up in the air and landed and he swayed from side to side but
his eyes were closed and there was something like a smile on
his face. And he turned around and around and jumped into the
air and there was nothing in the world for him but this. And the
smile spread and his face looked light and happy and simple. It
wasn't like laughing at someone, and it wasn't like when they
would swear together and it wasn't like anything the boy had
ever seen. The boy wished he could have it. He wished he could
take it. He wished he could grab him and tear it out of him and
make it his. It looked like sleeping. Like happy dreaming, standing on his feet. Spinning and jumping. The boy didn't want to
make a sound.*

*When the bell rang Satch stopped and steadied himself on
his feet. He saw the boy and the smile drained away. It was gone,
inside of him, where the boy could never get it. He saw the boy
and he went back to looking like nothing at all. He looked down
at his feet and walked out of the room.*

‡

Ben waited to leave until the woman had been gone for almost
an hour. He wanted to leave as soon as she did. He hated being in the
apartment, and as long as he was there it was like she was still there,
and every second was like her sitting and watching him and looking
at him and hoping for something from him. But he couldn't risk that
she would see him. He couldn't risk that she would follow him, or
that she would find a way to stop him.

Being out on the street felt better. The air was cold and it moved against him as he walked and he could walk and look and stay close to the shadows and do all of the things that he had practiced so that no one would look at him. Now he was doing what he was supposed to do, and it felt better.

It was still too early, and he didn't want to stay in the same place for too long until it got later. He walked back and forth through the streets. He let himself walk by Maria's apartment once, and then again an hour later. To make sure they were home. To see the lights on and know that they were home and that he still had a chance. When he saw the apartment and saw the lights he put his head down and kept walking and walking. It was still too early. It couldn't happen now.

When it was later, past midnight by the clock running on a scroll under the sign of a bank five blocks away, he went back. He walked quickly like he might already be too late, but he knew he couldn't be too late. He stood in the middle of the dark block near Maria's apartment. Far enough away, but so that he could see it, and watch the lights and watch the door. There was one light still on. In the living room. Because she knew, just like Ben did. She knew this had to be the night. She felt it like he did. It couldn't be any other night.

He stood and he watched. He didn't know for how long. An hour. More. He stood in the shadows and he watched the people that passed and he watched to see if they would notice him, but all of them walked past him like he wasn't there at all. They didn't want him to be there. They made themselves believe he wasn't.

And then he saw the man. Mark. Maria's ex-husband. Ben knew it was supposed to be this way. The man was walking quickly, but unevenly. He was determined. Walking through the dark blocks before Maria's apartment. He walked past Ben without noticing him. The man looked away, like everyone looked away. Ben was only a foot or two from him. Ben could have touched him. But now wasn't the right time. The man wasn't clear, but he was driven. He was moving quickly. He had an idea. There was something he needed to do. He was going to Maria's apartment. He would talk to her. Scream at her. Threaten her. Ben knew that it was all the man could think about. Walking the way he was walking, determined like he was, the man would push through Ben. He was still big. Too big to stop when he was moving like that. It was better to wait. Maria would be all right. She would get him away. Then the man would be different. And they would be all right.

He watched the man at Maria's door. Ben could see his body pulse as he pressed the buzzer. Again and again. Ben saw a light come on in Maria's apartment. The one closest to the front hallway. She didn't want to wake Sophia.

The door opened. She stood on the landing at the top of the stairway and stared the man down. Ben could hear them, even from two blocks away. He could hear enough. She yelled at him to go home. She said she'd already called the cops. Ben knew she hadn't. She never did. But the thought of it did something to the man. It wilted him. It confused him. Some of the power in his chest and in his arms seeped out of him. He yelled. But he wasn't clear. He wasn't certain. The idea wasn't right. He slouched. He wasn't sure. He wasn't sure of himself. After a few minutes Maria had backed him down one step. Then another. He yelled at her one last time and Ben knew it was really over. The man turned and walked down the steps. Maria stood and watched him go. Stood and watched him for one block. She would go inside before he got close to where Ben was standing. She always did. When the man crossed the street on to the second block, she went back inside.

Ben watched the man walking now. Toward him. He was walking slow. His shoulders and his head were low. There was nowhere else to go. Nothing else to do. Now there was nothing. He walked slowly and looked down at the sidewalk. There was no rush. No push. No determination. It was gone. Now he was barely awake. When Maria went inside he was barely a block from Ben, and walking slowly toward him.

Ben could feel the chill of fall like a shade over the very last warmth of summer. He could feel the concrete under his feet. He could hear the sounds of the man. His breath. The shambling way he walked, and the crisp sound of the brush of his suit pants and shirt. He could hear the sounds of the city. The sound of traffic from blocks away. A siren. The buzz of the power lines along the street side. The anonymous hum of all of it, together, like one living creature. All the lives and hopes and wants and hurts all gathered into one, come together in a dull chorus that they'd learned not to hear and not to see.

The man didn't see Ben. He didn't pay any attention. Ben waited until the man was close before he moved at all. Ben turned toward him with his head down. When he was a few feet away, Ben stepped toward him with his left hand out. Dirty. Shaking in a worn brown cotton glove. Begging.

The knife was out of its sheath, under his jeans on his right front hip. It was easier to draw from where his hand naturally rested, and it would be harder for the man to see it. He held the knife in a forehand grip, the blade extending forward from his thumb. He had practiced a thousand times. Since he was a kid and would steal the knife when his father was out of town and practice again and again. Imagining one enemy after another. Imagining a girl that only he could save. In the dark and in the shadow, with nothing left to imagine, he drew the knife from his jeans and held it tight in his gloved hand.

Ben stepped to the man's left. There was more room on the right of the sidewalk. Where it was darker. The man hesitated and shifted to walk around Ben, to the right. Not looking at the hand he held out. Not wanting to touch him. Looking at the sidewalk. Looking away.

With the man almost past him, Ben struck like he was throwing a punch. Angled up beneath the rib cage at the solar plexus. Ben heard the sound of the breath forced from the man's lungs as the hilt of the knife pinned his sternum. The man looked at Ben. Trying to understand. By the time he had some idea, he couldn't breathe to cry out. His look was dull. Glazed. He would die without knowing what it was that had killed him. But it didn't matter. Ben didn't need revenge. He didn't need a show. He only needed the man to die.

The man fell to his knees and Ben let go of the knife and pushed him over onto his back. He was alive when Ben took his wallet and his watch and pulled out his pockets for anything else that would be worth stealing. The man moved, and his heart still beat. But he wasn't alive. He wasn't a living man. He'd become a dying animal. Acting out instincts and rituals that had already failed him. Trying to pull at the knife. Kicking his legs like there was somewhere he could run.

Only the eyes were still the eyes of a man. Trying to understand. Trying to make sense, as if making sense of anything had ever saved a man. As if making sense was anything but a distraction from being helpless.

Ben put the wallet and the watch in his back pocket, handling them with his left hand that wasn't soaked through in blood. He pulled out the knife and wiped the blade as best he could with the bloody glove. He pulled off the glove and pulled it over the knife and held it under his coat, knowing that if anyone looked they would see the blood on his shirt. He stood back farther in the shadows to watch the man die. When the work was done and the man was still and limp, he walked away.

CHAPTER NINE

Ben walked a long, slow route back to his apartment. Twenty blocks into another neighborhood. One of the worst neighborhoods. He took the cash out and threw the wallet on the ground, in the corner by some trash cans. The gloves, the watch and the knife he threw into the sewer as he walked. Five blocks apart each time. He'd wiped down the knife before he'd left, so there wouldn't be any prints. He dropped the money on the ground where someone would find it. He didn't want it, but there was no reason to waste it.

He went home, put on cleaning gloves and put all of his clothes into a trash bag, and that bag into another. He poured a bottle of bleach into the bag, and enough water so that everything was soaked through. He showered and put on clean clothes. The next day would be trash day five blocks over. He walked there and found a trash can in a dark part of the street and stuffed the bag under the lid and walked slowly away, four blocks out of his way before he turned toward home.

None of it would matter if Maria told the cops. He didn't mind if she did. It was her right, and if she turned him in it would be fine. She had to know. It was important that she knew, and knowing was his gift to her. It was hers to use any way she wanted. But he didn't want it to be anyone else.

When he got home he was exhausted. But he didn't want to sleep. He poured a drink and it sounded and tasted and felt just the way he wanted it to. It smoothed over all of the edges. It calmed the noise in his mind. The look of the man. The look on his face. The whiskey calmed it just enough. And Ben was happy to feel clean, and to know that his work was done.

He sat back in his chair and he tried to think of nothing at all. He could feel the hurt and the old panic and fear and loss welling up in him. Not for the man. Ben didn't care about him. Now that he'd done what he needed to he didn't care about the man one way or the other. But the killing had stirred the old parts of his mind. Woken the hurt he could sometimes keep at bay. Woken it and made it all of his life, the way it used to be. He sat in his chair and he squeezed his eyes shut tight as the wave of all of it crashed over him and he felt like he'd be sick. It would be like this for a long time. It was okay. It was the price he knew he had to pay.

The sun was coming up later and later and he could see through his window the dark dissolving slowly into gray.

He'd done it for her. He knew that. He knew that made it good. That made it right. Whatever he had to go through. It was right. He'd done it for her. Done it for them. It was hard to keep his eyes open as he said it to himself, over and over, like casting a spell.

‡

The boy came late to school. After homeroom when they would sit and call out everyone's name and see who was absent for the day. He walked into the school when the halls were empty. He liked it like this. Quiet. Still. He wished it was like this all the time, and there was nothing wrong and all the noise and all the people were behind a door.

The boy wanted to run up and down the halls. To see how fast he could go and all the different things he could do with no one else around. He could do anything, and no one would stop him. No one would laugh at him. Nothing would be wrong.

He went into the bathroom and it was empty. He went into a stall and sat down without pulling down his pants. He wore his coat and it was too hot, but it didn't matter.

Kids would come and go while he sat there, and he liked it. Some of them would come in together and talk. The boy liked the sound of their voices. Like noises. Like the radio. He listened to them talk. And he listened to the water run while they washed their hands and it made him feel safe and alone. They could see his feet, but they didn't know it was him. They didn't know it was anyone. He was alone, and he could sit there forever and no one would care and no one would think about him or bother him.

He thought about the girl, and he knew he was stupid to still love her. She was always with them now. Always like them. She wouldn't listen to him, and she wouldn't know him. She would laugh the way they laughed. She would walk away. She would never want to talk to him. She was gone, and there was nothing he could do to save her. But he would try. He would try to be a man.

He held the gun in his hand and it still felt too big. The grip was deep red wood grain, and the metal was all black and smooth and even when he held his hand tight around the barrel for a whole minute the metal still felt cold. There was a scratch around the bottom of the revolving cylinder, along the back end where it would rub against the top of the frame. The trigger and the hammer and the sight were a different color metal. A deep gray, and there was a tiny insignia for Smith & Wesson over the rough wood of the grip. It was too small to see in the dark of the stall, but he stared at it for minutes and minutes and tried to look at it. It felt good to hold it, even though it didn't feel quite right. It felt good to hold it and be hidden behind the stall and know that no one could see him, and no one would ever know.

He thought that maybe this wasn't right. Maybe he was too young, and maybe he couldn't really be a man yet. But it was too late. It was too late not to try. It was too late to stop. There wasn't anything left. If he didn't try now there wouldn't ever be anything left. And if he couldn't win, it still wouldn't matter. He was already almost gone. It was always better to fight than to give up. A man would always try.

He knew it was getting close to time. He knew the class was almost over. He wouldn't go out in the hall before the bell rang, but he stood up. He put the gun in his belt, under his jeans at the small of his back. He practiced pulling it out again and again while he waited for the bell. He had practiced every night after school when he knew his father wouldn't see. It was still hard to hold it straight in his hands but it got so the hammer wouldn't catch on his jeans, and he could hold it steady as long as he didn't pull too fast.

He heard the bell ring and he put the gun back in his jeans. He stood and he pulled his coat down over his waist and he walked out of the stall. He realized it was the end. Being a boy, like he was, was over. It was ending now. He knew that it would be harder to live like a man. But he was ready. He knew that it would be harder every day from now on. He was tired of being little and stupid and no one ever caring about him. It was time to make everything change.

He walked slowly toward the door of the bathroom. He brushed his hand along the wall. He felt the smooth of the tiles and the rough caulk between. Like when he was with his mother driving on the highway and they could hear and feel the uneven seams in the road and they would drive for hours to the sound of thunk-thunk, thunk-thunk, thunk-thunk. They would drive away and drive for hours and wherever they were going would be someplace new and better. And they would listen to music and they didn't have to talk but they could watch the world go by outside the windows. And they would visit friends and relatives and people that the boy didn't care about, but he would see the different places. The places with more houses and cars, and the places that were warm and cold and the places that were cities and were close and dirty and scary but always exciting. And wherever they went they would drive and drive and the thunk-thunk-thunk would go on like the drums behind a song that would go on and on and on. But the wall ended and he pulled his hand away and he opened the door.

Everyone was in the hall and everyone was moving and pushing and yelling and laughing and all of it was wrapped up together. The boy walked by the wall on the edge of the crowd looking down at the tiles on the floor. He could feel their shoulders against him. Pushing past. He could feel all of it all around him, all of it one creature, but he couldn't look at them. He would do what he had to do and he would be a man, but he couldn't look at it.

He got to his locker and he turned the padlock and he opened the door and she was already standing there. He wanted to look at her. He wanted to see her. But he couldn't. He couldn't look at her. Not now. Not if he was going to save her. Not if he was going to keep his nerve. He couldn't look at her and get soft, and start to think and imagine.

The boy stood with his head in the locker, and he heard the girl's friends come over and laugh with her and talk with her. He heard one of them talk about him. "Look at the retard," one of them said. "What are you doing, faggot?" said another one. But they weren't different. They were all the same one.

"Leave him alone, you guys." Different faces of the same monster. And it all laughed at him. All of it together.

"Fuck you," the boy said, but he couldn't look out of his locker.

"What did he say? What did you say, retard? Come on, you guys, stop it. What the fuck's his problem?" They all talked over each other, but they were all just one, and it didn't matter what they said. "I mean it, you guys. Stop it." This was what they were supposed to do. This was how it had to happen.

"Fuck you," he said again, louder.

One of the hands pushed him. Another one closed his locker door. He was looking at all of them now. "Stop it, you guys." Looking at all of it. The monster was up close to him. Two of them close to him and standing over him. Pushing him. Others pressed in close behind them. All of them one. All of it one creature. And it thought it had him. The monster thought it was beating him. The way it had taken her and made her something she shouldn't ever have been. The way she was gone from him and she could never be kind. But now he was a man, and he wasn't going to let it win. It wasn't going to take him, and it wasn't going to win.

His hand slid under his jacket, and he could feel the cold steel against his back. "Leave him alone, you guys." The rough wood of the grip against his palm. He took hold of the gun easily, just like he'd practiced. He pulled it out in one smooth motion. It didn't catch. He didn't drop it, and he wasn't clumsy. He saw the looks on their faces. He saw the look in its eyes. It knew. It saw him. It saw the gun and it knew. "Get out of the way. Get away from him. I mean it." It was all one creature. Even as it changed in front of him. Even as it came to know him.

The boy held up his gun, knowing there were no choices. Knowing that nothing could change him. Knowing that nothing should stop a man from doing what he ought to do. His finger folded over the trigger and it still felt wrong in his hand. The butt of the gun too far back on his palm. His finger stretching for the trigger. And something else that didn't fit. That didn't make sense. Some voice. Some face. "Leave him alone." Some new face. Some face that he thought he'd known, but now it was too late for knowing. Nothing was like he'd planned. Nothing was like he'd imagined. But he wouldn't be weak. As he pulled back on the trigger he knew it was all over, and it was all beginning. The boy that died within him knew that he had finally won.

Ben felt the crack like thunder, and the shot that birthed him was like everything that had ever been and ever would be, all of it, all together, falling all at once. Ben squeezed his eyes shut against the world and the fury and he felt it all like an electric shock through his body. The gun flew back and pain shot up his wrist and the shot was so loud that it didn't stop. It didn't end. It started like thunder and it became yelling and it became screaming and it became the shock of pain and the push of hands and bodies against him. All of them running. All of them in a flurry of panic. Not all of them. And none of them were the monster anymore. It was gone like a child's fantasy and it wasn't the monster that shrieked and cried and gave itself over to the horror of everything lost.

Ben's life began on the ground at his feet. Ben's life began kneeling at her side. In the blood that wet his knees. In the few breaths she took, lying there. In the pull as she tried to take her hand from him. In the fear in her eyes. In seeing that she finally, truly knew him.

Born to the sacred duty of taking her hand. Holding on so tightly. Not letting her go. Watching her eyes go dim, and her chest still. Feeling her lose the strength to pull her hand away. Watching the hurt pass from her face and the fear drift away. Knowing that she wasn't with him anymore. Knowing that she would always be with him. And holding her and holding her hand like he'd wanted to when he walked down the hall, when they could have walked together and laughed together. Born into knowing that it was Ben that had killed her. It was Ben that killed her and he knew it and he felt it and he knew that holding her wouldn't change anything and in seconds he saw ahead for years and years and he knew that it was all over but that it wouldn't end and he knew that holding her couldn't change anything and he knew that Ben had killed her and she was never coming back. But he held her and held her and held her. He couldn't let her go.

‡

Ben woke late in the day. Too late to go to work, but it didn't matter. They said the last time was his last chance. Maybe they meant it, or maybe he would go another week without pay. Ben didn't remember falling asleep. He dreamt, but the dreams felt just like waking.

His hand hurt from where he'd killed the man. His wrist. He hadn't realized the adrenaline, and he'd hit the man too hard. Ben could remember the look on his face when he knew that he would never take another breath.

He should go out and get the papers. To see what the police said. There were lots of murders in this neighborhood and they never really paid attention. It would be worse because the man was white, but he was drunk, and Ben had taken his wallet and his watch and there was nothing else worth anything. He'd been robbed. It would be easy to think that, and everyone liked easy thoughts. He would get the papers and see what they said. He would call Maria later that day. That was all there was left to do.

Ben had been afraid that someone would find him ever since he'd gotten out. Maybe the fat woman would tell someone else. Maybe this was just the start of one person after another. Maybe it would happen again and again. Or maybe it was over. The memories were back. The dreams. They'd never left, but now they were behind and above and beyond everything he saw. Everything he thought. Every dream he had. Seeing her body. Seeing the crowd form around them. Everyone looking at him. None of them knowing what to do. All of them watching him. Watching him hold her hand until the bones cracked and broke. Thinking he was crazy because it was all he could do to keep her alive. Seeing he was a murderer because he couldn't.

Ben didn't care about killing the man. He could see it in his mind but it didn't bother him. It was something that needed to be done. It was right.

Maria was the only one who would know. She would know. She had to know. He would tell her if he had to. Maybe getting Maria back didn't matter. Maybe it wasn't important. But Ben felt like he should try. Felt like he should try not to let go of them.

He didn't like waiting around. Doing nothing. It would be a few hours before Maria got home. He wanted to talk to her. He only wanted to call her once, and he didn't want to leave a message. If she didn't want to talk to him, or if she wanted to turn him in, he didn't care. He'd done what he was supposed to. He'd protected them. And he wanted them back. But that wasn't his choice, and maybe it was better if they left.

He sat back in his chair and waited. He didn't want to go out. He didn't want to go walking. He would get the paper later. He felt sick from drinking too much before he slept, but he poured another drink. The bottle and the glass were sitting by his chair. The Maker's tasted the way it always did, and he was happy drinking it. For a few minutes he just thought about the taste of the whiskey.

The hours passed in a mire of minutes and seconds, lived and re-lived, over and over. He poured whiskey when the glass went dry but he didn't feel it at all. It didn't make any difference.

Ben stood from the chair when it was close to four and he thought Maria would be getting home. He could feel the whiskey, but it would be fine. "Hello, Maria," he said aloud. He hated the way his voice sounded, but he couldn't hear the whiskey. He would be fine once he'd walked for a while.

He took a shower and shaved and put on clean clothes. He brushed his teeth and used mouthwash. Once, before he showered, and again after. He felt good and clear by the time he was ready to leave, and when the memories came he would press his eyes closed as if there'd been a flash of light. But only for an instant, and then it was gone. He walked out toward Maria's apartment.

He stood on the street, away from the direction she'd come from work. He stood until he saw her walk up her stairs and through her door. He walked back to a pay phone he knew that was close. He stood by the phone and waited for what he thought was about fifteen minutes. He knew Maria would be tired after work and she liked to have a few minutes to rest.

He dialed her number and it rang once, twice, and the sound of her voice made everything break loose, and all of it crash over him again. He squeezed his eyes shut and he kept from screaming because he never wanted to make her hear it.

"It's Ben."

"I know."

"I want to talk to you."

"What did you do?"

"What I had to do. You know that." It was stupid to say it that way, but there was no other way to say what he meant. "I want to see you."

"No. No. You can't."

"Just once. I just want to see you once, then I'll leave you alone."

It was quiet on the line. Then: "When can you get here?"

"Whenever."

"Sophia gets home from her friend's house at six. You have to be gone by then."

Ben hung up the phone and walked toward Maria's apartment. He didn't try to think about what he would say. It never worked when he planned anything. He just needed to see her. He walked around the block a few times so that she wouldn't know how close he was, and rang her buzzer. The door clicked open, and the door to her apartment was ajar. He walked through it and into the living room. The shoes he had left behind stood together on a floor mat, lined up neatly, but bigger than Maria's or Sophia's.

Maria was in the kitchen making coffee. She didn't say hello. He stood in the living room and watched her pour herself a cup. "Do you want some?" she asked.

"No." He wanted a drink, but he didn't ask for it. When he looked at her she was all he saw. Nothing else. Nothing else. No memories, except of her. He could feel his heart shake his chest. Shake his body.

She walked to the kitchen table. "Sit," she said. She stood over the chair at the head of the table, and he pulled out the one to the right of it. She moved over so she would be sitting across the table from him. They both sat. "What did you do?"

"You know what I did."

"Why?"

"I had to. You know."

"I never told you to do that."

"I know."

"I didn't want you to…" She wasn't crying. Ben was glad she didn't cry. He hated the wet, swollen look of a woman's face when she cried. Her face was smooth. Sharp. Hard, but beautiful. She hadn't always been hard. "I didn't tell you to do that."

"I know."

"Why did you do that?"

He didn't want to talk about him. Not this way. Not like it was wrong. It wasn't important. She already knew why, as well as he could ever say. It wasn't important. It wasn't supposed to be like this. "How is Sophia?"

She didn't answer. She didn't make any sign that she'd heard him.

"How are you?"

"You're a murderer."

The sound of the word made him dizzy and he pressed his eyes tight together. He felt everything go loose, but he opened his eyes and it came back together. He could kill her. He knew that. It would stop her. He knew he couldn't or he wouldn't but it would stop all of this. "It wasn't murder."

"Then what was it?"

"I had to do it." He could tell her how it felt to kill a man because he had meant to. He could tell her it was like doing work. He could tell her it was like killing an animal. He could tell her the feel of blood soaking through his gloves. He could tell her that the muscles of the man's trunk contracted around the knife and how he could feel it up through his arm like holding a stick in rushing water.

He could tell her about standing and watching the man die and feeling no regret, and knowing that he'd kill him again and again and again if that was what he had to do. He could tell her about killing justly. He could tell her that the man's blood on his hands felt like hers, and he could tell her that the work he'd had to do had woken his demons and his dreams and his devils as if a day hadn't passed in thirty years.

"You had to do it? You had to kill him?" The way her voice sounded made him feel stupid. Dumb. Like he didn't understand, but he knew he did. He knew he did. "Is that how you thought you'd get me back?"

"I had to do it to protect you. To protect both of you."

He said it too loud. Maria stared at her coffee but she didn't drink. She wrapped her hands around it and held it close to her. "What did you do to Sophia? That night. In her room. What did you do?"

"I was dreaming. I had a nightmare."

"I didn't ask that."

"I don't know." The room rolled and sank and swelled and the words in his mind were confused and he didn't know how to say them.

"Then just get out," she said. She wouldn't look at him.

He tried to think of how to say it. "I didn't hurt her."

"In her room? In the middle of the night? She was screaming."

"I didn't hurt her. I would never hurt her." He was getting louder and louder. He had to make her understand. She had to understand. It was the only thing he would never do. He saw in her eyes that she wouldn't listen. Wouldn't understand. He saw her so far from him and he couldn't reach her and he couldn't make her understand. She wouldn't let him reach her and he felt everything spin and he felt the sound of Sophia screaming and seeing in her eyes that she thought he could hurt her. It was the only thing he knew he could never do again. No matter what. "I didn't hurt her."

Maria winced in her chair and pulled her cup closer under her chin. Ben realized his cheeks were wet and he wiped them but his hands were shaking. He knew he was making it worse, and it was falling apart. He couldn't reach her. He couldn't make her listen.

Ben heard the door before Maria did. He saw it open, and he saw the light come from the hallway. He saw Sophia. She saw him. She didn't smile, and she didn't fear. She dropped her backpack and hung her coat on a hook by the door. Maria stood from the table. Ben was standing, too, and the girl walked toward him. Ben couldn't speak and he couldn't breathe. He couldn't walk toward her. He didn't dare do anything to stop this, anything to change it. He didn't dare laugh or smile. He didn't dare cry out his joy and his amazement that she was here, and she was alive, and she was walking toward him. Maria hadn't moved, but the sight of her daughter so close to him stirred her. She tried to come around the table but the girl was there, there within reach, there where he could touch her.

"How do you do?"

She held out her hand and before Maria could stop him, and before it was gone or he could see that it was all a dream, he took her hand in his. He could feel it. Warm, and alive. He could see her, and see the life in her. Not fading. He could see that she was life and he thought of pulling her close and holding her close and tight where nothing could ever hurt her and nothing could ever take her. Holding her so that he could sob and laugh into her skin and feel her breath against his ear. Hold her so that he could take everything back. Now, here. Take everything back that he'd lost. Take everything back that he'd destroyed. Warm himself in her life, and hold it and crush it to himself like a treasure, like salvation, and he would never, never, never let her slip away. He heard Maria and he felt her pulling on his shoulder, pulling at his arm and at the hand that held her and held her life and coveted her and that could have all of her forever. He could see in her eyes that she didn't know. She didn't know what she had. What she was. She didn't know that her life could rebuild him. That it could wash away every wrong thing. All of his dreams. Everything his life had destroyed. For a moment he felt weightless in the truth that he knew. Weightless in knowing that if he pulled her close enough and held her tight enough and never let her go and never let Maria take her or anyone ever take her and if he clung to all the life she had he could finally be free. If he could hold on to her so tightly that he would never have to let her go. He knew that if he could keep her, and hold her, and have her as much as he needed her, and have her life and her joy and her safety, then he would be free.

And he let go.

ACKNOWLEDGMENTS

First, my thanks for the time and insight of the folks who reviewed this novel and gave me guidance at various stages.

For his superior editorial sense in making this book read as I hoped it would, Paul Vargas has earned my unending gratitude. Without his talent, enthusiasm and friendship this book could not have come to life.

Finally, to Mary Di Biase and Carly Behr, my wife and my stepdaughter. They are my foundation of hope; they are my beautiful visions and my home in this world. Thank you both.